SAINT VALENTINE'S FLEET

BY

M HOWARD MORGAN

SAINT VALENTINE'S FLEET

THE THIRD ADVENTURE IN
THE JACK VIZZARD SERIES

BY

M HOWARD MORGAN

www.Penmoreprepress.com

Saint Valentine's Fleet:M. Howard Morgan
Copyright © 2024 M. Howard Morgan

This is a work of historical fiction. While based upon historical events, any similarity to any person, circumstance or event is purely coincidental and related to the efforts of the author to portray the characters in historically accurate representations.

ISBN-978-1-957851-28-0(Paperback)
ISBN 978-1-957851-27-3(e-book)

BISAC Subject Headings:
FIC014000FICTION / Historical
FIC032000FICTION / War & Military
FIC047000FICTION / Sea Stories
Editors: Lauren McElroy, Chris Wozney
Cover Design and Painting by:
Acknowledgements to   Geoff Hunt PPRSMA,
 illustrator and artist for permissions
Covers: Emilija Rakić PRB.Emilia'sWorld of Design
All correspondence to:
Penmore Press,
920 N Javelina Pl,
Tucson, AZ 85737
First published in 2014

'He that outlives this day, and comes safe home
Will stand a tiptoe when the day is named
And rouse at him the name Valentine.'
—- Colonel John Drinkwater Bethune,
A Narrative of the Battle of St Vincent

AUTHOR'S ACKNOWLEDGEMENTS AND DEDICATION

All writers of nautical fiction owe a debt to those who have sailed the seas and oceans before them. Be they academics or kindred spirits who, like I, marvel at the feats of men from bygone eras living and working and fighting the great wooden walls of the tall ships, who conducted trade or fought to protect them. Some of the best stories are those involving the mighty ships of war fighting each other in bloody combat, whatever the motivation or circumstances of conflict may be.

Amongst the writers of nautical fiction, the names of Marryat, Pope, Reeman/Kent, Stockwin, Muir, O'Brian, Forester, and Woodman litter the shelves of my collection and have each played a part in entertaining me and shaping my understanding of the Great Age of Sail. More recently I have come to enjoy the books of new writers such as Alaric Bond, Chris Durbin, Phillip King, and Antoine Vanner. From the world of academics, I enjoy; Nicholas Rodger, Andrew Lambert, Brian Lavery, Edward Brenton, and Sam Willis as reliable and informative sources and whose works occupy much of my shelving.

The letters and journals of officers and ships' logs, less readily available, make for fascinating study too. As an example, during research for this novel, I spent a long and enjoyable day at University of Cambridge library reading several of the journals kept by a frigate captain, Graham Moore, (the brother of John Moore of Corunna) who features in this novel. The thirty-two volumes he wrote during his career had not been removed from the university's vaults since deposited there in approximately 1832, until I tracked them down and requested them! I am grateful to the library staff and Frank Bowles, its Archivist for the assistance so freely given to me.

For the Battle of Cape St Vincent itself, I relied on the contemporary eye-witness accounts of Colonel John Drinkwater Bethune, the journal of the Nelson Society, the correspondence of Sir John Jervis, several volumes of The Naval Chronicle, and the letters of Horatio Nelson, who, like his commander and mentor, was a prolific correspondent.

A rare and very valuable resource was found in the 'Biographical Memoirs with Critical and Explanatory Observations' by John Charnock FSA, published in 1806 and which I discovered in the Library of Congress placed there courtesy of Harvard College. It was Charnock who alerted me to John Clerk of Eldin, Scotland and his 'Essay on Naval Tactics' published in Edinburgh in 1776. Not a sea officer Clerk nevertheless advocated a challenge to conventional naval thinking by arguing that a fleet that could 'cut the line' of an opposing fleet and create a tactical advantage. It certainly influenced Jervis, who had been given a copy and the tactic was used at

St Vincent, and via Jervis, it almost certainly found its way to Nelson. That great naval hero never publicly acknowledged the fact, so I cannot be certain. However, it made me rethink my received knowledge of the man and the innovation sometimes attributed to him.

I thank them all for their contributions to my writing ambitions. My scribbling has been greatly enhanced and undoubtedly improved by the expertise and insight poured generously into the text by two wonderful editors. Tessa James in the UK and Chris Wozny in the USA. I am very grateful for their constructive work.

For the freedom to indulge my interest in maritime history and in the craft of writing I am indebted to and with love dedicate this book, to my beloved wife, 'She Who Must Be Obeyed'.

MHM

CHAPTER 1
Melampus

'Captain Vizzard, you'll be wanted on deck, sir,' the wardroom servant, Noah Cooper, said, his visage devoid of expression. 'Compliments of the First Luff, sir.'

'Very well, Cooper,' Jack Vizzard replied. 'My respects to the first lieutenant and I shall attend on him presently.' Swiftly scraping the bristle from his sun-stained face, he listened to the sounds of increased activity on the deck above: feet running, a bosun's call singing in its shrill voice accompanied by an officer's bellowing tone. The blade swept neatly across his left cheek as the deck of his cabin heeled and water from the wooden bowl slopped over the rim to the forever-mobile floor. It was an uncomfortable experience. At home, Mary would ensure he had hot water for his morning shave and some Paris Pearl Water to make the quotidian task more pleasant. It was a preparation he had long resisted until Mary finally purchased some, persuaded him to use it, and he realised that continued resistance was futile in the face of her determination. It had pleasantly surprised him and he'd quickly adapted to it.

There had been very little sun to warm the crew during the last week as they laboured incessantly in the permanently wet rigging. Fingers became numb and chafed, barefooted sailors suffered, clothes were permanently damp and mouldy; this cruise was very discomforting and tedious. Jack shivered as he woke to the sounds of the watch changing and the shouts of the midshipmen and bosun's mates rousing the men from their hammocks.

The cold had permeated his breakfast, unappetising and stale. The toasted bread was dry and hard, the butter was on the turn, the small beer was musty, and the servant was patently sour faced and more miserable than usual. The cold turned faces pale and lips blue. His own fingers were stiff, and his shaving water was cold. In short, the officer commanding the marines on board the frigate was in low spirits and a mood to match the conditions.

'He wants you right away...' The servant trailed off into silence as Jack's eyes drilled a warning glance. 'Yes, sir. I'll tell 'im, sir.'

A Turkish towel dried his face and removed the excess soap, as well as adding to the sense of wellbeing that comes to a man with the simple act of hygiene. His shirt was damp to the touch and crumpled. A black-spotted stock hung from a protruding trenail; Jack ignored it, pulled down the uniform coat from the blackened brass hook, adjusted his shirt and picked up his hat. After a brief glance in the cracked and dirty mirror, he combed his fingers through his black hair, extinguished the fluttering candle in the lantern with a strong blow from a pursed mouth, and ducked out of the cabin to climb the gloomy, pitching companionway and reach the quarterdeck just as a Channel squall heeled the frigate steeply to larboard.

'Ah, good day to you, Vizzard,' shouted the first lieutenant, Richard Rynne. 'Thought you should see what we are about. The foremast lookout reported a sail some minutes past, and we are set on a chase.' He returned the large brass telescope to his right eye. 'Off to larboard half a point, perhaps a league-and-a-half or two distant, or so says the American at the foretop. I'd say a little more.'

Rynne was prudently dressed more appropriately for wet weather than Jack, with a long oilskin coat and a battered fisherman's hat which had once belonged to his father. The moderate, persistent drizzle threatened to increase in volume as Rynne strained to focus the glass and swayed with the rolling deck. The sea was a heavy, dark grey with spindrift flying as the waves rose, meeting the wind. 'Damnation. I can't see a thing in this muck. Where's that mid?' he growled. 'I want him and his young eyes up the mainmast.' Turning about he shouted an order at a luckless on-watch midshipman, which sent him scurrying up the shrouds with the long telescope slung across his back.

Jack held tight to the lubber line and planted his feet as firmly as he could while the spray plucked at his hat. The waist was awash with hissing foam, and a dozen agile seamen more practiced in the skill of movement on a wet, rolling, pitching deck, were heaving on sheets and trimming sails to keep the swift frigate on course. *Melampus,* carrying topgallants on her fore and mainmasts, with staysails and jibs, averaged nigh on seven knots in this sea, which Rynne thought could be bettered if the rain would only clear.

'Bit of a blow coming, do you think? Will we find her in this?' Vizzard asked, eyes straining forward, seeking to penetrate the curtain of rain. 'I'll be damned if I can see anything.' Sprayed with cold, sharp drops of seawater that felt more like needles lancing his skin, he wiped his face with the back of his hand. His tunic absorbed the rain that penetrated his shirt and underclothes, and he regretted his undue haste; he should send for his canvas cloak.

'Captain Moore is determined to do so. He's gone below to inspect the gun crews,' Rynne shouted back, grinning. 'This is but a squall, Vizzard. I had you marked as an experienced sailor!'

'I am, Dick, but before we can catch our fish, we first have to find him,' Jack replied, 'and this one is particularly slippery and elusive.' He grinned through streaming salty spindrift that stung his face.

Jack had sailed on many ships; his longest voyages had been to New Holland back in '87 and the happy return some three years later. He had never been seasick, yet never quite achieved that sense of balance and ease of movement of the experienced able seaman.

His Majesty's frigate *Melampus,* of 36 guns, ship-shape and fashioned in Bristol by James Martin Hillhouse and Company, dropped into a trough, throwing spray over the fo'c'sle and soaking the gun crews readying the two nine-pounder bow chasers. Vizzard squinted at the men.

'We shall not engage anything in this weather, surely, Dick?'

He stumbled as the frigate pitched heavily again, her bows biting deeply into a wave, and grabbed at a deadeye to steady himself.

'There could be work for your lobsters, Vizzard,' Rynne shouted back, then bellowed to the quartermaster's mate, 'Mind your heading, man!' He turned and grinned at Jack. 'If we can catch her, the captain means to take her. That is where you and your Vandals will prove their worth, I trust. Better get your lads prepared.'

Jack Vizzard's detachment of marines were unorthodox fighting men, regarded by some line regiments as little better than scum. They were, however, respected by the crew of *Melampus* who had gradually come to hear of their exploits in France and of their fighting prowess against the French 74, *Vengeur du Peuple,* two years before in June '94, when Jack and a small detachment had served in Howe's fleet.

The wind had veered since the last turn of the glass and was now pushing hard from the west-southwest, directly onto the frigate's larboard quarter, so that the wave tops were ripped from the sea and sprayed across the ship's waist. One of the hands slipped, sliding into the base of the main-mast. The crack of a breaking arm was heard on the quarter-deck, the man's scream taken away on the wind as a mate bent to help him below to face the ordeal of the surgeon.

He might lose that arm, Jack thought. *Poor bastard.*

Clenching his jaws at the thought of losing an arm or leg, he squinted through the spray as a shout from the foretop confirmed the sighting of a sail. 'Where is she?' bellowed Rynne, using the speaking trumpet with a rasping authority and failing to conceal his growing anxiety. Jack did not clearly hear the sailor's words, distorted as they were on the wind, what sailors called a topsail wind, blowing harder now from the southwest and finding its way to his skin. He decided to go below to find his cloak.

As he made to return below the captain of *Melampus* stepped onto the quarterdeck and made for the weather side. Quickly taking in the condition of the frigate's sails and rigging, the captain allowed himself a slow smile of satisfaction.

Jack raised a hand in token salute, which Captain Graham Moore failed to notice or chose to ignore, too intent on managing his ship as it ploughed its way through the foaming grey-green and white water. Jack shrugged and lowered himself down to the darkened lower deck and to the mess allotted to his sergeant and the ship's marine detachment. Little light reached this cramped and crowded part of the ship even with the main deck hatches open in fair weather. In a blow, when the hatches were battened down and gunports closed, the only light came from pairs of lanthorns swinging from the low beams. He made his way past shadowy figures along the gun deck.

'Sergeant Major Packer? Where are you, Joe?' he called into the gloom. 'Come on, wake up, you dozy bugger!'

A ripple of laughter ran around the mess where a couple of dozen marines, in various stages of undress, sat on the deck or swung from hammocks. Realizing it was Captain Vizzard, the chatter stopped, and men stood as best they could, keeping heads low.

'Silence on deck!' Vizzard shouted. 'Joe Packer, stir yourself and show a leg. I need a word.'

The recipient of his order was his senior non-commissioned officer, right-hand man and friend of nearly a decade. Packer had been assigned to the young, newly commissioned Second Lieutenant Vizzard shortly before they joined one of the four companies of the Corps of Marines providing escort to the first fleet of convicts to New South Wales.

'What is it you're wanting now, sir?' growled a deep voice from the gloom. The bulky form of Vizzard's trusted sergeant and friend stepped into the dim light, pulling a shirt onto his powerful shoulders.

Packer detected an imminent sense of more work in Captain Lieutenant Vizzard's tone, and was not disappointed when pulled toward the bulkhead by his commander.

'Captain Moore will be ordering us to quarters afore long, Joe.' Jack's voice dropped as low as the deck-head above his stooped body. 'A sail has been sighted, very likely a Frenchie, and Captain Moore is engaged in a chase. Likely as not the privateer we have been hunting for some weeks.'

'Very well, sir. I'll get the lads ready. Thanks for the warning.' Packer grinned, now properly awake after two full hours in his hammock.

'I'm told Captain Moore is keen for a prize, so we must prepare to board once we close.' Vizzard stumbled as the frigate rolled suddenly, her heading altered. 'We've changed course. I'll see what is happening. Best make a quick visit to the blacksmith and get an edge on those weapons, Joe. Draw extra ball and powder for the lads, too.'

Joe Packer made a concealed gesture with his stubby fingers, an informal salute which made Vizzard laugh. The tough sergeant, whose head resembled a large pale cannon ball which glowed pink when he became angry, was the only man in the Corps who could get away with such mild insubordination to his commander. Mutual respect and an unlikely friendship crossing class boundaries had developed between the two, born of the privations of New Holland back in '88, and of the respect Vizzard earned from his subordinate and the other marine guards in defeating and humiliating their then commanding officer, Major Robert Ross, in a duel. Ross had been a belligerent man who bullied his way through the commission and made life hell for Lieutenant Vizzard and miserable for others in the nascent colony.

Vizzard ducked into his screened-off cabin in the gunroom and pulled on his oiled canvas cloak before returning to the deck and the sound of Captain Moore growling under his breath. Thinking he should not distract the captain, he remained aft near the taffrail and listened, sensing something amiss as men scurried forward, scaling the wet and greasy ratlines. As his eyes followed them, he saw the foremast tabernacle had splintered, threatening the topmast and topgallants.

'Get that fished and secured quickly now, Mister Masters,' Rynne thundered skyward to the bosun, who was leading his mate and another hand upwards to the wounded mast. 'I need that fixed within five minutes!'

The bosun waved acknowledgement as he reached the swaying foretop, quickly getting to work. Within the stipulated five minutes he raised a thumb towards the quarterdeck. Anxious faces staring up from the deck started to relax.

'I trust that will work, Mister Rynne,' said Captain Moore, immediately regretting the unnecessary formality. 'I must press on and catch our prey. Let's test it with the course and stun's'ls, Richard, but take in topsails; all of them, if you will.' Moore stood with hands laced together behind his back as his premier shouted a series of orders, sending the watch on deck into orchestrated activity. He allowed himself a thin smile as the foremast took up the strain of the additional pressure and the topmast held. 'Very good, Richard, very good. Now let us press on. Masthead there!' he bellowed, 'Report what you see.' Moore scanned a wide arc of the horizon, knowing the lookout would see anything before he could.

A silence blanketed the deck as men waited for news. Two dozen pairs of eyes stared to the lookout on the maintop, urging the man to sing out.

'Nothin' yet, sir, the American voice rang out after an interminable delay of fifteen seconds. 'Looks as tho' the squall is passin' so I'll keep m'eyes peeled, sir.' He continued to sweep the horizon methodically from starboard to larboard and back. The man spat and wished he was back ashore, back in Norfolk with Abigail.

Nothing more spilled from the American's mouth before the watch changed, although his prediction of the rain easing proved correct. The western horizon appeared to darken to a deep purple hue as a thin, early December sun eased its way into the dark ocean. Stretching across the western horizon, great, dark-grey clouds were massing and moving in various directions; flashes of lightning pierced the gloom, and an increase in wind was plainly discernible, even at this distance from the storm.

'I want all lights out, Mister Mansell,' Captain Moore instructed one of the midshipmen of the watch. 'Complete and total darkness, and I want the galley oven extinguished.' Clapping his hands together for emphasis, he continued, 'Please see to it for me.' He smiled genially at the young man, now eighteen years of age and eagerly anticipating his board examination for lieutenant. Moore had supported the youngster since taking over command of *Melampus* a year previously. Moore thought highly of him; he was conscientious, quick-witted, and already commanded respect from hardened sailors on the lower deck. Quite unlike his messmate, Bedington, the son of a senior officer in the 1st Foot Guards whom Moore's brother, a colonel, wished to reward in some manner. Bedington was a fool and would never rise to lieutenant if Captain Moore had his way.

Graham Moore brushed aside the minutiae of his command and turned his mind to his orders to seek out and take, or destroy, any privateer he found operating in his patrol area, generally from the Cherbourg Peninsular to Brest on the Atlantic coast. Too many East India merchantmen had been attacked, taken as prizes, damaged and foundered along the French coasts, so he and other frigate captains had received orders to hunt and destroy the privateers operating there. The Navy deemed the ports along the Brittany coast to contain nests of vipers, to be destroyed whenever one should venture out.

And he had been successful. Two privateers had been caught and one wrecked attempting to evade the determined Moore. The crew benefitted from his tenacity and courage, becoming well-drilled, skilled, determined, and keen for prize money. Weak and hopeless cases were removed from *Melampus,* transferred to outward bound ships of the Mediterranean fleet, or to the Indies. Two had been flogged for an 'unnatural act' and, after a time in the ship's prison, had been provided with the opportunity, fortunately taken, to desert the ship and be accordingly marked R in the crew muster record. But Moore had a more difficult task in ridding the ship of officers he did not respect, and young gentlemen of no potential value. He would have to find a solution to Bedington.

Moore had taken command of *Melampus* in September of '95, a little more than a year before, and had quickly transformed the frigate, and crew, into an efficient, happy ship. There had been gunnery drills, sometimes with the finest powder he could afford, more usually without firing. When weather permitted, he ordered sail drills, training the ordinary seamen and teaching the landsmen and boys. The son of a physician and Scots born, Moore had been in the Navy nearly twenty years, since '77, and had a brother in the army, Colonel John Moore. He had reached post rank eighteen months previously, but *Melampus* was not his first command. A tall man, his greying hair was starting to thin, and his brown eyes gazed on the world with intelligence and, perhaps, a degree of compassion. He loathed floggings and rarely awarded them unless necessity required it.

Moore paced across his quarterdeck, periodically halting to stare at the maintop, willing the lookout to hail the deck with positive news. The man's glass traversed the horizon rhythmically from starboard to larboard and back again, never pausing to hint at some object of interest. When the lookouts remained silent, Moore continued his pacing of the deck from windward to leeward and back, mirroring the lookout's above, clenching his firm jaw tight and controlling the growing frustration within. He heard the thrumming of the sails, the creaking of the deadeyes and the soft groan of the deck timbers beneath his feet, the slap of the sea as the frigate's bows cut through the roiling water. Near total darkness blanketed the frigate.

* * * * *

The night watches passed without a storm disturbing the routine of the crew. They expected the strange sail to have long disappeared and the traditional Sunday routine of a religious service, with Captain Moore officiating, to commence the day, followed by the repetitious reading of the Articles of War, plus some free time to indulge their private interests. A period of 'make and mend' allowed the sailors time to undertake repairs to their clothes, or work with scrimshaw, or carve an offcut of wood into a figurine. Instead, they were ordered to see to their equipment.

Jack Vizzard finished cleaning his sea-pattern musket and stared down the reversed barrel. Satisfied with the internal condition of the weapon, he returned the bayonet to its rightful place, having had the blacksmith carefully hone a keen edge to each of its three edges. He placed it on the temporary rack that Chips, the carpenter, had made for him, and wondered if it would be needed in the following hours.

From the relative silence on deck it appeared unlikely, so he pulled the letter from his trunk, found the stub of a pencil, and resumed writing.

It is now Sunday morn, my dearest Mary, and I expect Captain Moore to order the usual service cancelled, for we sighted a strange sail late yesterday and are now bent on finding it in this endless sea. The men are in good spirits, and Joe Packer begs I send you his best respects. He has been drilling with the men this morning, and I declare I am near satisfied with their progress. Many of them deserve the name of Vizzard's Vandals; one or two have yet to achieve the desired standard. If all goes well, my love, they may have the opportunity to practice their musketry on the French afore long.

The captain

'Deck there!' The shout from the maintop penetrated the silent ship and made Vizzard jump from the chair, thumping the top of his head on a beam. 'Topsail, a point off the larboard bow! Two leagues or more distant, sir!'

As Jack raced up the rear companionway, the ship around him came alive with men cheering and, without waiting for lieutenants to order them, racing off to their stations unbidden. On reaching the quarterdeck, Captain Moore smiled a greeting. 'Helloo, Vizzard. Appears we may have located our quarry at last. Are your fellows ready, do you say?'

'Certainly, they are, sir. This may be the rendezvous we have all been waiting for.' Vizzard fingered the pommel of his sword. 'My lads are spoiling for a fight. They have pent up energy to spend.'

'Indeed, Vizzard, I do hope so. I have wearied of catching this fellow; the *Hasard* is the rascal I believe her to be, curse the damned vessel. If I am correct, she is responsible for nigh on a dozen of our merchantmen in the last twelvemonth. I am determined to take her, Vizzard, and you and your rogues will help me.'

'You may rely on us, sir,' Vizzard assured him. 'How long, do you think, sir, to catch the Frogs?'

'The First Lieutenant advises a full glass—possibly more— and that only should she keep to this course. The villain has given no sign of having spied us thus far.' Moore looked at the sky. 'I shall have to hang out more canvas, I fancy.'

As he spoke, eight bells sounded and the men on watch lingered at their posts, reluctant to go below, which meant having to pass the baton, and the excitement, to eager shipmates.

Captain Moore strode across to where the second lieutenant stood marking up the traverse board and explained his requirement. A moment later Lieutenant Weaver shouted an order sending men scurrying to the t'gallants to shake out additional canvas. As the sail area increased *Melampus* surged forward, her pitch more pronounced as she met the seas, rolling a little more as waves passed beneath the coppered hull, which Moore deemed to be in poor condition and in need of repair, even replacement. The skilled helmsman, fingers calloused from years of experience, kept her course true, familiar with the rudder's responses to his sensitive touch as if it were an extension of his muscular arms.

Routine work continued. Up forward, near the larboard cathead, a bosun's mate worked at a new log and, with the help of a young volunteer, attached the knotted line, matching the knots against a rule to check the accuracy of spacing. The last one he made had been lost to the depths. A carpenter's mate finished work on a hatch cover that had been damaged during loading, tapping with a mallet to bring the mitre joint together. On the main topgallant yard seamen were rigging new reefing tackle. A gunner's mate was inspecting number four gun with its captain, who was troubled by the sound it had made during the previous week's drill. He peered into the touchhole and grunted audibly.

'I'll note that, Will. I reckon it might needs reboring, which means it'll be taken out. It'll be all right, I reckons, but I'll takes a closer look when we're done wiv this chase.'

'Deck there!' An urgent shout from the foretop. 'Sail two points to larboard, south of east. Hull's down an' she be 'bout three leagues.' The murmur rose around the deck as the watch came alive, stopped whatever tasks were in progress and dozens of eyes strained to the direction indicated.

'Silence on deck,' yelled the officer of the watch, Lieutenant Simon Weaver. 'Attend to your duties.' He strode to the larboard shrouds and leaped to the bulwark, climbing rapidly to the mizzen top, a glass swinging from his back. Reaching the futtocks he leant backwards, hauling himself onto the top. Grasping the mast for balance, he pulled the long telescope over his shoulder, steadied his feet apart and trained the telescope in the reported direction.

'What do you see, Mister Weaver?' Captain Moore growled, arriving on deck.

The horizon tilted, slipped, and rose again in a misty haze of dark-wine rolling waves, topped with foam that disintegrated as the wind lifted it from the sea. The low dark-grey cloud was inclining to cluttery weather and, for a time, Weaver could see nothing as he swept his glass across two cardinal points of the compass. As *Melampus* rose so did a sail, only a topsail, which hovered in the lens for a few seconds; just enough for him to make it out.

'Corvette, sir,' he bellowed down to the quarterdeck, 'and French, sir. No doubt about it.' He started his descent to the deck.

Moore smiled. *At last, I have him*, he thought. After weeks of cruising the Channel, beating against contrary winds and chasing shadows, she was in his sights. He had to take her this time.

'Helloo the deck, sir,' bellowed the American lookout on the foretop. 'Sail fine on the larboard quarter.' The voice hesitated for a long time before continuing with more certainty. 'Brig, mebbe three leagues, sir, and she's British!' *That woke them up*, he thought. All eyes were on the chase to starboard, and only he had performed his duty fully by continuing to search in every direction.

The officers spun to their rear and stared. There was little doubt, another vessel was coming up with all possible sails thrown out. Moore pulled open a telescope and, adjusting the focus with care, steadied the image. A brig she was, and British too.

'The brig-sloop *Childers*, gentlemen,' he announced, recognizing her. 'Commander Stephen Poyntz is in command of her. You may recall she was the first of our ships to be attacked by the French back in '93, when Martin Barlow commanded her. She will be very welcome, I fancy. Useful to have a pair of hounds when the fox is on the run.' He ordered the recognition signal hoisted, then noted the acknowledgement that broke out from her fore within half a minute; Poyntz was evidently alert. 'She will be up with us within an hour; why, she must be making a handsome ten knots or more.' Moore watched her shortening the distance between them.

'Have you any orders at this time, sir?' enquired Lieutenant Weaver, landing heavily on the deck.

Moore switched his attention to the French corvette ahead, now little more than a league away, with every sail she had and flying as fast as she could to escape the determined British warships.

'I believe, Simon, ...' Moore paused, rocking with deliberate slowness on his heels, enjoying the moment, '...you may now clear for action,' he finished quietly.

Weaver stared at the apprehensive drummer standing ready. 'Well, boy. What are you waiting for?' he said unkindly. 'You may beat "clear for action".' The boy's hands flew as the rat-a-tat rattled out the long-awaited command. The interior of the frigate exploded into activity, while from below came the sounds of screens being brought down, furniture being stowed and men running with purpose. Each of the twenty-six 18-pounder cannons on her upper deck was brought to readiness within two minutes, each gun crew ready, waiting on the order to load and fire. Splinter nets were slung from the yards to protect men from falling rigging. Mainsails were hauled up to reduce the risk of them catching fire from the guns.

'We should fight, and afore long, sir,' Weaver urged. 'She's making for the harbour of Barfleur; should be just off our starboard bow, and this wind will—'

'I am sensible of the risk of a lee shore, Mister Weaver.' Moore was becoming increasingly concerned and wished for more sea room. He had to get close soon or lose the opportunity; it was unnecessary for Weaver to remind him. 'Captain Vizzard!' he called, looking about for the marine officer. He spyed him at the rail, watching the approaching brig, and called across, 'Your men are ready I trust, Mister Vizard?'

'Yes, sir. I'll have the men deployed immediately.' He grinned, anticipating the captain's intentions, and ran forward to call down the companionway. 'Sergeant Packer!' he shouted, knowing his NCO would be waiting. 'To the foc's'le now, with your best marksmen, if you please.'

'Then you'd better join us, sir,' Packer replied, joining him on the deck 'You're still the best shot in the division, I reckons.' The rest of the detachment were filing up from below and running along each side of the frigate. 'Take your positions, lads,' Packer shouted. 'You knows what we're here to do. And for Gawd's sake, try and 'it your targets for once.'

The end of the afternoon watch rang eight bells for the start of the first dog watch; all hands were already at their allotted stations. The men going off watch were unwilling to go below, so they found weapons and prepared for a boarding fight, most with cutlasses, some with axes, and a handful of pikes for those who preferred to attack and skewer their victims from a distance. Several armed with both a pike and cutlass.

'Make ready, Joe,' said Vizzard, 'we'll be opening fire with the forrard guns any minute now.' Even as he spoke the order came, and the two fo'c'sle nine-pounders opened up a second apart, their thunder rolling across the narrowing space. Vizzard stood watching the arc of the balls and the splashes at the stern of the corvette. He levelled his telescope at its stern; *L'Etna*, he read. 'She's *L'Etna,* sir!' he shouted back to the quarterdeck.

Captain Moore frowned. So once again, he was thwarted; this was not *Hasard*. But still, it was a French ship, and a prize was a prize.

The corvette hurriedly returned fire from a pair of stern-chasers, the shots falling short and wide. The British crew shouted derision at the French crew, unheard as the wind, blowing onshore, snatched voices from mouths and carried the words away. Within minutes, *Melampus*' bow-chasers fired once more, one ball smashing its way through the enemy's stern, sending lethal splinters of timber scything through the French ship. The screams of the dying drifted back to *Melampus,* whose men replied with a cheer at the prowess of their shooting.

Vizzard watched as *Melampus* yawed closer to the wind and showed her broadside; the French vessel kept to windward, fired all her guns with little attention to aim and, surprisingly, then lowered her colours.

'By God, Joe,' Vizzard said. 'She's surrendered to us.'

'No wonder, sir,' Packer answered. 'Must have heard Vizzard's Vandals are after her arse!'

They laughed together as *Melampus* backed and came into the wind. A ship's boat was being readied to send Lieutenant Weaver across to take the prize, when suddenly the corvette caught the wind and cut across, making swiftly for the shore and the ancient port of Barfleur.

Moore ordered the starboard guns to fire, but *Melampus,* being low on stores and water, heeled too far and only three cannon were ready. Spitting fire out into the squall, they fell short. Moore, observing the falling tide at the approach to the small harbour, reluctantly decided to abandon the chase. Another few minutes and he would be unable to manoeuvre safely. Moore was aware of the rocks at the approach to the port and of the battery at Havre de Crabac. He had taken off émigrés in a clandestine operation only last summer. He dared not pursue the corvette further and put *Melampus*, and her crew, at notable risk. 'It's no good, Dick. We cannot follow her. I am sorry, but we must abandon this.'

'Hell and damnation,' cursed Jack. 'She was as good as taken, Joe. As neat a prize as we've seen in a twelvemonth.' He stamped aft toward the quarterdeck, his frustration painted across his face, eyes heavy with disappointment, mirrored by those he passed.

'Captain Vizzard,' said Captain Moore, as Jack climbed to the quarterdeck. 'Sorry to disappoint you. It would be folly to pursue her further. I fear we would founder or come under fire ourselves, were we to take the chase onward.'

'Aye, sir. The bloody Frogs did not fight fair. She had surrendered to you. That captain is a man of no honour, sir.'

Moore's disappointment was written on his face for all to see. 'We shall continue the cruise.' He turned away to issue an order. 'Mister Weaver, please now secure the guns,' he called across to the equally despondent lieutenant. 'You may return to our previous course and patrol area,' he commanded as he headed for the solitude of his cabin. Moore, unlike some of his contemporaries, was not given to unprofitable risk-taking. His was a more calculating, cool-headed mind; pursuing a chase into her home port against a contrary tide and a hostile battery was not a risk to which he was willing to expose his ship or his crew.

The wine he poured tasted corked, but he drank it anyway to remove the bitterness he felt.

CHAPTER 2
Berkeley

The cold early winter of 1796 saw Jack return home to his family, all of whom were suffering. Young Freddie had been the first to succumb when, shortly following his third birthday on Guy Fawkes' Day, he became ill, so ill indeed that Mary Vizzard summoned not one but two physicians to treat the boy. Their greatest fear was to lose another child. The previous winter, the infant christened Elizabeth had slipped away from life, breaking hearts throughout the household and beyond to the close-knit community in the village of Woodchester.

The present malady spread upward through the family to Annie, the daughter they'd adopted in Sydney Town when her mother died, to Mary, who'd insisted on nursing both the children personally. Jack's old nurse-turned-housekeeper, Maddy Neave, cared for the bedridden. Fortunately, they all recovered in time to enjoy the Yuletide festival.

For Jack, Christmas festivities were a welcome hiatus from the tedium of beating about the Channel, with little in the way of French vessels to chase, fight or capture. The weather inhibited the enemy from venturing out, and Captain Moore had abandoned the patrol when the next severe storm stove in the hold, spoiled much of the remaining stores, and sprung his foretopmast. It had taken the determined crew a day and a night to repair the damaged hull and pump the flooded hold, allowing Moore to retreat to Plymouth. Jack had taken the opportunity of leave for Christmas and travelled to Woodchester, a long and tiring journey along frozen rutted roads that all but shook the teeth from his head and made his bones and muscles ache. The coach travelled east through Devonshire, then north through Somerset. Towns and villages passed by slowly, the country draped in frost. As the coach journeyed north to Bristol, increasingly heavy showers of snow dusted the trees and hedgerows, and the wind found its way into the coach, adding to his general discomfort. His travelling companions were equally miserable, except for a naval officer traveling to Bath with whom he was able to share a few anecdotes and discuss similar experiences. They exchanged details and undertook to meet again, knowing the likelihood of doing so was remote. Eventually the coach passed into Gloucestershire, much to Jack's great relief, making its sluggish way along the Stroud road. It came to a halt in Woodchester, allowing Jack to alight and trudge on foot up the hill to his home.

Jack and Mary decorated the hall and reception rooms of Lampern House with generously draped holly boughs spotted with red berries, and hung a wreath on the front door. Friends and family members visited and enjoyed their hospitality, in the main providing Jack with some diversion, but occasionally only tedious conversation with Mary's brothers, who had nothing in common with an aggressive marine officer. Nor did they have much, other than blood ties, in common with their sister, who had risen from her humble origins to become a respected lady of the county, sought for her conversation and vivacity by many of the hostesses of the larger houses in Gloucestershire and Wiltshire. Mary loved her brothers but found conversation with them, beyond the well-being of their respective children, difficult. The brothers attempted to be sociable but felt uncomfortable in Jack's grand home.

A supper with Louise Mountjoy, widow of Jack's deceased childhood friend, Giles, proved painful and evoked unwelcome memories of happier times. Both Mary and Jack attempted some match-making to inject some entertainment, if not real attraction, between Louise and a young naval commander, a resident of nearby Stroud, who had amused them with tales of voyages to distant worlds. He had fought the Americans and the Spanish with some distinction, but Louise remained aloof and disinterested in any amorous relationship.

'I am sorry, Mary,' she whispered, when away from the menfolk, eyes moist and heavy with ongoing grief, 'there is no man in the world to fill the void in my heart. Giles was my whole life, and now, now I have the children, yes, indeed I do, but ... I'll not seek another husband, Mary, ever. I am content to remain a widow, with my memories.' She looked pointedly at the wedding ring on her finger and played with it as her mind thought of the man who had put it there. Mary understood her friend's feelings, yet she wondered if Louise truly would endure a life of widowhood, for she was a young and beautiful lady.

They returned to the dining room just as the door from the kitchen opened and Madeline Neave, the Vizzard's housekeeper, a ruddy-faced dumpling of a woman, waddled to the table. 'Will you be wanting a puddin', mistress? Only I've made a pair of apple pies for Ned and the children, and there's aplenty left. I could quickly make thee a sweet sauce to 'company it,' she said with a smile.

'Yes,' said Mary. 'Yes, Maddie, that will suit very well. Thank you.'

'You have a butler, do you not, Vizzard?'

Jack looked at his guest, or more correctly his wife's guest, as he had not met the fellow before and said, rather tartly, 'Yes, Commander, but he's not very proficient in the preparing and baking of apple pies, whereas Mrs Neave is particularly adept at the, ah, art of apple tarts. And for pies, Commander, you will find Mrs Vizzard is a champion pie-maker.' He smiled at the private memory. She returned the smile with her eyes.

'Then, sir, I do believe I shall be delighted to join you, if there is sufficient to spare, that is,' said Commander Shellard. 'Will you be returning to sea, Captain Vizzard?' he enquired.

Mary's eyes dropped as a shade of sadness crept into her heart.

'Yes, I will, in due course. With Captain Moore of *Melampus,* like as not. Do you know him?' asked Jack. Given that Moore was viewed by some as a rising star in the Navy, he thought it likely.

'Only by his reputation. He is said to be an excellent seaman and a hard but fair captain.' Shellard hesitated. 'He is thought well of at the Admiralty, I hear. You will have a chance of prize money with that man, as seizing prizes features large in his plans, it is rumoured.'

Mary interrupted him. 'But, Commander Shellard, surely that makes him a danger to his men, does it not?'

'Oh, William please, Mary. "Commander" is so formal,' he said. 'You might be forgiven for thinking such. However, many officers, and even more common seamen, would relish the prospect of serving a lucky captain, one who gains prizes, which may lead to promotion. A captain who is fortunate in the matter of prize money will usually find no shortage of volunteers when he needs to recruit additional men.' He smiled and raised a glass to Mary. 'Why, I learned of a captain in the last war who was awarded three eighths of a valuable prize, which equated to some £30,000. A king's ransom indeed. Your husband, madam, may find both honour and sizeable wealth serving under Captain Moore.'

'I would be content if he took the life of a country lawyer, as I once thought he would, Commander ... er ... William. However, the captain is a soldier first, a lawyer second. And the quiet life as a country gentlemen, I fear, is not an occupation that appeals to him,' answered Mary. 'More is the pity.'

Vizzard looked at his wife, his eyes softening. 'There will be time enough for rural life, my love. But while we are at war with France, I cannot neglect my duty.'

'I understand, dearest, that you would rather die than be accused of that,' said Mary.

Commander Shellard could not fail to detect the undercurrent of marital discord, and thought to divert the couple to a different topic. 'You have a fine house here, Captain. Have you lived here very long?'

'I was born in the drawing room, Shellard. One very cold December evening a few days before Christmas. Sadly, my dear mother—that is she in the portrait above the fire—died birthing me. I was raised by my father and Mrs Neave, our housekeeper. My father inherited the original house from an uncle and added to it, to his own design. He also designed and laid out the gardens himself. It became something of an obsession for him in his later years; the lake was created shortly before he passed away.' He smiled kindly at their guest, grateful for the distraction.

All eyes turned to the portrait of a beautiful lady with swirling dark chestnut hair and bright, shining eyes. Mary's heart softened. 'She was most beautiful, Jack. So sad you never knew her. I wish she had lived to be here with us now.'

'Indeed, Mary. How she would dote on the children. My siblings both have memories of her and tell of her great love of children. My dear father never really came to terms with her passing.' For once Jack could not fully suppress his emotions. A close observer would have seen a slight tremble of his lower lip, and eyes welling with tears. Mary certainly noticed.

'If I might say so, Vizzard, you have more than a passing resemblance to her. I raise my glass to her memory.' Shellard held up his glass, now much in need of filling, which Jack, mindful of the hint, proceeded to do.

'What of your service, Shellard?' Jack's interest turned to his guest's career. 'Do you have a ship at present? Or are you waiting on their Lordships' pleasure?'

'Ah now, Vizzard, here's the thing. The Mediterranean is becoming untenable for the fleet. Jervis has requested reinforcements and it is said—I hear from a friend in London—

that their Lordships may consent to find a few more ships for the old curmudgeon. I hope to secure a command of a cutter or brig, perhaps. I … er … brought a prize back from the Caribbean last month, and if she is taken into service, I hope to receive a permanent commission as her master and commander.'

'We wish you all success, Shellard, don't we, Mary?' Jack raised his glass in salute. 'Your captain must have confidence in your suitability for command to entrust you with a prize.'

'Well,' Shellard coloured noticeably, his cheeks turning a pale shade of red. 'I was fortunate in the boarding party I led. We lost a few good men that day.' A shadow passed across his eyes, and Jack deduced the man had lost a friend. The commander's next words confirmed his thoughts. 'My friend, James, was impaled by a Frenchman with a pike. We had been midshipmen together. It was a dreadful thing to witness. He died slowly as I held him.'

He suddenly recalled where he was and looked at Mary. 'I do humbly beg your pardon, Mary. I forgot myself for a moment. I hope I have not caused offence.'

'I do understand the burdens of service to the King, William, and that in war good men die. I pray that neither of you suffer in such a manner. Now, please may we move to more pleasant matters? I find such talk to be distressing.'

The conversation turned to more mundane subjects, including the current cold spell, which was producing harsh frosts, with reports of the upper reaches of the River Severn frozen over and being enjoyed by children, and their parents, skating on the ice. It was less popular with the fishermen or the ferrymen, who made a living moving people and animals to and from that part of Gloucestershire across the wandering, silver river.

* * * * *

The door to Jack's study, lined with bookshelves and overlooking the lawns and parterre to the rear of the house, opened suddenly, interrupting his reading of the *Gloucester Journal* news sheet he had received the previous day. This contained an item of interest concerning reported movements of the Spanish fleet.

'Oh, Jack, you will not believe our good fortune, you simply will not believe our luck!' said Mary, out of breath from her rapid descent from the bedroom. 'Do guess what has happened!' She held her hands behind her back as she leaned into her husband's studious face, his mind still focussed on the article and its implications for the Mediterranean fleet and the Corps of Marines.

'Hmm? What is it my love? Have you inherited a fortune from a hitherto unknown rich relative, or been invited to court to meet His Majesty, or … I do not comprehend?' Jack smiled at his wife's glowing, beaming face, the sparkle in her eyes, and enjoyed the broadest smile he had seen her wear for many weeks.

Mary hopped and skipped across the room and deposited a large gold-edged card on the smoke-stained stone mantel above the fireplace. 'You silly man. No, not a fortune and not an invitation to be presented to King George either. But something very nearly as exciting.' She skipped back towards Jack to grasp his hand as he rose from his armchair, put down the news sheet, straightened his back, and strode across the worn carpet to read the copperplate printing. It was unusual to receive a gold-edged invitation card, embossed with a family crest.

'Oh,' Jack said.

'Is that it? "Oh"? Is that all you can say?' said Mary, laughing. 'Why, what were you expecting? A knighthood or promotion to major? It's an invitation to a dinner, a special dinner, with very special hosts. We are to dine with the Earl of Berkeley and his lady at Berkeley Castle. Surely you know of the event!'

He moved to the window, stared at the lengthening shadows, and saw another frost forming on the grass. It was a fine garden which he enjoyed when at home. His father had it laid out after a particularly large fee was paid by a grateful client. Jack was forever thankful that his father had established trusts for his brother, George, his sister, Charlotte, and himself, trusts into which large lodgements had been made. The trust was the source of the wealth that supported them.

Knowing only a little of the Berkeley family, his curiosity was certainly piqued. He attended dinners in barracks or in London when required, but this was a social occasion which would see the wealthiest of the county and surrounding areas attending, the thought of which brought him a measure of discomfort.

Turning back to face her he said, 'I know of it certainly, my dear, but I do not know the Berkeley family. Attendance requires full regimentals, my dear. That certainly means a new gown and shoes for you, and probably a few other items. My uniform is stained with salt and mould, so I will need a new uniform coat complete with new buttons and braid, new breeches, probably new boots, and my sword will need some attention, for the scabbard is dented. It's an expense we should avoid, my dear.'

'I hope you are not suggesting that we decline, for Heaven's sake. Anyone who is interesting in the county will be there. Some, naturally, will be less interesting, I fear. Oh, but Jack, this will be the highlight of the Christmas festivities. Imagine, you and I dining in the Great Hall at Berkeley Castle at Christmastime. It rather means, I feel, we are becoming better known in polite society, even to the nobility. There must surely be no better place in the county to celebrate Christmas.'

He rubbed his chin and pushed a lock of hair from his eyes. 'What I find extraordinary is why, or how, an eminent earl of the realm, apparently a friend to the king and his brother, neither of whom I have ever met, should think to invite you and I to his Christmas dinner. He is one of the wealthiest men in the entire country, Mary; indeed he damn near owns half of it. I shall doubtless be the most junior officer present; the place will be littered with colonels and generals, probably even an admiral or two, and we will be pushed down to the end of the table amongst people of little consequence or interest whom we do not know, with nothing to offer other than tedious conversation about the price of sheep. I hardly see why you should be so excited, dearest.' Jack saw little to interest him in such a dinner, which would only bring inconvenience and additional expense during the Christmas festivities.

'Jack Vizzard, you can be quite a fool at times. Then you would not know that his wife, the Countess Lady Berkeley, was Mary Cole from Wotton way. My father and hers were friends when we were still at school. She obviously remembers me! I wonder what has put me in her mind after all these years.'

Mary all but danced from the room in search of Neave so that she could start forming plans for the event and write some letters to dressmakers in Bath and Bristol. Jack, resigned to the inevitable, shrugged, sat down at his desk, dipped the quill in the ink, wrote a letter of gracious acceptance, and started a list.

* * * * *

The brougham that Jack hired with a coachman for the evening joined three others lining up to enter the castle's grounds. Two immaculately attired sentinels stood in the front of the gatehouse on the western approach, directing the stream of coachmen on the manner in which to enter the courtyard, while the horses' heavy breathing formed clouds in the chill evening air. Their journey to reach the ancient castle by the River Severn had taken the better part of two hours. Jack had often spied its outline from further up-river at Frampton-on-Severn when he and his brother had borrowed a villager's boat, but Mary had never travelled so far, and to her it was a magnificent prospect. It was something to talk of to her friends, and to her children when they became old enough. Never in her imagination had she ever thought such an event would feature in her life.

Jack knew the Berkeley family had owned the estate for most of its seven-hundred-year history, and that Edward II had supposedly been murdered within its walls, a victim of

Queen Isabella and Roger Mortimer's plotting. Edward was laid to rest at Gloucester Cathedral, a tomb Jack had seen many times when he was a scholar and chorister at the adjacent King's School. He enjoyed regaling Mary with the tale during the journey; Edward's murder had been particularly brutal. Legend told how the townsfolk of Berkeley heard the king's screams and how his ghost stalked the halls of the old castle. Mary absorbed the history, storing it in the deeper recesses of her mind in case the subject should arise in conversation that evening.

The pale wintry sun kissed the ancient forest on the far side of the river, and threw shadows from the castle's walls as they entered the inner courtyard; there was the promise of another frost. Their brougham pulled to a stop behind a large town carriage, hauled by four heavy horses. Jack noticed the doors carried an armorial bearing, painted in blue and gold. The details eluded him, but he rightly assumed that it belonged to a personage of some rank.

'This may prove to be an arduous duty, my dear. The place will be full of Lord Such-and-Such, and Lady This-and-That.'

Mary whispered to him to be quiet.

'And we shall be announced as Captain Nonentity and Mistress of Nowhere Important,' he continued. This time Mary tapped his ankle, which made him wince.

He assisted Mary down onto the cobbled yard, where she gathered her gown to prevent it becoming soiled, while a footman took the invitation from Jack's hand, turned on his heel, and indicated for them to follow. He led them across to the lobby of the Great Hall, entering through an arched doorway, where they joined a short line of guests waiting to be announced. Jack stamped his feet as the cold penetrated the soles of his boots. The footman requested Mary and Jack's cloaks, revealing Jack in his bright red coat with the fresh white facings put in by a tailor in Gloucester to replace the former tar-stained and frayed ones. He unclipped his sword and handed it to the footman. His new bicorne hat and boots looked as though they had just been delivered by their makers, as indeed they had. All the bills were on his desk, and he had rolled his eyes when the dressmaker's account had been delivered. All matters for another day.

The warm light in the lobby came from four brass chandeliers, with other lighting provided by coloured glass oil lamps along the wainscoted walls. The Berkeley family were evidently prepared for the Christmas season, with holly branches placed around the walls and sprigs of mistletoe suspended from the glittering chandeliers to welcome the winter solstice.

Mary glowed with barely contained excitement, her deep-crimson velvet gown complementing Jack's immaculate uniform. Her hair was fashionably long, with falling ringlets and a chignon bun carefully prepared at the back of her head. Madeline Neave and her granddaughter had worked most of the day to achieve the perfect appearance, and Mary felt more like a countess than the low-born aspirant governess she had been when first she met Jack Vizzard at the vicarage nearly a decade ago. She risked standing on tiptoe to gain a better view of the ladies present.

'Do I have the honour of dining with Captain Vizzard of His Majesty's Corps of Marines?' boomed a voice from the entrance to the Great Hall. Jack saw a large, ruddy man in the dress uniform of a Naval post captain, striding towards him, rolling as if still on a man o' war. 'Why, indeed I do. Good evening, Captain Vizzard,' he grinned. 'I would be delighted if you and your charming lady,' he bowed in Mary's direction, 'would do me and my dear Emilia the honour of dining with us.' Noting the lack of recognition on Jack's face, he continued.

'You look all aback, sir. Of course, you would not know me from Adam. I am George Berkeley; the earl is my elder brother,' he explained in tones that most in the hall could hear. 'You and I served under Howe at the First of June. I have heard something of your exploits that day. I had the *Marlborough* then, amongst the van commanded by Tom Pasley. Our soldiers were good men, but not marines. We fought the *Impétueux*, were raked by the *Montagne*, and lost some good sailors—and one or two officers. My word, that was a bloody day.' He touched the scar on his head unconsciously, sighed, and played with the gold medal awarded to distinguished captains, hanging around his neck. Jack stared at it momentarily, taking in the figure of Victory, standing on the prow of an antique galley and placing a wreath of laurel to Britannia.

'I saw what was left of your ship that day, sir: nothing more than a floating hulk. It's a wonder you were not all killed.' Jack remembered the sight quite vividly.

Berkeley beamed as he grabbed Jack's arm, 'My dear Vizzard, it's a wonder *you* survived the carnage on that Frenchie,' he retorted, advancing Jack and Mary to the head of the line, collecting his wife Emilia *en route*, and striding in a seamanlike manner towards his elder brother, Colonel Frederick Berkeley, the Fifth Earl.

'Freddie, my fondest greetings to you and your lady at this festive time.' His voice was still at the volume he used from the quarterdeck. He nodded towards Lady Berkeley. 'Countess, may I present Captain Jack Vizzard and, er, Mistress Vizzard,' he barked, and coloured a little, having forgotten Mary's Christian name. 'He and I served together in Howe's fleet at the First of June, back in '94.'

The Earl opened his mouth to voice a greeting, but Lady Berkeley interrupted. 'Welcome, Mary, welcome indeed! It has been too many years since we last met, and, my, how our circumstances have changed since our childhood.'

Mary made a modest curtsy. 'I am surprised you remembered me, m'lady, but I am delighted to have received your kind invitation. We both are.'

'Oh, nonsense, my girl. The Earl may have made a countess of me, but I've not forgotten my origins, nor that my father often served ale to your father and brothers. I am only embarrassed the years have separated us and precluded us from being friends all this while. It was only by chance I recently heard of you living in Woodchester with Captain Vizzard. The Earl knew your late father-in-law, it seems. I am very happy to have the opportunity to renew our friendship, my dear. Please, sit with us here before we dine.'

The years seemed to fall away as the two became engaged in reminiscing over their respective childhood years, while other guests looked on, curious as to the identity of the attractive young lady now in exclusive conversation with the talented mistress of Berkeley Castle. It became an animated conversation, punctuated by bursts of girlish giggles, which the onlookers strained to hear.

Jack was gradually drawn away from the small group of smiling ladies, some of whom continued to glance coquettishly at the tall marine, who stood a full head above the stout and somewhat brash naval captain—a man inclined to shout at people rather than engage in conversation.

A short distance from them was a group of mature gentlemen, one in the uniform of a colonel of the South Gloucestershire Militia, and all elegantly dressed. Jack did not recognise any of them. A tall, well-dressed man, with sharp features and dark, brooding eyes below thin, untidy eyebrows, separated himself from the group and strolled nonchalantly towards Berkeley.

'It's George, is it not? How do you do? I am Harcourt. I have been advising your brother on some investments in India and elsewhere, and he kindly invited me for the weekend.' he said, extending a hand.

'Yes, I am the younger brother,' Berkley replied, a trifle sharply. Turning towards Jack, he introduced him as, 'My special friend, Vizzard. We fought the French together under Earl Howe back in '94,' before asking pointedly, 'You are a gentleman of business then, Harcourt? Not one of armed service to His Majesty?' It was becoming clear to Jack that Berkeley had difficulty in dealing with the civilian population, much preferring the company of kindred spirits, of military men.

'I believe gentlemen of business serve the country in other ways, Berkeley,' Harcourt replied. 'Trade is the lifeblood of the nation, is it not? Some men are born to wage war on the seas, while others are more suited to be merchants and traders, whom the Navy exists to protect.'

'Delighted to meet you, Vizzard.' Harcourt nodded towards Jack but did not extend a hand. 'Yes, however, my only son holds the King's commission and lodges in Portsmouth, awaiting a ship.' He failed to conceal the barely perceptible sigh of a disappointed father.

'I doubt he will have to wait long, Mister Harcourt,' said Jack. 'Jervis will have need of more ships afore long, in my opinion. Indeed, I anticipate returning to duty early in the New Year.' He glanced towards Mary, relieved she was out of earshot. 'There was an item in the *Gloucester Journal* recently as to how the Dons have driven Jervis from Toulon.'

Harcourt's smile did not reach his eyes. 'It's *Lord* Harcourt, Vizzard. I am made a baron.' He spoke tartly, peering along his nose in Jack's general direction. 'His Majesty graciously ennobled me last year. He too, has gained some benefit from my investment advice.'

'I do beg pardon, *m'lord*, I was not aware,' Jack returned with emphasis, his mind drifting away with thoughts of another Harcourt.

'Your son, Harcourt, which was his last ship? Perhaps I know of it,' asked Captain Berkeley, mulling over a list of officers he had been asked to consider employing by a variety of acquaintances, and failing to recall the name. 'I have spent a good deal of time in Portsmouth of late.'

'I forget what Russell tells me. It was an old guard ship as I recall. Possibly you might have occasion to help him, Captain Berkeley. I would be most obliged for any assistance. Would you know who has the disposition of officers for sea duty? I do believe he is in need of some time at sea. It would be of benefit to him.' Again, that barely concealed sigh.

The man has a problem with his son, thought Jack. *I wonder why and what it is?* He studied Harcourt's face for a time as Harcourt conversed with George Berkeley, then found himself talking to his hostess, Lady Berkeley, who had moved to speak with her brother-in-law, only to find him quite monopolised by Lord Harcourt.

'Captain Vizzard, is it not? I am so pleased you were able to attend our dinner. Your wife is an old friend from childhood, our fathers were quite well known in Gloucester and Mary will be a firm friend now we are grown.' Seeing Jack's concerned face scanning the Great Hall, she spoke to allay his worry. 'She is helping my mother with some minor domestic matter.' Her smile showed true warmth.

'It will likely involve your children, m'lady. When you are ready to dine, please send a servant to recall her, for she is apt to forget the passage of time when with children,' he laughed.

Lady Berkeley had taken particular care with her appearance for the occasion of the Christmas dinner. She was dressed in a full gown of cream ivory silk, the front panel of which was exquisitely embroidered, all of which supported an intelligent face from which deep blue eyes sparkled with the simple pleasure of social contact, possibly enhanced by her new status in society. Her fair hair was prepared in the fashionable manner with ringlets bordering her petite face, her hair and neck decorated with many fine diamonds. She smiled warmly at Jack.

'She is charming and shares my views on so many subjects, Jack. I may call you Jack, I hope? I feel I know you well already. She has grown to be a beautiful, amusing lady. Mary has told me of your adventures,' the countess lowered her voice, 'of her deportation to New Holland, and how you were reunited there. It was quite heart-warming, so full of romance. I felt a pang of jealousy as I listened to her account.'

Before Jack had chance to question that comment, her ladyship's footman announced the commencement of dinner, and slowly the three dozen or so guests filed into the Great Hall to take their places at the horseshoe-arrangement of tables. Jack gazed at the stained-glass windows along the north wall depicting various alliances of the Berkeley family, and the enormous fireplace at the head of the hall, whose dancing flames threw shadows around the expansive hall.

To their surprise, Jack and Mary found themselves seated at the head table with the Earl and Countess of Berkeley. George Berkeley was to Jack's left, and Mary was sitting next to the countess. Jack learned that the rather animated neighbour to his right was Dr Jenner, a physician born in the village and now practicing as a family doctor and surgeon. Catherine, his wife, sat on Mary's left. The tables were furnished with receptacles of exquisite porcelain and sparkling crystal, complemented by the gleaming Berkeley silverware reflecting the finest white Egyptian cotton covers that Jack ever seen. Each of the dozens of pieces laid out for the occasion were marked with the family's crest.

Jenner was talking of an academic paper he was preparing for discussion by colleagues at the Fleece Medical Society in Rodborough. His voice, tending to stridency, was beginning to dominate the table's conversation and irritate Jack, who found his attention to the discourse on cowpox-infected milkmaids and farmhands in the Severn Vale begin to wane. Meanwhile, the doctor's attractive wife was deeply involved in conversation with Mary. Overhearing their discussion, he learned she was originally from Kingscote Park and had met Jenner when the doctor had force-landed his hot air balloon in the grounds of her father's estate.

'These dinners can become quite tedious, do you not find, Vizzard?' George Berkeley spoke into Jack's ear. 'I know I do. Much rather be dining at sea with a mess full of like-minded fellows where one can sing and tell risqué tales and spill wine with no consequences. These country folks can be a narrow-minded lot. Take the good doctor on your right, for example. Sound chap he is, and looks after the family and the towns-folk right well, I hear. But he will go on about cowpox and milkmaids and how the blasted cuckoo is misunderstood and how we will all be flying in hot-air balloons and what not and the various experiments he is conducting. People fear his experiments will result in malformations, that we will start developing udders and suchlike.' He laughed loudly at his own wit.

His brother glared at him. 'What are you about, George? Another of your salty sailor's tales, I fancy. Not at my table with the ladies present, if you please.' Colonel Frederick Berkeley, the Fifth Earl, felt he that he was being ignored by his closest guests and decided it was time to put himself at the centre of conversation.

'Hah, Captain Vizzard,' he cried. Jack started at the mention of his name. 'It would appear our ladies knew each other in childhood. A happy coincidence, what?' The earl chortled and took a large slug of wine from a fine crystal goblet. 'Are you armed this evening, Captain?' he asked a little too loudly, creating the silence he wished. Noting the slightest inclination of Jack's head, he continued, 'I counsel you to be so and to stay alert on your homeward journey. There are rumours of a new highwayman at large on the Bristol Road.'

One of the ladies gasped audibly.

'I have always declared that anyone might without disgrace be overcome by superior numbers, but we should never surrender to a single highwayman.' He had their attention now, and paused to take another drink. 'As I was crossing Hounslow Heath one night, on my way from here to my house in London, my carriage was stopped by a man on horseback who put his head in at the window and said, "I believe you are Lord Berkeley?"

'"I am," said I. "And I believe you have always boasted that you would never surrender to a single highwayman?"

'"I confess that I have," said I.

'"Well," said the blackguard, presenting a pistol in my face, "I am a single highwayman, and I say, your money or your life!"'

Berkeley half sniggered before continuing. '"You cowardly dog," said I, "do you think I can't see your confederate skulking behind you?" The rascal, who was really quite alone, looked hurriedly around, and so I shot him through the head!'

The men who were in proximity laughed loudly. A women gasped and muttered a barely audible condemnation of the Earl's behaviour. Jack had become vaguely aware that there were very few ladies at the tables, other than Mary, the Countess, Mrs Jenner, and another whose name he did not know. He wondered why so many guests were not accompanied by their ladies.

'I thank your lordship for your counsel and, indeed, your wit,' he said. 'I trust that I will not be tested in a similar way this night.' He raised his own glass in salute to the Earl and smiled. 'However, should we have the misfortune to be so assaulted, I do assure your Lordship that I believe myself to be your equal as a marksman.'

'Ha-ha,' laughed the Earl. 'If you are seeking a duel or a tournament game, I will have to disappoint you, Captain Vizzard. I know you to be a marine, and your reputation is known to my younger brother George next to you. I am not so foolish to take the bait of a wager, although George might be willing to oblige.'

George Berkeley was shaking his head but smiling. He raised a glass in his brother's general direction, then proceeded to work through the third course of the evening's dinner, a particularly plump pair of roast ducks swimming in a sauce made from oranges and honey. George was very fond of duck, enjoying its darker, more flavoursome meat, and the sauce appealed to his sweet tooth.

As Jack casually surveyed the guests between forks of food, he noted a servant at the rear of the hall who had evidently been staring at him for some time, turning away just a second too slowly. Jack's gaze moved on, thinking little of it, his eyes moving in a slow arc much as if he was on the quarterdeck scanning the horizon for an enemy vessel.

'You are wondering why the Earl's guests include so few ladies, Captain Vizzard? His neighbour, Dr Jenner, interrupted his thoughts. 'I believe I read your puzzled expression. The answer is quite simple. Her Ladyship has few friends in the county,' he said quietly. 'It is sad in truth, as she is a fine, caring woman who has served the Earl and his interests very well. Indeed, she all but runs his estates, which, as you may be aware, are extensive. She has improved his lands to the family's benefit, and similarly improved the lot of many of his tenants.'

'It crossed my mind, doctor, that the fair sex is poorly represented this evening,' said Jack as diplomatically as he could.

'There is the making of a scandal there, I regret to say. It has been said he married her years ago, in secret, but questions are whispered as to why, if that is so, they married so publicly in Lambeth last year. I foresee a legitimacy dispute in the years ahead. The Earl and Countess have several children, but the eldest, William Fitzhardinge Berkeley, was born out of wedlock.' Noting Jack's raised eyebrows, he continued. 'You see what that means for the title, for the earldom? The boy may have a *moral* claim to the title, but the legality ... do you see, Captain? The House of Lords would simply not allow it. The boy will not inherit the earldom.'

Jack had no knowledge of the world of the aristocracy, neither did he wish to learn more, but he was surprised at the Doctor's assertion.

'It is not my place to comment on such private matters, Doctor, although my own wife was a little surprised to receive an invitation from the countess.' Jack looked at the ceiling to disguise his irritation at what he saw as tittle-tattle. 'Matters concerning the aristocracy are of little interest in my world.'

'But your own father was a baronet, was he not? I met him in Gloucester. Fine lawyer. He helped many people, and did exceedingly well in business. I am surprised you have not claimed the baronetcy for yourself. I met him again shortly before he passed on. He was proud that he had a title to hand down.'

Jack half choked on his wine. He stared at the doctor, wiping wine from his chin with a crisp napkin. 'What on earth do you mean, sir?' he said, softly.

'I am no herald of arms, Captain, but if I understood your father correctly, the baronetcy is hereditary. You should seek advice, Captain. You need to enquire of … what it is now? Ah, yes, I have it: the College of Arms. Hah, perhaps I should be addressing you next Christmas as *Sir* Jack Vizzard. Splendid, quite splendid.'

Sensing Jack's discomfort, Doctor Jenner changed the subject. 'You must see many wounds, Captain Vizzard? Have you been in many battles?' Jenner inclined his head in polite enquiry as he leaned back in his chair.

'Yes, Doctor. I cannot deny that I have seen some dreadful sights and … ah … have been responsible for some of those I have seen. It is my duty, after all, to dispose of the King's enemies.' He smiled slowly, but without humour, his mind spinning with the doctor's last comment. Could that happen to him, a humble marine? What should he do? Should he discuss the matter with Mary? No, not yet. The doctor was mistaken. *He must be*, thought Jack. Even if true, any title would pass to George as the eldest son. Unless George was, as he feared, already dead.

Doctor Jenner stared at him momentarily. He was a man dedicated to saving lives, looking at a soldier whose ultimate duty was to take lives in the name of the king. 'I studied surgery at Saint George's Hospital, you know,' he said at last, 'with the eminent John Hunter of Glasgow. I performed several amputations on some sailors, when one of His Majesty's boats berthed in London. The vessel was without a surgeon of its own, sadly.'

Jack spent a little time explaining to Dr Jenner that only line of battle ships would ordinarily have a warranted naval surgeon, and that smaller vessels were considered fortunate to have one. Often, the captain of third rates and smaller vessels would make do with a surgeon's mate or a pair of loblolly men, lacking the knowledge and skills to properly treat injuries or disease.

So engrossed were they in their conversation that guests were starting to leave before they realised the table was clearing. Mary looked pointedly at Jack and stifled a yawn, her clear signal that she wished to return home and that he was to have no more wine. Having taken their leave of fellow guests, they expressed their appreciation to the hosts, bade a farewell to George Berkeley, and instructed a footman to summon their brougham. The footman disappeared into the courtyard, and a few moments later their coachman pulled up in front of the entrance. Jack's mind now flashed back to the footman and the man's hard stare. That and Doctor Jenner's comments about his father. He had very mixed emotions swirling around his mind as he helped Mary into the carriage.

The night had grown colder and Jack shivered as the chill air quickly stripped the warmth from his face before finding its way to his lungs. A sharp hoar frost had formed; frozen puddles in the rutted road from Berkeley across the heath to Dursley sparkled in the bright moonlight. They made steady progress and turned north onto the Gloucester Road. After a mile or more, the road turned right onto the Dursley Road; the coach's pace slowed to a crawl up Tait's Hill, the horses snorting with the effort required. As they turned a dark bend in the road, a sharp voice called out, 'Halt there, I say. Stand fast, coachman, and hold your ground.'

Mary looked alarmed. Jack grasped the pistol from its hiding place beneath the seat and concealed it beneath his heavy boat cloak, his hand clasping it firmly against his chest.

'Captain Vizzard. Get out if you will, smartly now,' the voice growled.

Jack gripped Mary's hand, offering silent reassurance. He swung open the door, stepped onto the frosted mud and stared at the silhouette on the horse. 'Who are you and what do you want with me?' He spoke quietly but with real menace in his voice, taking a step forward.

'Stand still, Vizzard; do not move, or I will shoot you,' came the command. 'Why, Mister Vizzard, a pleasure to meet you at last. I have spent much time searching for you, and now I have you. As to my identity, you need not know that. And what I want—I would have thought that to be obvious. I'll take your purse and Mrs Vizzard's jewelery. None of your tricks if you want your pretty wife to keep her good looks.'

At that Jack bristled and was preparing to leap at the figure, when he saw the pistol in the man's left hand.

'Quite obviously, you dog, you know who I am. If you intend to shoot me, I believe I have a right to know who you are.' Jack risked a glance to the interior of the coach and was surprised to see that Mary was not in sight. The horses snorted steam from flared nostrils and stamped their hooves. He wondered where the hell she had gone.

'You don't know me, Vizzard. Perhaps I should simply kill you, with anonymity, then I could take my pleasure of your lovely lady.' He coughed. 'However, I should let you know why I am going to kill you and make it a slow and painful death, for you do not deserve to die quickly.' He paused to emphasise his threat. 'You knew my father. He was your superior officer, Captain Vizzard. I have been waiting a long time for this meeting. Do you still not know me? I should show my face.' The coughing restarted, but this time there was a noise behind one of the horses and the sound of the coachman's whip, whistling through the air with a loud crack, diverted the man's attention for just a moment.

It was enough. Jack pulled the pistol from beneath his cloak and in a swift movement fired upward, the ball striking the man's left shoulder with sufficient force to dislodge him from the saddle as his horse reared, throwing the man off its back. The highwayman fell heavily on his back, his pistol discharging itself harmlessly into the night sky, causing his horse to bolt. His fall broke the already damaged shoulder bone; blood oozed slowly onto the frozen ground. Opening pain-filled eyes, he saw the tip of Jack's sword hovering and circling above his heart.

'I will know your name now, you bastard.' The point closed on the man's bloody chest. 'Or, if you wish to die without confessing your name, I am happy to oblige.'

'No, Jack. Do not kill him, please.' Mary appeared from behind the brougham with the coachman's whip in her hands. 'He cannot harm us now. Let us take him back to Berkeley. Dr Jenner can assist him, and the earl has a dungeon where he can rot.' She was breathing hard from the fear that turns warm blood to iced water.

'My name,' the man hissed, 'is Squires. Arthur Squires.' His breathing was slow and laboured, and his words spilled out in painful gasps. He lowered the mask with his good arm. 'I see you recognise the name. As you should, for it was you who killed my father. Killed him, probably with that sword. My mother died of a broken heart.'

In a moment, Jack's mind went back in time to a cold, windblown beach in northern France, where Major Squires, his superior officer, revealed himself to be a traitor to England and to the Corps of Marines. Squires had gone on to kill Jack's friend, Giles, his special friend from boyhood who had thrown himself into the path of the pistol ball that Squires fired at Jack.

The memory stung, and Jack raised his sword as if to thrust it into the man's chest. 'Your father was a traitor to his country. He betrayed the King, the Corps, and England. He was also a murderer; he was responsible for the deaths of many fine men. He murdered my closest friend. In short, your father was scum of the lowest kind. Had I not killed him, he would have hanged at Tyburn as befits a common criminal and a traitor. I rather fancy that once the good Dr Jenner has repaired your wounds, it is to Tyburn you will go as a common highwayman. Alternatively, I could hang you myself for the attack tonight, and the fear and distress you have caused my lady wife. I doubt you would be missed by anyone.'

The coachman, fearing he was to be a participant or a witness to a lynching, now jumped down from his seat and suggested he and Jack put the man in the seat next to him and tie him down with some rope. Jack found a length of cord in the storage box, and with the coachman's help they raised the cursing, groaning man into the seat and tied him to the frame. As he tightened the rope, Jack had a thought.

'Answer me this, you turd. How did you know where to find me? What is your connection with Berkeley?'

'I knew your residence was near Stroud. Some discrete questions led me to Gloucester and a bootmaker, who confirmed that you were attending a reception at Berkeley.' He coughed, and his face contorted in pain. 'Some coins to a loose tongue in the village found me a footman at the castle; a few more and he alerted me when you would be leaving.' He leaned his head back and swore. 'I left the castle moments before you. I knew you would make your way up Tait's Hill, where your carriage would have to slow. I should have shot you immediately, but you had to know why, damn it.'

With Squires firmly secured next to the coachman and safely back in the carriage, Jack turned to Mary and said, 'That was very brave of you, my love, to take the whip and distract the blackguard. He might have shot back at you.' Jack placed his arm around her.

'I hoped to make his horse rear up, but it made him look away from you. I knew you had a pistol at the ready, and prayed you would shoot him. I was never so frightened ...' her voice tailed off, thinking of the night at the Vicarage, all those years ago. Her shoulders shuddered at the memory.

It was quite late when they pulled into the castle courtyard once more. A sleepy servant was sent to fetch Dr Jenner. Jack learned that the Earl and Countess had retired for the night, so another servant was sent to find the town watchman to take Squires to the town lockup. Jack agreed to return and assist in transporting Squires to the magistrate's court. He wished to prosecute the man himself, but decided it would be better to engage another attorney to do so.

'Mr Vizzard,' said Dr Jenner, 'I fear the Earl's servants are ill-prepared to accommodate you and your lady this night. Given the late hour, may I offer you both the hospitality of my home? It is but a very short walk from here.'

'We would be delighted, Doctor. I was, I confess, not enthusiastic at the prospect of the long journey home to Woodchester.'

They walked the short distance to The Chantry, Jenner's home, adjacent to the village church, passing the rustic hut at the end his garden where, as Jenner explained, he used to treat the poorer citizens of the Berkeley vale. As they walked, he talked of the experiments he was conducting with cow pox. Jack was glad of the darkness to hide his rolling eyes. 'I call my hut the Temple of Vaccinia. The Reverend Ferryman built it for me with logs. I shall show it to you in the morning, if you would like to see it, Captain Vizzard?'

Jack muttered an appropriate word or two and was grateful they had reached the entrance to the house, bringing any further discussion of experiments on milkmaids and farm labourers to a halt. He was tired; tired of wearing his full-dress uniform, tired of listening to the doctor, tired from an excess of wine and the excellent port Lord Berkeley had shared, but mostly his body was reacting to the threat posed by Squires' son. He had escaped death again and, Christ on the cross, the man had threatened to violate Mary. It brought the past immediately into the present, along with all the hate of that dark night before he left Woodchester and set out on his journey with the Corps of Marines.

Jenner's wife, Catherine, having been disturbed too, was waiting in the expansive hallway with lamps and mugs of hot chocolate their maid had heated for the guests.

'It's very kind of you, Catherine,' said Mary. 'What a day this has been.'

3
Portsmouth

The Christmas season over, Jack returned to Portsmouth, a long and tiring journey along frozen, rough roads. He spent three days in barracks at a desk, wrapped in a heavy woollen cloak in a dark room with ice forming patterns on the interior of the windows, writing mind-numbing returns of stores and supplies and drafting reports for the colonel's approval before dispatching them to the Admiralty.

He was in a black mood, the cause not melancholia, nor even anxiety about his family, but the tedium of duty as adjutant. The colonel had discovered, during a casual conversation with another subaltern, something of Jack's personal history. Colonel Souter decided that an Oxford graduate in jurisprudence, and son of a successful lawyer, would be an eminently suitable candidate for the post of adjutant, recently vacated due to the premature death from influenza of the previous incumbent. Jack loathed the work. He had joined the Marines to get away from such tedium.

The work of the adjutant had increased, too. Following the execution of Louis XVI some three years previously, an

Order in Council required the Corps to raise another thirty companies. Portsmouth now had thirty-five of the one hundred companies forming the Corps. Jack's own company had increased its establishment. He commanded two first lieutenants, two second lieutenants, five sergeants and five corporals, four drummer boys and eighty privates. His officers were adequate, but no more than that. He was satisfied with the sergeants who had benefited from Joe Packer's training and influence.

He started suddenly, and stopped thumbing through the pile of correspondence. Before him, in a precise, copperplate hand, he read an order naming him. A broad smile spread, all but cracking his face as the sun melts frosted grass, and a light appeared in his eyes, reflecting the lambent candle on his desk. In the way that one's own name always catches the eye, so he noticed the order, signed by Evan Nepean, First Secretary. Addressed to Colonel Souter, Commandant of the Marine Division at Portsmouth, the order confirmed Vizzard's appointment to the Mediterranean Fleet under the command of Sir John Jervis. His orders were to take his company to join one of the ships sailing to reinforce Jervis, whom Jack guessed to be blockading Cadiz following the recent alliance between France and Spain against Britain.

'Packer! Sergeant Major Packer!' he bellowed, 'Get your drunken arse in here! Now, if you'll be so kind,' Vizzard added with friendly, mock sarcasm.

'Yes, Captain Vizzard, sir. I am right 'ere at your service, sir.' Packer stamped to attention in front of Vizzard's battered mahogany desk, throwing an exaggerated salute and a toothy grin. 'And 'ow may I be of service to you, this freezin' mornin'?'

Jack looked up at Packer with something approaching affection. He owed his life to the tough sergeant, and his sergeant owed him a similar debt. The two men shared a bond their difference in rank and background could not break. They had shared the privations of Sydney Town; fought the French ashore in Brest and on the sea; and fought to the point of exhaustion when *Brunswick* battered *Vengeur du Peuple* to a sinking hulk back in '94, a bloody battle that had cost Vizzard's detachment of marines a heavy price.

'The company has received orders, Joe,' he muttered in a low voice. 'Keep quiet, though, even Colonel Souter has yet to hear of it. We are to reinforce Sir John Jervis in the blockade of Cadiz. What say you to that, eh?'

Joe Packer pulled up a chair and sat. 'No great surprise, and it's about time, sir. That's what I say. You were never one for garrison duty, and you've had a face as long as a wet week in Wales ever since your leave, sir. Not that I have been to Wales. When do we take ship?'

Jack read again the perfectly formed words of the Secretary to the Admiralty Board.

'A matter of weeks only, Joe. We are to be distributed aboard a squadron of vessels fitting out in Deptford.'

Sergeant Packer moved to the window as the morning's thin cold light crawled through the glistening panes, bringing form to his lined face. 'Very good, sir. Between you and me then it is. The men will be 'appy at the news, even if it does mean losing out on their allowances. Wot wiv the deductions for uniform, clothes, the Chatham Chest and wot not, the tuppence farthing a day mounts up. Their Lordships must do something about the lads' pay and deductions, sir, in my 'umble opinion.' In fact, Packer anticipated a moan or two from the company. Times had been very hard for everyone since the food price crisis of '95. The men would often have a grumble about their pay and the deductions made from their pay. Packer sighed and changed the subject.

'Will you be takin' leave of duty and seein' the family, Mister Vizzard?'

Jack rose from the chair, pushing it back and glancing at the piles of paper littering the desk. He stretched his arms and yawned. 'I fear not, Joe. There is no time, and I cannot see the Corps granting further leave so soon after my Christmas absence. I shall write once I've spoken with Colonel Souter.'

"Ave you had word from 'ome, sir? Are the young 'uns well?'

'Nothing this last week.' He smiled. 'And you know the frequency with which Mrs Vizzard corresponds.'

The sergeant grinned. 'You 'ave more letters than the colonel, sir,' he grunted. 'We all knows that. Now me, Mister Vizzard, I ain't got no one to write to and none to write to me, neither.' He sighed. 'You're a lucky man, sir.'

Packer had known Mary Vizzard in Sydney Town, but had met her only once since the detachment returned from New South Wales, where she she turned heads amongst the convicts, civilians, and the military alike. The tough sergeant sighed audibly. He was married, but only to the Corps. The Marines had taken him in as a youngster and made him into a man; a hard, efficient fighting man respected by his men and the officers above him.

'Yes, Joe, I am very aware of my good fortune.' Jack clapped his friend on the shoulder. 'Who knows, Joe, there may be a woman just around the corner, waiting to take you on.'

'Not for me, sir,' he replied. 'There ain't such a woman born would take a shine to me, 'cepting a Portsmouth doxy. But I ain't unhappy, Mister Vizzard. Now, best you report to Colonel Souter and let him know what's afoot, sir.'

'You're right, Sar'nt Packer. The bugger had better not object or try to block this. I fancy we are too cold sitting here in barracks and could all do with some Spanish sun and wine!'

He stamped his way out of the building, to the sound of Packer chuckling at the best news the company had received in months.

* * * * *

'Well, Vizzard,' rumbled Colonel Souter, 'if my Lords of Admiralty so command, who am I to object? Jervis is a fine admiral. If anyone can bring the French to battle and defeat them, it is he.'

Souter received the news with equanimity. His function was to deploy his marines wherever so ordered by The Admiralty. But he did, occasionally, wish for a major campaign requiring the entire division, which he commanded. *Perhaps it will come with this present war,* he thought.

'So I am to await further orders concerning the ships to be despatched,' he muttered. 'Wonder what they have found to bring into commission.' Souter shuffled some papers on his desk, searching for a letter of some relevance he thought was there. Failing to find it, he continued. 'Well, you are a favoured man, Jack. There are many officers who would want to take your place. Nepean appears to have requested your company specifically.'

Jack had called on the Admiralty last year. He'd met Evan Nepean at the request of Earl Howe, who had spoken of Vizzard during a dinner when he and others had been discussing the deteriorating situation in the Mediterranean.

Nepean had taken an interest in Vizzard as far back as '94, when he became Secretary to the Board of Admiralty following Howe's victory against the French, although Jack never knew it. Nepean not only advised the government and its ministers on Naval policy, but also, sometimes, implemented their policies, even before ministers had decided what those policies should be.

'Sir, you know me as one not to seek favour or interest. I cannot deny I am pleased to have been selected for service, and my men will be happy to get away from garrison duty, I have no doubt.'

'You will be free of garrison duty for a very long time, Jack,' said Souter. 'The situation has become more serious than the country or the government is willing to acknowledge; with the Dons now allied with the Frogs, Admiral Jervis will be outnumbered and outgunned when he does encounter them. Our resources are still limited.' The colonel paused as he watched Vizzard's face for any response. 'If, or when, there is an engagement between the fleets, Jack, it will be a bloody battle. I believe it is a large fleet they have.'

'And an important battle at that, sir,' Jack answered, 'for they will have a fleet to bring an army to our coast; one we would be unable to match. The country needs time to increase the fleet and prepare our defences against an invasion. Such a thing cannot be allowed to happen, sir.'

'Hah, I have it now,' said Colonel Souter, flourishing the letter. 'Seems Captain Moore is to be detached from Strachan's squadron. He and a Captain Peyton in *Minerve* are to escort three Indiamen as far as Gibraltar. You will go with them, Jack. There you will receive fresh orders from Admiral Jervis. Moore is thought well of at the Admiralty, I am told.'

'A fine officer, sir. It will be good to sail with him again,' Jack replied. 'Exceedingly keen for prize money; I hear he wishes to acquire capital with which to support a wife, but he has declined to identify the lady in question.' Jack grinned.

'Well, Jack, not all have a manor sitting on half of Gloucestershire. As for the lady, that is none of our business.'

Jack's grin slipped. 'I am a fortunate man; I acknowledge it, sir. And I have benefited from his success, too.'

'Your good fortune may continue then, as I have little doubt that he will distinguish himself and his ship yet further,' Souter said drily. 'Be that as it may, Jack, I have other news affecting you.' He smiled at Jack's surprised expression. 'In view of your recent promotion, and especially now given your forthcoming deployment, I judged it appropriate to assign another officer to your band of vandals! A young gentleman from Bedfordshire, of all places. Always thought of that county as a trifle dull myself, but not too distant from London....' Souter plucked another letter from the pile on his desk. 'Here it is, I have it, one Lieutenant Martin Hale. I understand his father to be a senior official at Chatham. The youngster comes to us with a commendable reference as '*one with much promise'*. I'll have him report to you on his arrival.'

* * * * *

Three days later, the freeze having thawed, during a rowdy bayonet-practice period in a wet and muddy field adjacent to the barracks, a smartly dressed young officer, accompanied by a sergeant, approached Packer and spoke sharply. 'You there, Sergeant. I am Lieutenant Hale and am told I may find Captain Vizzard here. I see no officer supervising you, however.' He spoke airily, looking about for a fellow officer. 'I'd be obliged if you would come to attention when addressed by an officer,' he snapped. The subaltern glared at the NCO, then grinned at his companion, the sergeant, whose arms displayed new golden stripes.

Sergeant Packer stretched to his full height. He glared at the youth, took in the newly acquired dress uniform, noting that it must have left its tailor within the last few days, as indeed it had, and, still not blinking, called out, 'Mister Vizzard, there's some toff-looking bugger for you, ... sir,' he added, following a deliberate pause.

The young man flushed, looked about him, but saw only a group of dishevelled marines in a heap on the grass. One separated from the heap, wiped the mud from his sweat-stained, mud-streaked shirt, and strode toward him.

'Good morning, Lieutenant. I am Captain Vizzard. You are to join us, I understand.' Jack pulled on his uniform coat. 'Then you must learn one thing before all others; Company Sergeant Major Packer here,' he nodded towards the NCO, 'is the finest marine in the Corps, bar none, and you will, at all times, treat him with respect. Then you may, in time, earn *his* respect'. Nodding towards the second man, he asked, 'Who is this?'

The young lieutenant came to attention and saluted. 'I understand, sir,' Hale replied, his jaws flexing. 'This is Sergeant Docherty, sir. Patrick Docherty. He was persuaded to accompany me on transfer to Portsmouth.'

'I doubt you do, Mr Hale, but in time you may. Welcome, Sarn't Docherty. Please join Sergeant Major Packer over there,' Jack said, while holding his gaze on Hale. The young man in front of him was tall, fair haired, with an intelligent oval face from which gazed a pair of sparkling, bright blue eyes. Jack saw how he stood confidently, unintimidated to be facing his commanding officer for the first time. 'You may have heard from Colonel Souter that I am, shall we say, unorthodox?' Hale had heard this from various sources, and he nodded confirmation. 'My men can drill as perfectly as the rest of the division, Mr Hale, but they fight dirty, with extreme violence, an array of weapons, and with more initiative and guts than other companies. They will expect you to do so, too; and to lead them, not push them from behind. Do you understand me?'

'Yes, sir. I intended no offence to the sergeant major; I assure you.' He nodded in the direction of Packer. 'Sir, you should know I sought a transfer to Portsmouth; your name is spoken of in Chatham and at the Admiralty. My father is held in some esteem by the First Lord, and, well, my Lord Spencer and the Permanent Secretary arranged matters so that I should be placed under your command, sir.' Hale shifted his feet, embarrassed at the confession and the admission of using influence.

'Did he, indeed?' said Jack, looking afresh at the young man before him. 'Then we had both better make the most of the opportunity, had we not? Welcome to the company, Mister Hale. Work hard, learn quickly, do as I say, and all will be well.' Jack spoke firmly because he meant every word. The young subaltern held his gaze, revealing just a hint of defiance.

'Aye, sir. I trust you'll find little to complain of, sir.'

'I trust, Mister Hale, I find *nothing* to complain of. My men are the best in the Corps, and if you are to lead them in battle you must be better than they. We have no time for training you in all my methods or ideas of using infantry when fighting ashore, but I will see your shooting,' Jack continued and, turning to his friend, 'Sergeant Packer, set up a pair of targets if you will, at, say, seventy paces, and have Jamie prepare a couple of muskets. I wish to see how well our new subaltern can fire. But let's make it an interesting exercise.' He smiled, enjoying the challenge he was about to set. 'Let us shoot from over there,' he said, and pointed at a mound surrounded by muddy water through which the remainder of his troop slipped and slid towards patches of drier ground. 'And you men throw mud at us.'

Dirt-stained faces broke into grins with a ripple of laughter, quickly silenced by a look and a growl from Sergeant Packer.

Within four minutes, a marine, Jamie Hay, approached bearing two muskets and cartridge pouches. 'Your weapons, sirs,' he said with a straight face, 'each as fine an instrument as the Corps can provide, sirs.'

'Very well, Mister Hale. This is what I call my mad minute. Four shots in less than sixty seconds. If you manage four, I shall pay your mess bill for the month. If I manage four, you pay my bill. The line regiments regularly manage that, and some of my best men can fire five balls a minute, but you and I will not attempt that today. I am more interested in accuracy and a cool demeanour under distracting circumstances. Do we have a wager?' Without waiting for an answer, he continued. 'Now, let us see just how poor you are.'

Jack picked up the cartridge pouch and strode onto the mound, oblivious to the mud, planted his boots and squinted at the target seventy paces away. Hale, less confident, squelched into position to Jack's left, emulating a stance like that of Jack's as best he could.

'Mister Packer, you will act as timekeeper, please,' shouted Jack. 'And Corporal Clutterbuck, use my telescope to call out the strikes, if you would.'

The non-commissioned officers grinned and, in concert, called out agreement, taking up positions behind and upwind of the two officers.

Vizzard steadied his weapon. 'You may call when ready, Sergeant Packer,' he shouted.

'You must fire a minimum of four shots. Each man to fire at will and each shot must hit the target to count,' intoned Packer. He knew Vizzard could out-shoot any man in the division, had not been defeated in swordplay that Packer had heard of, and could run faster than any man he had seen in his life. 'Make ready!' he bellowed.

Jack pulled the lock fully back and studied the flint. Satisfied, the weapon was grounded, cartridge end bitten off, powder poured down the barrel and the paper and ball rammed into position. To his side, Hale imitated Vizzard. Jack grunted in appreciation. 'Not a complete stranger to the weapon, I'm pleased to see,' he said.

'Take aim!' bellowed Packer.

Weapons rose rapidly to waiting shoulders, eyes squinted along cold barrels.

'Fire!'

Smoke and flame spurted from muzzles, startling some seagulls. Packer's eyes narrowed, and Corporal Clutterbuck lowered the telescope and marked a piece of paper with the stub of a pencil, lightly chewed at the end. Several men shouted and threw clods of mud at their officers with undisguised enthusiasm.

Jack moved with inspiring speed and had his weapon up to his shoulder for the second shot as Lieutenant Hale's rod started to ram the charge home. Once more the crack of firing crashed across the field, and smoke blew into the officers' faces. Mud splattered Hale's face with a sting and his eyes blazed. He stole a second to glance at his new commanding officer, who was oblivious to the mud flying around his head and splattering his uniform. Clutterbuck lowered the telescope and again pencilled marks on his paper.

Hale was faster with his third shot, firing nearly simultaneously with Vizzard. He grounded the stock to reload. A heavy lump of mud and stone struck his left cheek, hard. Distracted, he loosened his grip on the musket, which slipped from his hand and fell to earth. Jack, oblivious to the error, rammed home his fourth ball and swiftly fired. 'Shit and corruption,' he cursed, knowing he had rushed it and the ball was low on the target.

'Fifty-seven seconds,' bellowed Sergeant Packer. 'Mister Vizzard wins.' Hale had recovered and managed his fourth, but a good five seconds later.

'Good work, Mister Hale. You would benefit from some practice, but all in all a very fair and creditable demonstration of your ability. Welcome to the company. I suspect you and I will get along very well.'

'Thank you, sir,' Hale replied, breathing hard. 'I might have bested you had I not dropped that damned thing! But a wager is a wager, and I shall honour the debt. Now, may I request permission to share a glass or two with you? Once we are refreshed and changed, that is.'

'Sir, sir,' called Tom Clutterbuck, the youngster in the company, as the officers started to leave. 'Doncha wanna know how good the shooting was?' he asked, running up waving his piece of paper.

'Ah, yes indeed, Tom, thank you,' said Jack, 'I was forgetting.'

Young Tom gulped some air. 'You hit the bull three out of your four shots, sir,' he blurted 'and one left outer.' He grinned. 'And Mister Hale here,' he grinned with a nod, 'well he hit three bulls and one inner, sirs!' Tom hopped from one foot to the other in his excitement. No other officer had done as well to his knowledge, and he saw how surprised the men in his section were at the news. 'That's bloody good shooting, Mister Hale!' he concluded.

Jack roared with laughter. 'Hah, Martin,' he said, 'shared honours then. If you agree, I release you from the wager!'

'You are very efficient with the musket, sir,' said Hale. 'I must admit that.'

'The advantage of practice, Mister Hale. Practice, practice, and yet more practice. With muskets, swords, knives, pikes; in fact, any weapon and with no weapons. I have the men fight with themselves—but never when the buggers have been drinking. I'll not have that.'

'No, sir, I would hope not,' Hale grinned.

'Your job, Mister Hale, is to lead your platoon. The men will accept you if you behave like an officer. That is, to behave as an officer should, by taking the lead from their front, standing up for your men, showing them how to fight, and, if necessary,' Jack paused to emphasise his belief, 'how to die.'

'That, sir, is a sobering sentiment. I sincerely hope I don't have to do that. However, I will show them how I intend to lead them and help them survive a fight.'

'My hope, Mister Hale, is that they soon will have a battle to fight. That is what these men need; they are becoming a little stale.'

They walked from the field, leaving Sergeants Packer and Docherty to bring the men back to barracks.

* * * * *

Wispy smoke issued from the log fire in the mess, projecting dancing shadows on the walls as servants hurried about the gloomy room clearing tables and carrying bottles and glasses. The two officers, legs stretched towards the crackling fire, exchanged details of their histories.

'I never truly grasped the Greek or Latin, sir,' said Hale, in response to some comment of his superior. 'My interests leaned to mathematics and matters more scientifical.'

'But at the King's School!' exclaimed Jack. 'Hah! I also attended the King's School, only that at Gloucester.' Jack drained the contents of his glass and continued. 'Now, Hale, tell me true; why the Portsmouth division and not, say, Plymouth? From there you might find yourself in America or the West Indies.'

'The truth of the matter is as I said this afternoon. Your action against *Le Vengeur* is still remarked upon by senior officers in Chatham. If I am to see action against the French, I reasoned I should be with a company that has a reputation such as yours. And there is a rumour that your company has been selected for a very particular purpose, sir. More than a rumour, if the truth be told,' he added quietly, eyes levelled at Jack's. 'I heard it from Nepean directly.'

Jack's eyebrows rose perceptibly. So, he knew. Clearly there was more to Hale's transfer than mere youthful zeal. He must have influential friends. That or Admiralty orders were being carelessly disseminated.

'We are to join the fleet under Jervis, once the required vessels have been made ready, but within the week we will be deployed to *Melampus*. I sailed with Captain Moore until she returned for refitting before Christmas. He's a fine officer and a sensible commander, not one to rush into danger without evaluating the risks to his ship and his men. That said, the man is keen on prize money, so there is certain to be some action. We would be wise to prepare accordingly. I'm receptive to any ideas you may have, Hale.'

Lieutenant Hale spoke to the fire, wringing his hands. 'You mentioned the Greek wars earlier, sir, and I confessed my failure to grasp the fundamentals of their language. However, one aspect of their civilisation I did take an interest in was that of the Spartans.' He glanced toward Jack as if to gauge his reaction. 'They took boys as young as six or seven and trained them in the martial arts until they became warriors. Their leaders instructed and trained them to become healthy and athletic for the wars the Spartans had to fight.'

'You will find, Mr Hale, that my men are healthy beyond the normal requirements of the Corps,' Jack said flatly, 'but you are at liberty to try some ideas of your own. Bear in mind we will be at sea in a week.'

'Yes, sir, I know that,' said Hale in a voice now partly affected by wine, as his words slowed and became a little slurred. 'What I have in mind can be undertaken at sea, almost anywhere, in fact. We will not require a great deal of space.'

Jack stood, tugged on his right ear, and yawned, the fatigue of the day taking effect. 'Very well, Hale. Have the men parade in the morning, then we will proceed with your ideas. I hear tattoo has sounded, so for now I will bid you a good night.'

* * * * *

Overnight the air had become warmed, but the sun failed to make an appearance. Instead, Portsmouth citizens tramped through sheets of rain and sleet driven by a strong sou'wester. Those few taking an interest in the activities of the marine garrison observed fifty or more men of Jack's parade company marching at seventy-five paces to the minute along Southsea Common in old and worn uniforms, carrying full, and evidently very heavy, knapsacks.

Hale proceeded to exercise the company in a variety of ways: singly, in pairs, in groups of four and all together. He had them running, squatting, jumping, crawling, and wrestling until their bodies steamed and faces turned red with exertion. He rested them and repeated several exercises. Throughout, Lieutenant Hale was a participant; slowly, grudgingly, the marines stopped cursing him inwardly and became more determined to keep to the pace he set.

Sergeant Major Packer swore quietly. His heart was pounding, as was his head. Joe Packer took pride in honing his fighting skills; he practiced daily with a musket, keeping his weapon clean and in the best condition possible. He threw tomahawks and knives at a target until he could hit the bullseye with every throw. However, his method of killing enemies did not include running, squatting, or wrestling. He thought Lieutenant Hale's drills to be a waste of his time.

Jack, bent double, hands resting on his knees and panting, slowly raised his head towards his subaltern, 'My God, Hale, that was demanding work!' Rain streamed down his face, and he was ready to bring the exercise to a conclusion.

Hale, breathing heavily, gazed at the sea and at an inbound 74, heeling in the wind. 'Sir, that was merely a preliminary; I wish to repeat this every day. The battalion's weekly field exercise is of value to the requirements of drill, but your company, may I say, are unlikely to benefit from such exercises.'

'You may say so, Mr Hale, as I find I am in agreement with you. My Vandals can do all that the regular companies can, but I prefer they fight with a certain cool-headedness and willingness to endure more than their fellows.' He straightened his back, his tired muscles protesting after the weeks of sedentary duty in the Field Adjutant's office. 'You have done well, but I think it time to get the men back for their dinner. They have earned it this day.'

CHAPTER 4
Harcourt

Sergeant Joe Packer spent his leave of absence in Portsmouth. His orders restricted him to the town, and he had no wish to travel to his old home, a small village in Essex; there was nobody he wished to see, nobody there who wished to see him. He was not minded to waste the little money he had on futile and unnecessary travel. Neither was he willing to waste the time involved. If the news sheets were to be believed, the country was half-starved, the last harvest having been so poor. The roads were cluttered with people moving in search of food or employment, usually both. Footpads and highwaymen preyed on lone travellers, or families, or anyone that might have anything of any value.

Instead, Packer became an explorer. He explored most of the taverns in Portsmouth Town and in several of the closer surrounding villages. He also explored several willing ladies of the town. Too long away from ship duty, he turned restless and irritable. Then, to make matters worse, he got seconded to assist the despised Impress Service, which needed to find men for the fleet. Packer was given a gang of tough sailors, a bag of coin, and instructions not to return to the rendezvous without the required number of men.

'None of your useless landsmen, Packer,' the lieutenant had commanded. 'Bring me some prime seamen or I'll have you on report!'

The young bastard got away with nothing more disrespectful than a scowl from Packer, who was not about to lose his stripes to a snotty toff, newly commissioned. Packer recognised the freshness of the face and the gilt of the glistening single epaulette: neither had seen much salt air. It would have been easy to knock the bugger on the head. The consequences would not justify the satisfaction, however, so Packer swallowed his pride and wished Jack Vizzard were present. Captain Vizzard would not have agreed to the secondment of his senior NCO.

Packer hated the work; he loathed the need for the service, despised what he was forced to do, and preferred any other duty to the shameful work of dragging a man away from his wife and family. Portsmouth was a Navy town, but good, experienced seamen kept away from the port and waterfront. The law allowed only sea-going men to be pressed, though some officers either ignored that or turned a blind eye, willing to bend the rules simply to acquire much needed men for the Navy. The new lieutenant was being a stickler for the rules, which Packer might have respected if the bastard weren't such an officious prick.

By a stroke of luck, the next morning Packer spotted and seized just such a man as the Navy wanted. The minor detail that the man was unwilling was irrelevant.

'You have no right to press a person of my distinction!' protested the man as he was pounced upon by the gang.

'Lor' love yer! That's the wery reason we're a-pressin' of your worship,' retorted the grinning gunner's mate of the press gang. 'We've such a set of blackguards aboard the tender yonder, we wants a toff like you to learn 'em some manners.' He laughed as he tied the man's hands.

The smartly dressed man had attempted to conceal his background with a show of wealth, perhaps with the benefit of prize money. But Packer had seen the hands; fresh soap had not removed the tar from his fingers. Furthermore, the cove walked like a seaman, and when taken, the affectation in his voice fell away and the language of the foc's'le returned in abundance. A slap about the ear from the gunner's mate and the man fell into a quiet sulkiness.

Packer chewed the inside of his cheek. Here was an able-bodied seaman; just what the Navy needed. But he was being dragged back to ship duty just when he'd made a new life for himself on land. Vividly, Packer wished that all the clerks who worked their safe little tasks at the admiralty could be assigned to ships, with himself as their sergeant.

He felt degraded, and yes, he admitted to feeling degraded. Pressing was like being a buggerer and a highwayman at the same time.

That evening, he shared a couple of pots of ale with a naval quarter-gunner, name of Clayton, a member of Joe's gang. The two had struck up a conversation during the day's patrolling, and over a couple of ales and a couple of tales they quickly become mates. They understood each other, the tough marine NCO and the equally tough, cheerful sailor.

Some good-natured exchanges of insults secured the friend-ship—that and a couple more pots of ale.

It was Tim Clayton who described an incident which served to illustrate the hazards of pressgang work.

'It were up in Chester, Joe, three years back. I was with Lieutenant Oakes, now deceased, sadly, and we'd had the devil of a job finding a rendezvous.' Clayton ordered another pair of ales from the serving girl, throwing a meaningful wink in her direction. 'We could find no landlord with the balls to allow us to hang out the flag; they were all as hostile as a 74 full of Frogs. Anyhows, we persuaded one to open the doors to us and we set to, knowing the townfolk were of a mind to cause trouble. They didn't want to lose their men, you see? There was a dozen of us, but we were no match for the hundreds that descended on the inn that evening.' He downed a large measure and continued.

'Hundreds of 'em, Joe, and a good many of them women. We barricaded the door and kept 'em out for nigh on a couple of hours; we reckoned they would murder us all if'n they got in. A couple of the lads went down from stones and rocks thrown through the winders. Eventually the door gave way, and in the bastards swarmed. It was a right battle, I can tell you. They beat us and threw us out into the street more dead than alive. The inn, well it was stripped bare, and I means bare. Not a stick of furniture was left, and the barrels all but emptied. 'Twas only the timely arrival some mounted militia troops that saved us.'

'It's hard and ugly work, Tim,' said Packer, 'that's the truth. I'd rather be at sea fighting the Frogs than hauling men off the streets. Half of what we take are no good and get sent 'ome again. It stinks, Tim, and the sooner Mister Vizzard gets back here and gets me off this duty the better I'll like it.'

'You ain't wrong, Joe. I wants a ship again. Word out there is that a squadron is being put together to join Jervis in the Med. Mebbe I can get a berth. Argh, I needs a piss, mate. Don't yous drink my ale!'

Clayton rose and swayed his way through the warm smoky noise of the taproom to the cobbled street at the back of the inn and stumbled into a dark corner. The stream of urine was steaming in the cold air as he steadied his aim away from his boots, when a nailed boot scratched on the stones behind him. He spun round. 'What the—'

His words were cut short as a belaying pin cracked on his temple and he fell.

The shadowy figure bent to rummage through his short jacket.

'Oi, you!' a voice shouted. 'Stand away this instant, you bastard ,or I'll shoot you where you stand.'

The footpad swung round with the belaying pin raised to attack. A big mistake. The large marine didn't hesitate; the pistol fired a blinding flash in the dark alley. The ball smashed into the robber's face, boring itself deep into the soft tissue of the man's brain before it removed much of his skull at the back and splattered his brains against the wall behind. He was dead before he hit the ground.

'Sweet Jesus Christ, Tim. You all right, mate?' Packer knelt and touched the gunner's shoulder.

Clayton groaned and tried to lift himself to his feet, knees buckling as he stumbled into Packer's arms.

'Let's get you out of 'ere smartish, afore we gets caught.' Packer's thoughts raced. *Before I get caught*, he reflected. *Why did I shoot the bugger? I could have downed him with one good fist and let the gallows man have him.*'

Slipping the sailor's arm around his shoulder, Packer supported him into the black, wet street, muttering oaths as he took the weight. As they passed the front of the Black Horse, a lieutenant and an older midshipman approached and stopped, blocking Packer's path. He grinned at the officers, throwing a clumsy salute while supporting his friend, very nearly dropping him.

'What's afoot, Sergeant? Where are you bound?' the lieutenant, a tall, fresh-faced man drawled while the midshipman smirked, enjoying Packer's discomfort.

'My mate, sir,' he said, inwardly cursing the interruption, 'had a bit of a slip and banged 'is 'ead.'

'Is that right, Sergeant?' The lieutenant turned to his junior. 'Do you believe that, Mister Cole?'

'No, sir,' the mid replied. 'I suspect both men to be incapable through drink, sir.'

'Not at all, sirs,' Joe tried. 'It's just as I said. My mate was taking a piss when he slipped on a turd or something.'

'A likely tale! I should have you clapped in irons.'

'No, sir, we're good and loyal men, sir. Senior men too. My mate 'ere is 'urt an' I needs to get him to 'is ship's surgeon. He was attacked by a footpad, sir, on me honour, sir.'

The officers looked at Clayton and then at each other. The lieutenant leaned forward and sniffed. 'He is drunk, you bloody liar,' he shouted. 'I shall have your stripes and put some others on your back, you filthy scum lobster.'

A red mist swirled across Sergeant Packer's eyes and his fist flew before his usually calm brain made any conscious decision. When it cleared, he found the lieutenant spread across the frosted cobbles, his mouth bloody and contorted with the pain of a broken tooth.

The midshipman jumped back, fearful of the marine's intentions. He pulled his dirk from its sheath, shouting for help, which arrived in the form of half a dozen sailors returning to their ship under escort of a pair of bosun's mates.

'I mean you know 'arm, sir. I dunno why I 'it 'im. I just saw red when 'e insulted the Corps.' Packer swore at himself and prepared for a beating, knowing many sailors had no love for the marines. Instead, he found his arms pinned behind his back and tightly tied with a length of rope, which cut into his wrists.

Staggering to his feet, the lieutenant stuck his face within an inch of Packer's. 'How dare you! I'll see you swing for this, Sergeant. Strike your superior officer, would you? I'll laugh as you piss your pants and swing from the foreyard, you bastard lobster.'

Packer wisely said nothing this time. *Shit*, he thought. *He's fuckin' right. Packer, you bloody fool. What a mess you've made of things.*

Clayton was pulled to his feet and similarly bound before the two were dragged off to the guard at the dockyard gate. Packer's offence was noted in the log by a marine corporal who looked askance, wisely said nothing, and escorted the naval party to the lock-up. He sent one of his men to report to the colonel that the famous and respected Sergeant Joseph Packer was locked in a cell, having struck an officer.

Poor bugger, thought the corporal. *He'll hang for the pleasure of of punching an officer.*

Packer sat in the gloomy cell of the port's lock-up, the stone floor cold beneath a thin scattering of dirty straw. He stared at the whitewashed wall and wondered how many days he had left to live. Swearing softly, he reflected on how he had destroyed his life with a single stupid act and let down the reputation of the Corps. *Shit*, he thought, *Captain Vizzard will roast me before they hang me.* 'Never thought I'd let the boss down,' he muttered.

* * * * *

The lieutenant lodged in rooms in a narrow back street behind the High Street, where it joined Broad Street, within spitting distance of the Sally Port. The house was in a terrace often used by junior officers on half-pay or waiting on orders in the hope of a ship. Its four storeys were uneven, with deflecting beams, the roof was in need of some retiling work at one end, the old and spalling brickwork showed a century of grime, and a few of the window frames were rotten.

It was occupied by a varied collection of inhabitants: a couple with a young infant; a clerk from the Navy Board; a young ensign from the 67th Regiment of Foot; and an old, loud woman who growled at every passer-by who crossed her path. She was dressed in clothes that, although not quite rags, were old and dirty.

Jack Vizzard knew all this, having spent two days keeping the house under close watch from various locations in the neighbourhood. He was not in uniform and varied his attire from that of a country gentleman of means to an injured sailor. He even gained entry one evening on the pretext of seeking a room, but his prey was 'not at 'ome' that evening. The officer 'as a room at the top of the house, at the rear, so he can look at the sea,' the loud woman told him.

Lieutenant the Honourable Russell Harcourt was a wealthy young man, related, Jack had learned, to a bishop in the north of England. Yet he was no friend to members of the clergy. Jack made it his business to discover as much as possible of his enemy, for Harcourt was most assuredly that now. And Jack knew what to do with his enemies.

Or did he? This evening he was undecided. He had killed in battle many times, even committed murder once. But that had been many years ago, before New Holland. Jack doubted he could do the same again, certainly not to a brother officer. But this Harcourt fellow had called his friend and close comrade 'filthy scum' and had ordered Packer thrown in a gaol, to await a brief trial by the Court Martial before being hauled up to the yardarm to be hanged.

Gifted to Jack by his mother and father, and acquired from the tutors at Oriel, was the power of persuasion. He intended to use it in a calm, reasoned manner to get Harcourt to withdraw his charge and admit to some error or misunderstanding. Thus, he was limping along the street wearing a dirty, torn coat with old boots borrowed from the barrack's cobbler. The swordstick he leaned on was on loan from a trusted friend in the division. All he wanted to do, however, was give the fop a beating he would never forget.

He watched as the loud woman left the house and, unwittingly, failed to securely close the rough, dilapidated door before she shuffled away. Jack waited until she had turned the corner before swiftly crossing the cobbled street and slipping inside. The top of the house was in darkness. He squatted in an alcove beside the broad rising chimney. If he was right, 'The Honourable' would return by six bells.

The front door slammed as a heavy-footed man stamped up the creaking, loose wooden stairs. Jack held his breath and pressed his body back into the recess as the lieutenant, breathing hard, his sweating brow illuminated briefly by a sliver of light from the attic window, groped in a pocket for his key, unlocked and opened the door to his room. He paused as he made to step inside.

A hard push to his back sent him sprawling. He looked up to see a shabbily dressed, hooded figure, with a blood-red kerchief tied about his face, standing over him, legs apart, pointing a pair of pistols at his head.

'What the devil are you ?' he spluttered.

'Quiet, Mister Harcourt. I suspect you are fonder of talking than listening, but it is the latter I would encourage you to do at this time,' Jack ordered.

'Who the hell are you, and what do you want of me? I have no money, as you might detect from my circumstances.' Harcourt glanced about the room, as if to emphasise the penury in which he lived. 'I am without means of any kind and am dependent on the charity of family and friends.' His words were at odds with the new, immaculately tailored uniform, soft leather boots, and fresh silk shirt he wore. When the shabby man standing over him made no move to attack him, he risked a slight smirk and started to rise.

'Silence, you lying bastard, and stay where you are,' Jack hissed. 'Move again and I'll put a ball into your knee. I told you to listen, Harcourt, you scum.' At that the lieutenant's smirk vanished. 'That's a word you understand, is it not, Harcourt? You know scum when you see it, don't you, man?'

An expression of puzzlement appeared on the lieutenant's face. 'What are you suggesting, you ... you scoundrel?'

'You have no idea as to my identity?'

'How could I while you hide behind that kerchief?'

'Perhaps I should keep it that way, scum!' Jack paused and watched Harcourt become visibly more scared. 'You are responsible for placing at severe risk of death a man whose boots you are not fit to lick clean. By reason of your arrogance and ignorance, a good man is charged with an assault for which he will hang. You, Harcourt, have the opportunity to save a life, a very valuable life, you worthless turd, by withdrawing all charges against the sergeant you insulted. He is a man with more courage than you will ever have, of far greater value to King George than you will ever be. You will formally withdraw your charge against the man. In return for that, your own life will be spared. Or do nothing and the day a noose is placed about Sergeant Packer's neck is the day you will die.' Harcourt's eyes showed the growing fear he felt. 'This I vow to you.'

The lieutenant stared in disbelief at the hooded stranger standing with pointed pistols in his steady hands, steel-blue eyes showing the strength of his determination. Harcourt knew in that moment he must agree to anything this bastard villain demanded, in order to save his own skin.

'And if you should think for one moment that a false, hollow promise will suffice, you are gravely mistaken, you cowardly piece of shit. You will report to the admiral this evening. When I receive notice of your contrition, you have my word your life is spared and you will never hear from me, or see me, again.'

The lieutenant swallowed hard and opened his mouth to swear a promise, then the tall, strangely dressed man spun on his heels, slamming the door as he left, and disappeared down the dingy staircase. Harcourt slowly, cautiously, moved to the door and, deciding it was safe to do so, ran after his unwelcome visitor, dashing into the street. He saw no sign of the stranger, who had simply vanished into the night.

He returned shakily to his room.

CHAPTER 5
Packer

'What's agoing to 'appen to me, boss?' Sergeant Major Packer looked tired and gaunt, and, he felt, if he was honest with himself, frightened. Never and ropemakers, carpenters and iron workers, coopers, and sailors, before had he experienced fear like this, fear that turned his insides to liquid. Nothing had ever scared him before. Facing death on the deck of a frigate or a 74, or storming a fort, he could master, but faced with the prospect of the hangman's noose on the fleet's flagship, he was overcome. He could not shake the thought of hanging from his mind.

He'd faced many trials in his life and was no stranger to suffering. Growing up in a cramped farm labourer's cottage shared with half a dozen siblings had been a trial. His father had died just as he turned twelve, leaving him to work in the fields with his mother and elder brothers. A few years later he'd made his way to Chatham, where he became one of the dozens of boys scratching a living in the dockyard.

During that time he'd learned from the artisans: the sailmakers and ropemakers, carpenters and iron workers, coopers, and sailors, and could work with rope and sailcloth and iron. Then he joined the Corps of Marines and found himself fighting for his life on board a man o' war at the relief of Gibraltar. His life had been a series of trials, but he had done well. He found his calling as a soldier. Maturity brought with it a natural ability in managing men and getting them to do his bidding. He wore his three stripes with pride and became a respected soldier; feared by raw recruits and tolerated by the officers above him.

Then Lieutenant Jack Vizzard entered his life and they shipped to New Holland with the first of the transported criminals. Those years in the new colony were hard but Lieutenant Vizzard led the men through the tough times and earned his respect as a natural leader of men. Both gladness and guilt therefore flooded his heart on seeing his superior enter the cell a few days later.'

'Your trial is set for tomorrow at noon, Joe,' Jack said, his tone sombre. 'It will be a brief affair as they can't be seen to acquit you.' Jack noted the effect of his words as Packer's face dropped. 'It will be nigh impossible for me to defend your actions. Death and damnation, Joe! What the bloody hell were you thinking?' For the first time since learning the news, Jack was overtly angry. 'I go home for a few days and in my absence, you ruin your life by swinging at an officer! A poor specimen of an officer but, damn me, he holds the King's commission. It is akin to striking the King himself.'

'I'm sorry, Mister Vizzard, sir. I just saw red for an instant and afore I knows it I've gone an' decked the bastard.' Packer stood, the chains biting into his ankles. 'He called me scum, sir. Me! I just have to throw myself on the court's mercy, won't I?'

Jack paced the small cold cell, arms folded across his chest. He felt sick at the sight of the anguish on his sergeant's face. 'There'll be precious little of that tomorrow, Joe. Like the story of John the Baptist and Salome, they want your head on a plate. Discipline would quickly disappear if they failed to hang you. It creates a dangerous precedent.' Jack sighed. 'I will speak on your behalf, naturally, although the colonel has all but thrown you to the wolves and damn near ordered me to let you hang and be done with you.'

Packer clanked over to the high window to suck in some of the cold, weak, salt air. 'I'd be obliged if you'd try an' stop using that word, sir.' He stamped to improve the circulation in his cold, aching feet then returned to the rough bench and slumped down in despair. 'I'm so bloody sorry to have let you down, sir. You been good to me over the years, and we've seen some things, ain't we?'

'Try not to despair, Joe. All is not lost,' reassured Jack, his voice a little softer, trying to lift his friend's spirits. 'You know I shall do all I can to see you free. There is always hope.'

'Thank you, sir. It means a good deal to me to 'ear you and to 'ave you in my corner, as it were.' The hard-as-nails soldier turned away to hide the moistness in his eyes.

Jack placed a hand on his shoulder and called for the guard.

He'd faced many trials in his life and was no stranger to suffering. Growing up in a cramped farm labourer's cottage shared with half a dozen siblings was a trial. His father died just as he turned twelve, leaving him to work in the fields with his mother and elder brothers. A few years later he made his way to Chatham where he became one of the dozens of boys scratching a living in the dockyard. Along the way he learned from the artisans; the sailmakers and rope-makers, carpenters and iron workers, coopers, and sailors, and could work with rope and sailcloth and iron. Then he joined the Corps of Marines and found himself fighting for his life on board a man o' war at the relief of Gibraltar. His life had been a series of trials, but he had done well. He found his calling as a soldier. Maturity brought with it a natural ability in managing men and getting them to do his bidding. He wore his three stripes with pride and became a respected soldier; feared by raw recruits and tolerated by the officers above him.

Then Lieutenant Jack Vizzard had entered his life and they'd shipped to New Holland with the first of the transported criminals. Those years in the new colony had been hard, but Lieutenant Vizzard led the men through the tough times and earned his respect as a leader of men. Both gladness and guilt therefore flooded Joe's heart on seeing his superior enter the cell a few days later.'

'Your trial is set for tomorrow at noon, Joe,' Jack said, his tone sombre. 'It will be a brief affair as they can't be seen to acquit you.' Jack noted the effect of his words as Packer's face dropped. 'It will be nigh impossible for me to defend your actions. Death and damnation, Joe! What the bloody hell were you thinking?' For the first time since learning the news, Jack was overtly angry. 'I go home for a few days and in my absence, you ruin your life by swinging at an officer! A poor specimen of an officer but, damn me, he holds the King's commission. It is akin to striking the King himself.'

'I'm sorry, Mister Vizzard, sir. I just saw red for an instant and afore I knows it I've gone an' decked the bastard.' Packer stood, the chains biting into his ankles. 'He called me scum, sir. Me! I just have to throw myself on the court's mercy, won't I?'

Jack paced the small cold cell, arms folded across his chest. He felt sick at the sight of the anguish on his sergeant's face. 'There'll be precious little of that tomorrow, Joe. Like the story of John the Baptist and Salome, they want your head on a plate. Discipline would quickly disappear if they failed to hang you. It creates a dangerous precedent.' Jack sighed. 'I will speak on your behalf, naturally, although the colonel has all but thrown you to the wolves and damn near ordered me to let you hang and be done with you.'

Packer clanked over to the high window to suck in some of the cold, weak, salt air. 'I'd be obliged if you'd try an' stop using that word, sir.' He stamped to improve the circulation in his cold, aching feet then returned to the rough bench and slumped down in despair. 'I'm so bloody sorry to have let you down, sir. You been good to me over the years, and we've seen some things, ain't we?'

'Try not to despair, Joe. All is not lost,' reassured Jack, his voice a little softer, trying to lift his friend's spirits. 'You know I shall do all I can to see you free. There is always hope.'

'Thank you, sir. It means a good deal to me to 'ear you and to 'ave you in my corner, as it were.' The hard-as-nails soldier turned away to hide the moistness in his eyes.

Jack placed a hand on his shoulder and called for the guard.

* * * * *

Lieutenant the Honourable Russell Harcourt had become increasingly worried as the Court Martial he had initiated approached. Towards his brother officers in the taverns and gaming rooms of Portsmouth, he presented a mask of the aggrieved party; confident in the course he had set, satisfied that justice would be served, and his honour maintained. He had no close friends but those officers who accepted him into the circle listened to his account of the assault. Without exception, they provided empathy for his circumstance. An enlisted man must never be allowed to attack an officer and expect to be forgiven. They were all agreed that the sergeant must hang.

When by himself, however, he shook with trepidation. The image of that stranger, with the audacity to confront him in his rooms and threaten him, kept returning to disturb his sleep. Then, as the day approached, came nightmares of what could happen—what would happen—if the stranger kept his word. The man had a wildness and intensity in his eyes that left Harcourt in no doubt he would die painfully at the man's hands, or on the point of a sword. 'Damn the man,' he thought. 'Who in God's name was he? What influence did he have to show such confidence?'

It crossed his mind to leave the town and become lost in London, but that would destroy his already weakened reputation. He should already have received a first step on the promotion ladder; at least to be appointed the senior lieutenant on a frigate, and from there, a short step to commander's rank and master of one of the Navy's smaller ships. He didn't understand the delay. Father was now a baronet and that should play a part, surely. As it was, he could find no suitable employment commensurate with his rank in life. Offered the post of third mate on an Indiaman by a desperate captain, he had declined: it was beneath his status. The Admiralty ignored his correspondence and the port admiral ceased granting him audience many weeks since. Perhaps he should abandon the Navy and work for his father at the bank after all. Harcourts was prospering and fast becoming a reputable bank in the City. He could become rich investing with other people's wealth, just as father had done.

Damn the menacing intruder again. What was he to do? Each evening he walked back to his rooms in fear, eyes darting in all directions, fearing he would encounter the wild-eyed stranger. Those bright, ice-blue eyes, cold as steel, seemed to follow him; he imagined he saw hooded spectres in every dark corner, in every alley, even on the busy street. The door to his room was locked and he now carried a loaded pistol as he ascended the stairs when returning to his room. He had taken to keeping a midshipman's dirk hidden in his coat, too, frequently fingering its shaft as if seeking security.

The night before the Court Martial, a note had appeared beneath his door. Not a sound had he heard and, unlocking the door and pulling it open, he heard no footfall on the stairs. The note contained a simple but stark message: 'Withdraw or die.'

Once again, he ran down the stairs, taking them two at a time, leaping into the street prepared to confront his antagonist, the dirk glinting in his hand. An elderly woman, shuffling on the arm of her daughter, screamed in terror. Panting in naked fear, sweat shining on his face, Harcourt's eyes were wide and his hands trembling.

He returned to his room, shaking, to sit alone in the frightening darkness.

* * * * *

Captain Vizzard sat in the cold of the adjutant's office, a single oil lamp illuminating a desk littered with papers and dusty books. Jack last looked at his law tomes—when? 'Oh, in New Holland,' he mused, 'when working as assistant to David Collins, the first Judge Advocate of the colony and secretary to the Governor, Arthur Phillip.'

He started with the Articles of War, displayed on every ship, and read to ships' companies weekly to reinforce discipline. Reading through the document he stopped at Article XXII:

XXII. Striking a superior officer. Quarrelling. Disobedience. If any officer, mariner, soldier or other person in the fleet, shall strike any of his superior officers, or draw, or offer to draw, or lift up any weapon against him, being in the execution of his office, on any pretence whatsoever, every such person being convicted of any such offense, by the sentence of a court martial, shall suffer death; and if any officer, mariner, soldier or other person in the fleet, shall presume to quarrel with any of his superior officers, being in the execution of his office, or shall disobey any lawful command of any of his superior officers; every such person being convicted of any such offence, by the sentence of a court martial, shall suffer death, or such other punishment, as shall, according to the nature and degree of his offence, be inflicted upon him by the sentence of a court martial.

That was unambiguous. A Court Martial would readily sentence Joe Packer to death.

He pored over the Naval Courts Martial Act of '79, noting that Sergeant Packer's offence had been committed ashore, and was thus subject to the Naval Mutiny Act. Whichever provision he turned to, the conclusion was identical. There was no sustainable, viable defence available to him and Packer would surely hang.

Unless Harcourt withdrew the complaint.

Yet the scum had made no effort to do so, as far as Jack was aware. His attempt to frighten the foppish officer hadn't worked. He had killed before. Could he do it again? Murder another man; a fellow officer who wore the King's uniform and carried the King's commission? He could not. He had threatened the man, convincingly in his opinion, but no, he could not kill a man for seeking punishment of an insubordinate soldier. Or could he? The desire to save the life and career of the man who supported him, taught him the ways of the Corps, and saved his own life for nearly a decade was overwhelming.

Jack was in despair. Packer had become more than a trusted subordinate. They had endured too much together; in New Holland, in France, in a major sea fight against the French back in '94. He trusted the man with his life; he *owed* the tough marine his life. Pulling open the drawer he lifted a bottle of French brandy from its depths, poured a large measure into a pewter tankard and enjoyed the fiery liquid as it passed down his throat. When he had drained the pot, he returned the bottle and stretched out on the canvas camp bed prepared by his orderly. He was asleep within the passing of only a few minutes.

CHAPTER 6
Queen Charlotte

The single crash of the cannon aboard the flagship *Queen Charlotte* announced two facts: it was noon and Joe Packer's Court Martial had opened.

Sergeant Packer stood rigid between the beams of the great cabin of Bridport's flagship as the admiral's clerk read the details of the offence in a clear, if sombre, tone. 'Where is Captain Vizzard?' he wondered. A young Second Lieutenant called Gunnersbury stood nervously flicking at some papers, uncertain as to what he could say to the senior officers arrayed in front of him. Packer had not met him until this morning. 'This is likely my last full day on earth,' he thought. 'Tomorrow, they will hang me.' With that thought, despair swept over him like a wave washing over a beach.

The admiral looked irritated, visibly angry that important business had to be interrupted for another Court Martial. Four post captains viewed the prisoner with a mixture of expressions. One had a show of pity, another clearly irritated at being unable to attend to the demands of his ship and the distraction from his duty, the third could not hide his disgust. The last showed cold disinterest.

At the door to the flagship's great cabin, two marine sentinels from the Plymouth Division, not the local garrison, stood with loaded muskets and blinking eyes, stealthily glancing at the naval lieutenant. Their fleeting looks conveyed cold anger that one of their own should stand condemned to hang from the foreyard of this very ship.

Wilson, a corporal and the stockier of the two, was resentful. He loathed officers. All they did was take all the glory and wasted men in the pursuit of 'honour', as they chose to call it. He loathed naval officers particularly, for their pomposity and arrogance and the floggings a few of them seem to relish. Wilson had a scar-striped back beneath his uniform; the flogging had been ordered by an officer like Harcourt when Wilson was a youngster, a new recruit to the Corps, and knew nothing. He didn't blame the sergeant one little bit.

Harcourt sat idly in a leather chair, legs crossed with the upper foot twitching in a kind of dance, as its owner nibbled on a thumbnail. His ears funnelled the muted voices of the captains forming the court and wondered how they would regard him. His eyes darted to the marine sentries, conscious of their silent enmity toward him. He wanted to challenge them, provoke them, to force a remark to which he could take exception and order another punishment. He stared coldly at the two men, immaculate in red coats and round black hats, pipe-clayed white cross-belts dividing their crimson coats. He was ready to pounce the moment either gave himself away. But they just stared ahead, carefully ignoring the lieutenant's eyes, mindful that even a casual glance in his direction would betray the loathing they each felt and bring forth a torrent of insulting or abusive language.

Footsteps on the companionway above his head caused Harcourt to alter his demeanour and assume the visage of an important officer. The dim 'tween decks concealed the identity of both the new arrival and the chief witness until he stood directly in front of Harcourt. The marine sentries straightened visibly as a Captain of Marines, immaculate in dress uniform, snapped at the man in the chair. 'Lieutenant Harcourt, tell me, why do you not stand and salute a superior officer? Is it because you are scum and are afraid of marines?'

The sentries snorted in disbelief, resuming a sombre expression when Jack threw a sharp glance at the pair. 'Silence on deck,' he growled. 'There is a Court Martial in progress.' Turning back to face Harcourt he stared. 'Well, answer me man,' he said.

Harcourt slowly stood, an expression of concern and puzzlement on his face. The striking blue eyes drilled into him like cold steel bayonets as understanding struck him with force.

'You!'

'Ah, recognition at last, Harcourt. Do you recall my terms, you dog? I am here to fulfil my promise to you.'

'I ... I've not forgotten, you devil,' he stuttered, 'I wait to be called.'

'I strongly urge you to march in right now and explain yourself to the admiral and do exactly as I instructed you. You know the alternative.'

The sentries exchanged surprised glances.

Harcourt stared at Jack for a long moment, taking in the hate in his eyes, took a deep intake of breath and knocked on the doors leading to the great cabin. Without waiting for a response, he stepped inside.

* * * * *

'You should have seen the admiral's face, sir,' Sergeant Packer chuckled as the jolly boat took him and his escort ashore through a cold, wet rain. 'I could not believe my ears. There I was waiting for the hangman and suddenly that arse Harcourt's standin' to attention afore the surprised captains and the admiral, bleatin' on about having made a mistake, that he hadn't been 'it in the face at all but slipped on the ice smacking his ugly mush and only thinkin' he's been 'it. He looked proper scared, he did.' Joe licked his lips, 'I could do with a wet, sir.'

'I suspect we'll be watched, even followed, Joe. The George might not be the most circumspect of taverns for us to celebrate your good fortune.'

'Have no fear, sir. I know of a quiet taphouse a little out of the main sea lanes as it were. Anyways, I'm a wanting a word with you about my 'good fortune' as you puts it. I don't believe in that, not for a minute.' He gave his officer a curious look. 'I 'ave friends on the flagship, and odd conversations 'twixt officers get passed along very speedily, like.'

'Sergeant Packer, fortune favours the bold, from the Latin *'Fortuna Audaces Iuvat*. I suggest you press me no further and enjoy breathing the air of freedom and thank whichever deity you pray to for your liberty.' Jack smiled, happy his threats had born fruit.

'I'm an unbeliever as you well know, Cap'n Vizzard, but I reckons I know who to thank for my reprieve from the noose.

I also think you should watch yer back from now on. Or I'll be watchin' it for you, I means, 'cos I reckon on a certain naval officer looking to seek revenge for the loss of 'is 'onour. The admiral was scathin' about officers makin' false accusations against 'respectable NCOs'! You should have 'eard him tear into the lieutenant for wasting senior officers' time. M'lord Bridport was furious. He'll be after you, sir, an' don't you doubts it.'

Jack snorted. 'Evidently Lord Bridport knows you ill, or he might not have been so complimentary, Joe! As for The Honourable Mister bloody Harcourt, I could not care less. It would give me pleasure to meet him any dawn, with pistols or swords, or for that matter I would fight him with bare knuckles. I doubt Harcourt has ever had a fight in his life.'

'I wouldn't trust 'im to give you the satisfaction of a duel, sir; 'is sort prefer to knife people in the back. That's why I tell you to keep an eye in the back of your 'ead like,' Packer replied. 'I reckon I'll be closer than yer own bleedin' shadow from now on, Mister Vizzard.'

The jolly boat bobbed and slowed as the midshipman in command ordered 'oars', whereupon the sailors raised their oars to the vertical and the boat nudged the steps, allowing Packer to disembark, followed by Jack. 'His sort of bastard don't fight fair, sir,' Packer offered. 'His sort come up behind ye in the dark, like the coward he is. Unless he's got a bunch of toughs in front of him.'

'By the by, Joe. I did not mention that I met the man's father at Berkeley. Hardly surprising that the son is as he is. The sins of the father are visited upon the son, as it were. Well, let him come. I made it personal. Just took a dislike to the fop as soon as I set eyes on him. Don't like the cut of his jib, Joe. He'll never make a good seaman, or officer, and, in truth, he probably owes his commission to money and influence alone.'

They climbed the slimy, concaved stone steps to The Hard and Jack risked a glance over his shoulder. He saw no evidence of pursuit and felt that Harcourt simply lacked the nerve to attempt any retribution or seek satisfaction for the wrong done to his honour. Nonetheless, as a pair of sailors hauling on a cart approached, Jack pulled Packer behind it and ducked inside the Keppel's Head.

'I think the Keppel's a mite too close, sir,' Joe hissed quietly. 'Too many officers, I reckon. No disrespect. There's a quiet place round the back of College Street. Small tap room. Friendly sort of place it is. Won't be any nosey parkers.'

Jack was watching the steady stream of human and animal traffic passing and re-passing. Satisfied, he grabbed Packer's arm and strode into the street. 'Where is this damned ale house of yours, Joe?'

The Brewery Tap was a boisterous ale-house, the haunt of sailors and marines alike, and thereby a place where brawls frequently broke out. Dockyard workers might occasionally pass an evening inside the old timbered building, full of smoke from the long-stemmed clay pipes popular with seafarers. Three men sat in a huddle by the inglenook fireplace where unseasoned logs were slowly adding to the smoke-filled atmosphere of the room. It smelled of tobacco and stale ale. The place was quiet, with only three or four older sailors enjoying a peaceful time, away from the busy dockyard drinking establishments.

Packer summoned the pot-man with a wave of his hand and, when the wooden tankard was full, he raised it in Jack's direction. 'I thank you sir, most 'umbly. I owe you my life, Mister Vizzard.' He drank deeply, the watered-down ale tasting like nectar from the Gods. He rubbed his eyes with his free hand.

'Promise me this, Joe. If you ever have the need to hit Mister bloody dishonourable Harcourt, you tell me first.' Jack took a mouthful. 'Then I'll hit him.' They laughed. 'I am serious now, Joe. If you ever strike a superior again, you put the entire Corps in the dock, not just yourself. It tarnishes us all and I'll not have that, not even from you. Especially not from you. Apart from that, the mere suggestion of a repetition is certain to see you swing from the yardarm. You will never have a second chance.' Jack stared at his sergeant and friend; the gravity of his words accentuated by his expression.

Two sailors, soaked and shivering from the freezing rain now falling heavily and with a great deal of noise, entered the alehouse. They hesitated, adjusting to the dark interior, only to receive abusive language from the other drinkers. Meanwhile, the pot-man returned with a pitcher of ale to refill tankards. 'Now drink up, sir, I fancy another afore we head back.' Joe's heavy hand brought the tankard down hard on the table.

* * * * *

Captain Graham Moore looked at the certificates the man in front of him had delivered on coming aboard *Melampus*. Nothing remarkable in any of them; the man had not distinguished himself in any degree at any time for anything since receiving his commission. Then there was the cryptic note from Lord Bridport, all but apologizing for foisting the man upon him, and requesting that he, Moore, endeavour to make something useful of him, or, as Bridport put it:

I am confident you will, in the manner of previous subordinates under your distinguished command, find the means to develop this officer's abilities and character so he may become of some value to the service.

Plainly the man had caused offence to someone or become an embarrassment and Bridport wanted him away from the Channel Fleet. Moore sighed; another ineffectual officer with influence and interest. It was not the first occasion he had been burdened with an admiral's cast-offs, but he was tired and frustrated at the continuing lack of commissioned officers of real ability and quality.

'What is a snatch-block?' Moore demanded.

'I beg pardon, sir?'

'Answer my question, please,' Moore insisted.

'Sir, you insult me! That is ordinary seaman's business.'

'Let us just say I wish to be humoured,' Moore replied with a soft smile.

'Er, it's used to take a cable off to an angle away from its, um, line of, er, force or to take a line around some, um, obstruction, I believe ... sir. Now why do you ask me such?'

'I sincerely hope any man holding a lieutenant's commission would know the most elementary matters of rigging,' snapped Moore, the smile instantly gone. 'I was more interested in the manner of your answer, sir! And I find it unacceptable and disappointing.' Moore glared at Harcourt.

'Describe to me if you will, the manner of rigging the jib boom. You should identify the requirements for the traveller, the horses, guys, and martingales.' Moore's searching eyes bored into Harcourt's, causing the lieutenant to become increasingly uncomfortable.

'Well, sir, I think one must, er, put the guys onto the jib boom first, I believe. Is that correct?' Harcourt managed to blurt out.

'You clearly have an inadequate knowledge of rigging, Mister Harcourt. You would do well to spend some time with the bosun. Now, I suggest you find the first luff and see to your duties.' Moore bent to a ledger on his desk and returns from the gunner and the sailmaker.

Harcourt stood straight, arms by his sides, fists clenched tight. His mouth moved, as if to form some words of protest but none spilled out and he turned on his toes and strode from the cabin.

CHAPTER 7
Orders

L ieutenant Dick Rynne had supervised the loading of stores as they were brought aboard, placing a pair of the more experienced midshipmen 'tween decks to keep a close eye on the passage of supplies down into the hold. There were men to be trusted on this ship, a great many of them, but there were several, particularly amongst the new-pressed men, whose trust had yet to be earned.

A couple brought aboard on Monday were a cause for some concern. One—Rynne thought him to be a Dane—had tried to bully a ship's boy until the bosun intervened. The other, a tough-looking Geordie, had already been on Captain's Report for swearing at the purser on his first day aboard.

Rynne, a short, powerfully built Yorkshireman of aristocratic features and a common seaman's tongue, was respected by the crew and Captain Moore. The burden of responsibility lay heavily on Rynne's shoulders, and he felt damned tired; the beginning of another cruise and already he was weary. The other officers appeared at first blush to be acceptable, until subjected to closer scrutiny.

Weaver was an affable West Country man of florid, rounded features but lacked prescience and natural authority and Rynne questioned the man's capacity for battle. A natural flair for leadership was not immediately apparent and a few of the people were privately scornful of his softly spoken manner of talking. It seemed to Rynne that shouting was anathema to Weaver; he engaged in conversation with the men. That aside, Rynne conceded Weaver was quietly confident and appeared competent in his watch-keeping duties.

Matthew Swinton, the senior midshipman, was younger, only twenty years old, and showed potential to make a good officer but—'There's always a but,' Rynne muttered to himself—Swinton's weakness was laziness. That and an emerging tendency to leave decisions to other, more experienced, men. Rynne thought he had lost confidence and made a mental note to work with him on that.

The other officer left the ship almost immediately after reporting on board and meeting Captain Moore last week. Rynne assumed the captain gave him leave to sleep ashore and thought no more about him until he crept aboard during the forenoon watch. Having skulked in his cabin since reporting on board, he was nothing more or less than a dandified fop, dressed in fine uniform with glistening thread and the smell of an expensive tailor about him. Rynne recognised him as such immediately. He sighed as he worked through the watch lists, allocating men to stations and trying, as always, to find a balance between unskilled ordinary seamen and reliable, able seamen. Experienced hands who knew the ropes and were able to work the ship and the guns could pass on their knowledge to the younger, less experienced men.

Now he had not one, but two marine officers joining his wardroom to consider. The Marine detachment returned on board at six bells in the afternoon watch and were busily settling into their allocated messes. Rynne knew Jack Vizzard from the last cruise *Melampus* had taken. The marine captain was very competent, obviously smart, cultured, well-educated and tough. If there was a prize to take or a fight to be fought, he need have no concerns about Jack. The man was good humoured and loved, yes actually loved, by that rag-tag collection of tough soldiers. Rynne had no direct authority over Jack and considered him an equal. He was glad the marine was aboard.

The Admiralty, for reasons best known to Their Lordships, added a junior subaltern to the ship's marine strength: Lieutenant Martin Hale. Though young, he appeared to be a leader and was confident when dealing with the men. Rynne watched him talking to that swaggering sergeant deploying his marines and detailing sentries. He would leave Hale to Jack's command.

Thank Christ in heaven he had Tom Marsters as bosun. The blunt Hampshire man represented the best the service could provide. Rynne had not met a more experienced bosun in the nigh on twenty years he had served. Marsters was resourceful, a necessary quality in a ship's bosun to keep a ship running smoothly, and he was quick-witted and fair with the hands. If they accomplished their jobs with skill, then Tom Marsters was satisfied. Those who did not were soon shown the error of their ways. Tom was content with those who learned quickly; to those who did not, he was a tough master.

A gunner's mate, Tim Clayton, had come aboard from one of the lighters provisioning the ship and volunteered. Rynne saw in the open, weather-beaten face and confident manner an experienced hand and took an instant liking to the man. He added him to the ship's muster and assigned him to the gunner's custody. Both men were satisfied; Clayton had found a berth on a frigate under a lucky captain who was seen as a rising star in the Navy, and Rynne found a gunner's mate for Mister Farragio, the warrant gunner, who was slowly losing his hearing. Deafness was a risk to the ship during battle when a man might not hear or fully understand an order repeated from the quarterdeck.

'Mister Rynne, sir,' the thin, nervous voice of Swinton called out. 'The captain is approaching the ship, sir.'

'Very well, thank you Mister Swinton,' Rynne barked. 'Have the side party ready. I shall be there momentarily.'

Rynne slipped some letters into a canvas case, pulled on his coat and, with his hat tucked under his left arm, bounded up the companionway to the weather deck. Jack was already there with half a dozen of his men, suitably smartened for the occasion, with Lieutenant Weaver and one of the midshipmen, Bedenham. From the waist, Rynne noted Captain Moore's launch being pulled by the strong crew through the swell. He risked a quick glance with the telescope, remembered he was hatless and quickly donned his best bicorne.

'He wears a stern expression, Jack. I wager he will want to be away on the next tide. I wonder what the orders are.' He quickly collapsed the telescope, tucked it under his left arm and glanced around the deck, thankful to see nothing obviously amiss that might incur the captain's displeasure.

Captain Moore had spent three days in London and sent word ahead of his planned return to *Melampus*; the letter arrived only with the morning's messenger. Rynne was occupied for the better part of the day ensuring the ship was, in all respects, ready for sea. The standing and running rigging had been tarred and ordered, six months' provisions had finally been carefully stowed in the hold and properly documented, and eight tons of powder carefully taken to the magazine to supplement the existing supplies—Captain Moore invested his personal funds into extra supplies of powder to have more resources for gunnery training. The sailmaker had been fortunate to secure two new courses for the main and foremasts, a full set of royals and two jibs, a flying jib and an outer, to replace those found to be wearing thin.

'It will be the Mediterranean, Dick,' said Jack. 'I'll wager a bottle of claret with you. The war in that sea is going to hell in a basket and we are surely reinforcements for the fleet there. Jervis commands and he is in need of more ships if he is to stop the Dons and the Frogs from combining and sailing for England.'

'We shall learn more shortly, Jack.' Rynne turned to the bosun, 'Ready, Mister Marsters?'

The bosun raised the call to his lips and waited for the ship's commander's head to reach deck level to shrill the whistle as Jack's marines presented arms with synchronized precision, surprising Rynne. Jack smiled.

'Welcome aboard, sir,' said Rynne, with a hand to his temple. 'I trust your journey was not too weary. I'll have your servant prepare some supper for you.'

'Good evening, Dick,' Moore replied with a warm smile. 'Be so good as to join me, would you? And you, Mister Vizzard, I would have you join me also. I wish to discuss our business with you both.' Moore noted the heightened interest in his marine captain's eyes. 'You will not be disappointed, Mister Vizzard, I do assure you.' Turning to his first he said, 'Call the hands, please, Dick. I wish to have a word with them too before we sail; the morning will see us busy.'

At a word from Lieutenant Rynne, the bosun ordered 'all hands to bear aft'. The bellow was repeated by his mates and within a few minutes the ship's company assembled between the main mast and the quarterdeck. As men came to understand Captain Moore intended to speak, loud voices fell silent. Men shuffled forward the better to hear what the Captain had to say.

The puzzled expressions of the crew gave Moore some satisfaction. Many captains put to sea with no explanation of the mission to be pursued. Moore's words brought forth a mix of emotions which, he was pleased to note, were principally positive. The odd scowl and a quiet murmur from heads to the rear were to be expected from any crew. The bosun called for three huzzahs for their captain, which were delivered with mixed enthusiasm.

The Mediterranean. It had been the area of operations that brought glory and honour to some, and prize money to others. Graham Moore looked forward to it with high expectation. It would serve better than the constant cruising of the Channel where searching for the enemy who played a cunning game of cat and mouse had been exhausting work and unrewarding.

He strode into his cabin wearing a broad smile.

Saint Valentine's Fleet

* * * * *

The crew settled for their supper leaving the harbour watch alone on deck, and a lusty musical entertainment in progress in the foc's'le, the strains of which filtered aft to the stern. Sounds from the deck were few; the lieutenant of the watch, Simon Weaver, paced rhythmically overhead accompanied by a midshipman. A cough from one of Jack's marines at the cabin door merged with the creak of timbers as *Melampus* rolled on a gentle swell.

'The Dons believe we are unaware of their plans; their ships may be disguised to blend with their fleet and will likely be shielded,' Moore recounted, almost verbatim, from his orders. 'When Jervis has found them, we and the replacement ships, *Prince George, Orion, Namur, Colossus* and *Invincible* will be detached and attempt to take them.'

'They will be worth fortunes, sir. If we can take them.' Rynne foresaw wealth beyond his dreams.

Jack attempted to introduce a sense of reality to the discussion. 'With all respect, sir, I believe they will be beyond reach,' he said. 'It will be nigh on impossible to get to them, sir, in my humble opinion.' Then he added prudently, 'And if we do catch them, sir, I will have need of more marines.'

'We shall make the attempt, Jack,' the captain responded. 'We shall try because what they are carrying will be of immense value to our country.' Moore was not a rich man, and the prospect of significant wealth was in no way abhorrent to him. After all, if he was to secure his lady, he would have to offer her a comfortable life. Some prize money would surely allay any fears she or her family might have. He also sought recognition and approbation from his superiors, as any ambitious officer would. A few of his contemporaries had acquired wealth beyond imagination from their defeat and capture of enemy vessels. He heard of an admiral whose share enabled him to purchase a large estate in Surrey despite not actually having been involved in the action concerned.

'What they are carrying will also make the flag officers and captains rich beyond measure, sir,' Jack commented, with oblique reference to Captain Moore's quest for prize money. 'Although the rules concerning that elude me, I believe a share is awarded to all other ships that may be in sight at the time?'

'In the process though, Jack,' interjected Lieutenant Rynne, 'we shall destroy the Dons before they can meet with the French and overwhelm us. The capture of the Spanish ships carrying that cargo will be worth Seven Cities of Gold, and the approbation of our King. God bless 'im, gentlemen,' he finished, raising a goblet of wine to his mouth.

'The matter will be discussed with Jervis once we meet him in Gibraltar,' Captain Moore added.

'I fancy the admiral will be more intent on destroying the Dons, sir,' Jack offered. 'From what I hear, Sir John cares little for prize money and more for ensuring he, and every officer and man, has performed his duty.'

'That may be so, Jack,' said Rynne. 'You may disdain gold and silver but I for one would welcome such a windfall.' Rynne was not ashamed of his humble birth but did nothing to advertise his straitened circumstances, aware that Jack enjoyed the status of master of a substantial property in Gloucestershire and a similarly substantial private income.

'Disdain, Dick? I think not. I have a growing family to support and, Oh Lord, Mary is set on repairs and renewals of the house. My late father put a new roof on the old place not too many years past, now my dear wife is set on adding rooms to the property, with fireplaces and chimneys, *and* changing furniture and all manner of expense awaits me. Gold and silver? I will gladly take my share.'

'Gentlemen, the ships in question are not identified. I sought your company and counsel as I have orders to seek out the information required to do so.' The comment caused two pairs of eyebrows to fly to half-mast. Jack's brain, soothed by a generous intake of Madeira and anonymous blackstrap, quickly awoke, sensing Captain Moore had a scheme to unfold. The Captain's next words confirmed his suspicions.

'A gentleman of affairs in London has some knowledge of the destination of the goods but could not identify the vessels. The Dons' ships will be making for Cadiz; I understand there to be a manufactory in the city where the raw material is, ah, processed. Should the ships concerned elude Jervis and the fleet, London wishes us to locate them in Cadiz and, er, relieve the Dons from the work involved. How we are expected to achieve that troubles me. It is the Dons' main base and if we must attack them in their base, it will need more resources than I have available. The material can then be transported to Birmingham where it may be, shall we say, utilized.'

'How are we to identify the ships, sir?' Jack enquired. 'And to cut them all out from Cadiz? That would be nigh impossible. As you say, Cadiz is a substantial harbour, the Don's main base. It will be very heavily protected, and we should require a substantial force, in my respectful submission.'

Graham Moore pondered the question, as he had when first he read his orders. 'To be candid, Jack, I have been worrying at the point all day, without an answer I am embarrassed to admit. I am hopeful we might identify them on sight. Your comments and suggestions are cordially invited, gentlemen.'

A prolonged silence filled the dim cabin and Jack, for once, had nothing more to offer. He drank to cover his confusion, as did the two naval officers, each occupied with their own thoughts.

'A conundrum indeed,' risked Lieutenant Rynne. 'We are to assume the subject vessels are—or will be—distinguished from their fellows in some patent manner to enable us to identify them across an expanse of sea and to capture them without the active intervention of the Dons,' he said. 'And this against some of the largest vessels in the Spanish fleet, no doubt.'

Jack cleared his throat. 'Would it be possible for *Melampus* to be disguised as a Spaniard and so infiltrate their fleet? Do we have any Spanish-speaking people who could be the 'voice' of the ship, do you think? Or as a neutral vessel ... perhaps an American ship? We have an American on board; I have heard him in the maintop.'

Captain Moore stared at his Captain of Marines. 'What are you thinking, Jack? That it is too difficult a mission? Formidable it may be, but I consider we have a duty to try.' He hurried on without waiting for any answer. 'While it might be possible to confuse the enemy for a short time, the

Melampus would eventually be seen for what she patently is —a Bristol-built man o'war. But yes, as a *ruse de guerre* it might give us the necessary surprise to get aboard one or more of 'em and cut 'em out of the fleet. Damn me, but what a risky enterprise it would be! It would need more than my *Melampus* to carry out such a task. We would need another frigate or, better yet, a 74.'

Jack voiced the obvious flaw in the scheme. 'The admiral will have to know of the plan,' he said, 'else our own ships may intervene and attack us, sir. Could we try to intercept them before they rendezvous with the Dons' fleet? Once they do, they will be shielded by some powerful vessels.'

'Indeed, Jack,' Moore agreed, 'Jervis will be fully aware of our plans. He may have intelligence to assist. We shall see when we meet him at The Rock, if not before. I look forward to talking through my orders with him.'

Rynne swallowed. 'I have yet to be honoured to meet Sir John, sir. I understand him to be a tough disciplinarian, but a fair seaman and commander.'

Moore smiled at his premier. 'Oh yes, Dick, he's a demanding man. He will not suffer fools or incompetents but is quick to recognize and reward meritorious service and loyalty.' He smiled at a memory. 'There is a story, reported as true by one who was present at the time, of a seaman who lost his pay from his britches when swimming. At the sight of the man wailing his misfortune like a washerwoman, Sir John told him to cease his tears and handed him seventy pounds from his own pocket! This is the commander slated for hanging a man on the Sabbath.'

Jack smiled. 'Then we have naught to fear, sir,' he said. 'Sir John will find no fault with *Melampus* or her officers.'

'The ship is in good order, Jack, according to the dock-yard, if their people are to be trusted, although I do wonder at some of the timbers and the copper is certainly in need of repair. We have a fresh set of canvas to bed in and the new heavier carronades. I am confident we will be a match for all but a line of battle ship. I am less sanguine that her crew is all it could be, however. Gentlemen, I must speak plain. I have full confidence in my senior officers,' he nodded at Rynne and Jack with a smile. 'However, we have a new lieutenant aboard who you would do well to watch. The man is not a sound seaman and I question, indeed I very much doubt, he will have the confidence of the people. I would be obliged for your support as I fear he is lacking, and may always lack, the necessary skills in several areas to discharge his duties.'

Jack took little interest in the line the captain's discourse was taking. The management of the ship and its officers was the responsibility of the captain and his premier. As his mind started to wander, he watched a fly crawling up the bulkhead behind Dick Rynne. He thought of his unfinished letter to Mary and whether he should recount Dr Jenner's remarks relating to his late father's title. On balance, he was inclined to keep that to himself until he could obtain more information. It would be better to discuss it with her once he was home, such a shock it would cause. There was still the question of his brother George. No word from him in nearly fifteen years ... Jack's mind drifted to thoughts of his elder brother and what might have befallen him. His father had never lost the grief of his leaving.

Rynne's voice dropped a little. 'The man reported to me on coming aboard at the start of the afternoon watch, sir. I have not seen him since. I still have the watchkeeping bill to complete.'

'Harcourt, yes, he's a very odd bird. Foisted on me by Lord Bridport, who I learned wanted him out of his command and as far from Portsmouth as he could be sent. Only son of Lord Harcourt, a banker associated with John Company, I gather.'

Jack Vizzard stared at Captain Moore. All pondering of his father's baronetcy disappeared instantly. His mind immediately returned to the encounter on the flagship before Harcourt finally withdrew his charge against Joe Packer. The atmosphere in the cabin was stuffy and warm, warmer than the mess deck. It felt heavy to Jack's lungs as he took in a breath.

'I know the man, sir. He is not a man to be trusted with anything, in my opinion, save possibly duplicity and treachery. And I have met his father, we were both guests of Lord Berkeley at Christmastime. We should all keep a sharp lookout for that man. I fear there is trouble ahead, for us all.

CHAPTER 8
Frigate Captain

'Deck there,' the American at the main mast-head, Nathan Forrester, called out. 'On the deck, I think I seen a sail, just off the larboard quarter, mebbe a point, and no more than two leagues off.' He paused and checked the horizon again. 'Yep, hull down but looks like she be close-hauled an' headin'.nor-east'

Harcourt had the deck as *Melampus* skimmed south under topsails and courses' in a fine southwesterly breeze beneath a cold, blue sky perforated with closely packed clumps of grey cloud rolling out into the Atlantic. The crew had seen only grey skies, heavy rain, and squalls since leaving Portsmouth. He stood, unhearing, gazing to larboard, fuming inwardly at the perfidy of senior officers.

Activity from his father and an uncle had gained him his commission. The uncle was a retired captain who had carried the young Harcourt's name on the last two of his sea-going commands, thereby giving the boy the required legal sea time. He passed his examination board with some difficulty; a friendly senior captain at Chatham, one in debt to his father, helped persuade the other members to pass the boy even though his answers to some questions had been weak and lacking conviction, according to one of the examiners.

Following a short cruise to Ireland on an escort brig, he was appointed to Portsmouth and the Impress Service, the Navy always in need of men, but there was to be no immediate sea-going commission for Harcourt. His previous certificate of service recording, in suitably ambiguous terms, that his seamanship knowledge was poor and his ability to command below average. The bitterness soured his mouth even months after learning the news. Now, at last, he had another ship, and a chance to prove his value. But he soon learned that his nemesis, a captain of marines and his insolent, insubordinate and intimidating sergeant, were aboard. Harcourt did not know how to deal with the situation. He nibbled on his thumbnail, staring ahead at the bowsprit rising and falling as the waves passed under *Melampus*.

A footfall brought him back to his senses and he spun on his heel to be confronted by a stern-faced Captain Moore.

'Why have you not reported, Lieutenant Harcourt? The lookout called you nigh on a minute past.' Captain Moore's voice was sharp and his face did little to contain his anger. 'Are you not familiar with my standing orders? That I am to be called whenever a ship is sighted?'

'I ... my apologies, sir, I was about to call you.'

'Not good enough, man,' snapped Moore. 'If I had not heard the call, you would have done nothing. Nothing!' He glared at the officer and noted several hands staring in surprise, waiting for orders. He had shouted at a subordinate officer in plain hearing of the crew. It was unheard of. Moore's unblinking, hostile eyes drilled into Harcourt's as he bellowed to the American. 'What do you see there, Forrester?'

'Can't see now, sir, but mebbe it was a small brig or sloop. It's gone now I reckon,' he shouted back. 'No doubt spotted us, turned tail and ran.'

'Keep to your present course, Cooke,' Moore said more softly to the helmsman.

The stocky man from Nottingham, whom Moore had promoted to quartermaster's mate during the ship's last cruise, nodded, and simply said, 'Aye sir.' To himself he thought, 'The cockwomble was daydreaming. He never heard the lookout's call.'

Captain Moore pulled the glass from the binnacle's side, turned, and strode to the weather shrouds, climbing rapidly to the futtocks, pulling himself over as *Melampus* rolled to leeward. He stood, feet apart, traversing the heavy brass instrument across an arc of ninety degrees. He could see nothing but white-topped rollers slowly journeying to the French coast. 'Likely a privateer, possibly heading to Nantes or Saint Nazaire, out of sight below the eastern horizon,' Moore thought. 'We may encounter Lord Galloway's squadron, Forrester, although his station is further south,' he said to the American. 'Please stay alert, Forrester. I wish to speak with His Lordship, should we meet him.'

'Bloody fool.' His mind had returned to the vexed matter of Harcourt. 'I should send him below ... but that would demean him in front of the watch on deck.' Moore sighed, swept the horizon once more and climbed down to the deck, replacing the telescope before striding to the flushed Harcourt.

'I encourage you, Mister Harcourt, to pay closer attention to your duty,' he growled at the red-faced officer, 'unless you wish to incur my considerable displeasure once more.'

With a glance towards the impassive helmsman, Captain Moore closed the door to his quarters calling for his servant, Dallow, a quick-witted man, too old now for duties aloft. 'A bottle of something, Dallow. I care not what.'

Slumping on the horsehair-padded stern bench, he resting an arm along the ledge, and looked at the foaming wake streaming behind *Melampus*. The light was slowly fading as eight bells rang announcing the end of the afternoon watch and commencement of the first dog watch. The evening sun, sliding below the horizon, caught the ascending nascent moon, casting orange and red beams along the sea. He registered the drumming sound of running feet on the deck and the calls and shouts of the petty officers as men ran to their stations, but his thoughts were with the lady, wondering what she was doing.

Dallow, ever sensitive to his captain's mood, entered the cabin bearing a bottle of brandy, one of a dwindling supply liberated by Moore from a French prize taken off Cherbourg the previous year. 'Shall I be lighting the lamps, sir?' he asked.

Moore looked back into the cabin willing his mind back to the present. 'I think you might, Dallow, but close the shutters first, please. I have several returns to study and a few letters to write.' He moved to the worn mahogany desk positioned against the bulkhead. It had once been his father's. Picking up the quill, he checked the barrel, dipped it into the brass well and pulled a sheet of paper from the bureau drawer. Pushing aside all thoughts of his junior lieutenant, his face softened as he turned his attention again to the lady. He wrote slowly, nibbling the feather's tip absent-mindedly while choosing his words with care, wondering when she would read it ... and what her reaction might be.

At length he paused, deciding to finish the letter later, and pulled his private journal from a drawer to bring it up to date. He wrote:

I left Portsmouth on the morning of the 23rd and returned by the place where my Goddess reigns. I am now over head and ears in love yet refrain from declaring myself; I was prevented by different circumstances but chiefly by the consciousness of my being in no condition to support her in the event of her consenting to share her fate with mine. I am in a painful state of suspense with regard to the state of her heart; she may like me, but I am sure she is not dying for any man. If I could be sure that she loves me, I could go to sea with satisfaction and increased ardour, founded on the hope of removing the only bar to the completion of my wishes by capture from the enemy, but if I were sure she were indifferent about me, I would be extremely indifferent about riches. I did not tell her how dear she is to me. Dear as the ruddy drops that warm my heart, but I think she must see it, and I do not think any of the family be ignorant of it. I am perplexed in considering the conduct of that most respectable and amiable family to me. If they see my love for this Dame their kindness to me must proceed either from the business not being disagreeable to them on the whole, or else convinced that I have made no impression on her heart and that as she is invulnerable to me, there is no reason for their altering their conduct to a man they esteem. I am afraid this last is the most probable. She appears every day more amiable and more exalted above the ordinary gay, insignificant creature that flutters about between Earth and Heaven.

It is worthwhile to live to gain the heart of such a creature; I am sure she cannot love by halves and I think her too delicate and too proud to submit to the meanness of giving her hand to a man who possesses not her whole heart.

* * * * *

Sergeant Packer had not ventured on deck in two days. He told himself the weather had not encouraged drill, which was true enough, but the whole truth was he did not want to run into the Honourable Russell Harcourt. Not through fear —Joe Packer feared no man—but because of his hatred for the man, and to avoid causing Captain Vizzard another problem. Having hit

Harcourt once, Packer worried he required little provocation to do it a second time, to avenge

the time spent in the brig and the fear and anxiety experienced when convinced he would hang. Packer kept below deck and left Lieutenant Hale and a corporal to drill the men.

But he could not stay there; Harcourt was surely aware he was on board as part of the marine contingent, and he would have to face the man at some point. It was odd the lieutenant had not encountered him during divisions, he mused, unaware Lieutenant Harcourt had been confined to his cabin for two days. 'Severe colic,' the surgeon's mate had reported to Captain Moore.

Packer heard raised voices overhead and recognised one as Jamie Hay, his NCO, a corporal from Scotland who Vizzard had promoted as reward for his work in France and during Howe's Action in '94.

'Bugger, now wot's 'appened?' he said to the deck-head and pulled on his jacket. Thundering up the companionway he reached the deck to see Corporal Hay on his back, his cap and musket on the deck and a red welt on his cheek. Standing over him, breathing hard, was Harcourt.

'What the bloody 'ell is going on 'ere?' Packer growled, looking down at Corporal Hay.

Harcourt stood, his chest rising and falling, arms by his sides with fists balled. In his right hand he tightly clutched a length of cane—a starter—and Packer understood immediately that Harcourt had used a bosun's rattan to strike Jamie Hay. Pulling himself up straight, he stared at the lieutenant and breathed slowly twice before he spoke.

'Might I ask this man's ... ah, offence ... sir?'

Harcourt continued to stand motionless, his face now wearing a mask of indifference. Packer continued to stare at him and then told Hay to get to his feet.

'Sir,' said Packer with forced courtesy, 'may I repeat my question? You appear to have struck one of my men. Please explain why.'

Harcourt turned slowly, his lips spreading a thin smile. 'The man was insubordinate, Sergeant Packer. You will be aware of what becomes of insubordinate and insolent scum such as your man there.'

'Report to Captain Vizzard, Jamie. On the double!' growled Packer. Turning back to Lieutenant Harcourt he spoke softly, his voice barely above a whisper, avoiding the interested looks of the sailors on deck. 'I'll thank you, sir, to refer any incidents of so-called insubordination to me, sir. You do not command my marines. I will deal with my men as I see fit.' Packer's self-control was stretched to its limits. His hands were clenched behind his back. 'And I ask that you cease referring to marines as scum … sir. It is a very dangerous word to use, as I thought you had learned.' As he spoke, Packer's face slowly moved closer to Harcourt's. 'Captain Moore will have to 'ear of this … sir. He might take a dim view of an officer striking a private soldier.'

A shout from the quarterdeck brought further discussion to a close.

'Is everything in order, Mister Harcourt,' the officer on watch, Simon Weaver, shouted. He had been aloft on the mizzen top with his glass and had not seen any incident.

'Nothing I cannot manage, Mister Weaver,' Harcourt replied with patent sarcasm. Then hissed, 'You will do well to keep quiet, Packer. I have not finished with you yet!' before striding to the rear companionway and the sanctity of his cabin.

'Nor I with you, you piece of shit,' Parker muttered softly under his breath.

* * * * *

'What the bloody hell happened, Jamie?' Jack asked after the Scottish marksman completed his report.

The quiet Scot looked confused and worried. Placing a hand on his marked cheek, he ventured, 'I dunnoo, sir. The

Lieutenant snapped that my salute was 'sloppy' and next I ken ahm doon on the deck.'

Jack shook his head. 'You must have done more than throw the nob a slack-handed salute?'

The marine protested his innocence assuring Captain Vizzard of his conduct. With the cabin walls closing in on him all he wished was to escape to the sanctity of the marines' mess and the camaraderie of his mates. But he was in front of the boss being quizzed repeatedly about a stuck-up, bullying English prick of an officer. The stripe on his cheek still stung and he yearned for a discreet session with a bottle of rum to ease the pain, and the humiliation.

'Get yourself forrard, Jamie. I daresay there you'll find some rum a suitable palliative. But hear me man; you mind your step with Mister bloody Harcourt. He'll be looking for trouble, with you, Sergeant Packer or others of the detachment. Know this and pass the word to all. Harcourt is not to be touched, under any circumstance, and I mean *no* provocation. Lieutenant Harcourt is my business, understand me?'

'Sir,' he said.

'And pass the word for Sergeant Packer to attend me as soon as it may be convenient for him.'

Hay threw one of the smartest salutes of his career, span on his heel and ducked out of the cabin, seeking the company of his mates.

Jack pulled a seaman's knife from inside his left boot, from a hidden compartment the cobbler in Gloucester fashioned on Jack's instruction, and rubbed his thumb across the edge of the blade. He decided it would benefit from a turn or two on the armourer's wheel.

A soft knock on the door announced the arrival of Joe Packer. 'Yes? Come in, Joe,' he muttered. 'I hope you haven't done anything I will regret.'

Sergeant Packer lowered himself onto a three-legged stool and slapped his hands on his knees. 'I ain't done nowt, sir. Not yet anyways, but we do 'ave ourselves a problem with that toff, Harcourt,' he said, putting emphasis on the H. 'Seems to me that 'e's set on provoking you or me by pickin' on the lads, an' I doesn't like it,' he sniffed. 'Not one little bit I don't.'

'Joe, it is vital that Harcourt's scheming be frustrated— his plan is obvious, you've hit the nail on the very head.' The knife in his hand pulled his attention as he noticed a scratch on the grip. He wondered if he would use it in anger. 'He knows we will be incensed, and the moment you or I retaliate he can resurrect a Court Martial against you,' he growled, 'or I.' He returned the knife to the hidden compartment in his boot, stood up, head between the deck beams and continued. 'Let us take a turn on deck,' he all but whispered. 'I need some clear air to think, and we might be heard here.'

They strode along the gun deck and encountered Corporal Munday with the gun captain of Number 4 Starboard gun, John Rivers, a loquacious, muscular man, with long grey hair worn loose.

'You see, Ned, iron corrodes at sea, unless we keep the bores clean and free,' Rivers was saying to Edward Munday. 'If we gets rust in the bore the bugger might misfire and blow me an' my crew to bloody smithereens,' he grunted. 'So, what we does is we clean an' paint 'em—keeps Cap'n Moore 'appy too.' His teeth showed in the gloom.

The sailor stopped at the approach of the marine captain and his sergeant. 'Carry on man', said Jack. 'This is of interest to my lads, as we are to work some of your guns.'

'Well, we makes up this mixture like; six ounces of lamp blacking and three pints of spirits of turpentine,' Rivers explained. 'Once the turpentine and black are well mixed we add three ounces of litharge and an ounce of umber, to give it a gloss, see?'

'Thought all you 'ad to do was wash 'em out wiv a sponge, mate,' said Munday. 'And what is litharge if you don't mind me asking?'

'Oh, we does that 'an all when we's in action, but this is for protection. Rust is a bugger, mate.' Rivers spat the remains of a quid of tobacco through the open port. 'An' the Navy don't want no rusty guns, nor do Captain Moore. 'E would have the first luff's family jewels and mine if 'e found any rust, you mark my words.' He wiped black spittle from his mouth with a grubby shirt sleeve. 'Since you ask, litharge is a kind of lead oxide, so I'm told. It be used in fine china and in glassmaking to reduce, um, stickiness, I think.'

The marines watched keenly as Rivers applied the noxious substance into the open barrel of the gun, spreading the mixture down with the rammer, before pulling it free with a satisfying thwack.

'Morning, Joe.' A voice from the gloom made Packer and Jack turn. 'Oh, and morning to you, sir.' Tim Clayton's face became visible by the light of the open gunport as he knuckled his forehead in salute.

'Morning, mate,' Joe replied. 'This is Captain Vizzard, our Commanding Officer. Sir, this is Tim Clayton, the man I was drinking with the night of the, er, trouble with Mister Harcourt.'

'That were a bad night, Joe. Not that I remember much of it.' Turning to Jack he said, 'Right pleased to make your acquaintance, your honour. Joe here saved my life that night. You probably know that. I heard stories about hows you got Joe here away from a meeting with the noose, sir'.

'The marine corps is a special place in the Navy, Clayton, and I would rather my men died fighting our enemies than at the hands of one blackguard. I'll leave you to get on with your duties,' said Jack.

Clayton stepped across to the gun and watched as Corporal Munday asked Rivers to teach him how to prepare the mixture before moving to the next gun. Jack and Packer walked toward the forward companionway and, climbing to the main deck, made their way to the fo'c'sle and greater privacy.

* * * * *

The light from the swaying lanthorns flickered over Captain Moore's table as his quill dipped in the brass inkwell, staining the paper in his journal with black as he recorded the bare, cold facts of the present cruise. He added his private thoughts, chiefly on the officers and warrant officers he commanded and on whom he greatly relied.

Lt. Harcourt is become more nuisance with each passing day. He dithers and is inattentive in his duty and is unobservant. The watch on deck is composed of patently capable

124

people, for which I am sorely grateful, but Harcourt fails to give adequate direction to their endeavours.

Moore nibbled the tip of his left index finger, then he stretched his arms, inadvertently dripping ink on the canvas stretched across the floor.

Now rumours reach me of a maliciousness in him observed by the crew that I had not detected in the man, and it concerns me greatly. I shall watch Lt H closely and, if I must, clandestinely.

His journal entry completed, Moore sanded the page and closed the volume with a clap, stowing it out of sight in his desk. Slipping on his coat he strode out of the cabin and onto the deck, breathing in the cool evening air. He paced across the beam of his quarterdeck several times, hands clamped behind his back, sniffing the air. There was a bank of thin, wispy fog off the larboard bow, some two leagues distant, slowly sliding across the oily sea and *Melampus* was heading directly for it.

The helmsman, Christmas Wilson, a muscular former shipmate from Moore's days in the 32-gun frigate *Syren*, sensed his captain's mood and kept his eyes fixed forward, hands sensitive to every need of the rudder. He avoided any eye contact with his taciturn commander.

'Christmas,' growled Captain Moore, 'how long have you been a bosun's mate?'

'That'd be nigh on seven years, Captain,' Wilson mumbled, suspicion rising at the question and more than a little troubled as to what was coming next. He glanced at the fore and main royals, nothing amiss there. Courses, similarly, reefed up to their yards and in order, else the officer on watch would have done something about them. The deck was orderly. Nothing amiss came to his notice.

'And how many years in the service of the King?'

'Man, and boy, sur, it be all of twenty now.' Wilson swallowed. 'What's he after?' he thought to himself.

Moore, apparently satisfied, continued his walk, descended by the weather companionway, and went forward. 'Seven years. Twenty,' he thought. Moore himself had twenty years' service. Men on watch nearby stopped talking and wondered why the captain had left the quarterdeck but continued about their tasks with possibly more alacrity and zeal than might have been the case had the captain not been amongst them. Moore sniffed the air again. There was something wrong with it. His nostrils twitched, his senses heightened, and he strained to listen. The air was smoky and now there was noise, a faint but increasing crackling alien to his ship.

'Deck there,' shouted the maintop lookout, 'there's a ship afire, off to starboard. Can't rightly make 'er, but she be well alight, sir. The fog's hidin' her, sir.'

Moore paused. Then ran to the main shrouds and, puffing from the exertion, hauled his aching back up and out along the futtock shrouds, pulling onto the maintop and surprising the mute lookout, who pointed a trembling arm out to a point off the starboard beam. 'There, sur,' he shouted, compensating in volume for his hesitation in alerting the quarterdeck.

The fog had thickened and at first Moore could not penetrate the murk until a flash in the darkness followed by the cracks of musket fire gave him a bearing. 'Beat to quarters, Mister Weaver, this instant,' he roared to the deck, annoyed with himself for delaying the order. Unslinging his telescope, he adjusted the ring and centred the lens on the faint glow slowly weeping out from the fog. There, he saw it. A dark shape beyond the glow, and it was ... he was not sure ... a brig of war possibly? He could not make out the vessel on fire. Too much of it was destroyed. As he watched, its foremast, ablaze from base to foretop, fell with a shower of sparks into the sea.

He looked at the backstay, thought about sliding down it as though he were still a young midshipman, sighed and made his way through the lubber's hole and, as quickly as his aches allowed, descended to the deck. Instantly calling for Vizzard, he made his way through the crew running to their stations. 'Captain Vizzard, we have a privateer to deal with.' He shouted an order to bring *Melampus* onto the larboard tack and beat towards the danger. 'I sense something very amiss with this, Mister Vizzard. Let us sharpen our wits and have your best marksmen prepared.'

'Yes, sir,' Jack replied. 'I shall make ready for a boarding too!' Without waiting for further orders, Jack ran forward shouting for Joe Packer. 'Joe let's have sections two and four in the tops with extra powder and ball. Targets will be officers first. The remainder to make ready for boarding. We are going to see some action after all.' He grinned in the increasing murk while the smoke gradually enveloped *Melampus* as she steadily approached the burning vessel.

'And don't you look pleased about it, sir,' grunted Packer, before mirroring his friend's enthusiasm. 'The lads are fair itching for a scrap, too.'

Discipline, never the strongest in Vizzard's Vandals when idle, had been severely tested; only that morning a tough sailor foolishly challenged a marine to a boxing contest in the hold and wagering led to arguments among the circle of on-lookers. Packer had stepped in but not before several tars collected broken teeth, a broken nose, and a cracked rib, the last probably caused by Sergeant Packer's personal interven-tion. 'They need to mix it with a ship-full of Frogs, sir.'

Moore bellowed from the quarterdeck and the main course rattled to its yard. The frigate heeled through three points smartly, Christmas Wilson bracing himself as the bows burrowed into the silky sea, before he eased the wheel and straightened her on the new course. 'Why did it happen on my watch?' he grumbled, well beyond earshot of the cap-tain, as the gentle breeze pushed his greying hair away from his leathery, sun-stained face.

The fog thinned a little and the first vessel, now blazing more fiercely, was drifting away to starboard. Brig-sloop, he now discerned, from what remained of her masts and rig-ging. Not a large vessel. Moore heard screams, shots, and shouting, then saw men jumping into the sea to escape the flames. His mouth tightened knowing that few sailors could swim, realising they had surely chosen drowning against the horror, the slow torture, of death by fire.

'Half a point to larboard, Christmas. Take me astern of the poor devils.' He could not bring *Melampus* to, in order to provide aid, not yet. He had to take the privateer before it slipped away in the darkness. 'Do you have her, Mister

Weaver?' he bellowed again, becoming energized at the prospect of profitable action after weeks of tedium.

'Aye, sir,' Simon Weaver shouted back. 'Ready to try on your order, sir.'

'Then let us get busy, Mister Weaver!'

The two 9-pounders in the foc's'le thundered out in near unison, their smoke drifting away as Moore waited for the report from the foremast. 'Short by 'alf a cable, sir.' The call directed at Lieutenant Weaver but noted with a scowl by Captain Moore.

The guns' crews were loading for the second attempt, the starboard crew, captained by Clayton, ahead of the other by eight seconds. Weaver, lowering his telescope, nodded at the gun captains. Again, the thundering crash. Again, the smoke. These were Blomefield's new design and Moore watched keenly to see how they performed in anger. The crews immediately set about swabbing out, preparing for the next firing.

'A hit, a hit!' The foremast lookout was hopping with excitement. 'That scattered the bastards,' he yelled.

'Belay that,' Captain Moore roared his disapproval. 'Attend to your duties, man.'

They were gaining. Moore's experienced eye measured the reducing distance. Estimating speed, distance, angles; three minutes or perhaps a little less, he judged. 'Mister Weaver,' he said more calmly, 'take a closer look at the jibs, see if they can be made to draw a little more, if you would.' Weaver dashed forward to speak with the people.

His frigate lifted as the jibs caught a breeze and steadied the bows, bringing *Melampus* back to the line Moore wanted. He peered into the dark again, lifting the glass to his right eye, the better eye he always thought. There was the enemy! A brig of war sure enough, and she was slowing even as Moore's eye found her. 'A Spaniard,' he thought.

The bow chasers spat flame again and men cheered as the brig's foremast splintered audibly and fell away, dragging her round as she lost way. Moore stared across and saw men working furiously with axes and knives to clear the wreckage. She would fight now; of that he was certain.

'Back topsails,' he roared above the growing noise, 'double-shot and with grape, Simon. Aim for her deck.'

Within a minute it seemed, the portside guns spat fire, smoke, and death across the closing expanse of sea, turning the brig's lower sails to lace and her deck to a butcher's shop. The second broadside was less disciplined, a little ragged, but further damaged the enemy who now found men enough to return token fire. Moore reckoned two or three balls hit *Melampus* that he knew but caused no serious harm. Then the gap between the two vessels closed with the groaning and splintering of timber and a great roar of voices: shouts of fear or aggression as well as derision passing between them.

'Take her, Mister Weaver. Go and board her. She's ours!' He glanced at Rynne who had drawn his sword. 'No, Dick. I need you here with me.' Lieutenant Rynne still held his sword but pulled a pistol from his belt and fired at the enemy, as an act of defiance at the order, the disappointment obvious in his pursed lips.

Weaver ran to the bulwark. Seeing Jack there backed by a dozen of his lobsters, he shouted, 'With me, Jack. Let's be at them,' with uncharacteristic volume.

But Joe Packer won the race, leaping across the narrow gap between the bows of both ships, his boarding axe swinging like a scythe in a field of barley. Jack was second, a fact that irked him, but soon he was too busy with his sword to think more of it. Face contorted, he lunged at a tall man dressed in blue, absently noting a ring hanging from the man's right ear. His opponent swung awkwardly with a cutlass that Jack parried calmly, driving the point of his weapon into the man's throat. Blood sprayed in a fountain of crimson. Amidst the rising noise, images of men moved slowly before him even as his sword flashed with the speed of lightning. He felt calm and master of his weapon.

As quickly as he despatched one, another appeared in front of him, and another. He side-stepped to the right, slashing, and catching a man across the face, evoking a curdling scream as the second closed with a pike. He stepped quickly into a gap on his left. Again, his sword swung down, severing the pike's head from the shaft, leaving its holder open-mouthed for a moment, until Jack's sword punctured his right lung, causing the man to collapse to his knees, frothy blood bubbling from his mouth, before he fell face down to the deck.

Weaver was to Jack's left, hacking at a pair of Spaniards intent on bringing down the English officer. Jamie Hay swiftly thrust his bayonet into the nearest, giving Weaver a reprieve and freeing a space for him to slash his cutlass hard onto the neck of the second assailant. The man screamed and fell against the bulwark, where another marine finished him with a bayonet.

Jack looked to his left, towards the vessel's stern, and saw the brig's captain. As their eyes locked, Jack knew he had to kill or capture the man if they were to take the vessel. 'Joe

Packer,' he yelled, 'with me.' He knew instinctively the tough sergeant would be close, even if not visible. Then he started slashing and stabbing as more enemy sailors pressed forward.

A marine's pike lunged forward impaling an older sailor who failed to avoid the weapon in the press of men, his face grimacing in agony as his innards spilled when the weapon was withdrawn. Jack pushed a man aside onto Weaver's sword as the *Melampus'* boarders pressed forward.

'We must get to the officers, Jack,' shouted Weaver, 'while those bastards live, they'll fight!'

Jack grunted. 'Kill the bastards, Simon. Just kill them,' he shouted. 'Spare none.' And in that moment, amidst the chaos, noise, and screams of wounded and dying men, Jack noted Weaver had, after all, proved himself to be a fighting officer deserving of merit.

Steel struck steel and steel struck bones and men screamed as they spilled their blood onto the filthy deck. More sailors and marines pressed through as the Spaniards and Moors fought like cornered beasts to keep their ship, and to stay alive. They fought the onslaught from the determined English sailors and faced the terror that Vizzard's Vandals, with their blood curdling screams, physical strength and vicious fighting skills, were creating. Jack's men appeared invincible, defeating all comers that stood before them.

He glanced to his left and saw Simon Weaver on his back, clutching his leg. 'Bloody hell, Simon. This looks bad.' A small Spaniard, with more courage than others, was moving forward, a wicked cutlass above his head. 'Oh no you don't,' yelled Jack and darted forward to catch the man under the arm with the point of his sword. The Spaniard shrieked in agony as the blade punctured his heart. 'Get back, Simon. Get back to the ship.'

A ball plucked at Jack's tousled, sweating hair. Spinning on his heel he pushed towards the brig's wild-looking captain, who had dropped to one knee and was busy reloading his pistol. Jack looked at him as he struck another Spaniard's knee with a violent kick and heard the joint crack, finishing him with a thrust of his sword. His pistol was empty, and he stared at the Spaniard. Quickly he bent and pulled the knife from his boot.

Packer was at his side again, a cutlass in one hand, a bloody boarding axe in the other. 'You goin' for him, sir?' he yelled, nodding toward the enemy's captain.

Together they pushed men aside, until Jack found his way forward blocked by a giant of a man, a dark-skinned Moor standing like a mountain in front of him. The man was a full head taller than Jack, with gleaming white teeth, a huge sweating chest, the most muscular arms Jack had ever seen, and a scarlet sash around his naked waist. A wicked scimitar swung lazily from his right hand.

If he wanted the captain of this privateer it would have to be through, or over, this muscular and very capable-looking warrior. Jack guessed he was the captain's bodyguard. He stepped forward, his sword raised, and the Moor swung the shining scimitar, glinting in the moonlight.

Jack feinted as his opponent's blade scythed the air in front of his face. The man's reach was short, just as Jack had calculated when watching him playing with the weapon moments earlier. Jack's sword flashed, the Moor moved instinctively, and Jack's blade skimmed the man's side, drawing blood which trickled down his leg. The gleaming teeth vanished, to be replaced by a snarl and a low animal-like growl. The Moor spat from the side of his mouth and stepped forward, just as Jack hoped he would. As Joe thrust his pike, with a sneer the man parried it with his scimitar but, in doing so, left himself exposed to the point of Jack's sword, which flashed and pierced his chest.

Withdrawing the sword, blood poured from the wound while the man stood motionless, a surprised expression on his face. Jack wondered if he had not thrust deep enough, and in the time it took for the thought to form in his head, concluded the wound was not fatal. He raised the bloodied sword when, suddenly, the Moor collapsed in a heap at his feet.

Jack found himself facing the Spanish captain just as the man straightened and started to raise the pistol. As Jack paused, the Spaniard stopped, lowering his weapon. He half turned and gave an order to a young man behind him, who cut the lanyard holding securely aloft the flag of the Kingdom of Spain.

'El barco está perdido, señor. Tienes tu victoria.' His eyes fixed on the sword in Jack's hand, now menacingly close to his chest.

Staring at the Spaniard, understanding he was surrendering, Jack was aware of the continuing noise behind him. 'Tell your men that, señor,' he said in English, nodding over his shoulder. 'They don't seem to understand.'

The man nodded and shouted an order, after which his crew slowly started to throw down weapons. Jack's marines and the *Melampus'* sailors pushed them into a group in the middle of the deck, remaining wary of the Spaniards and ready to immediately end the life of any who might have a treacherous thought.

'Joe, would you get them organized and hail Captain Moore. He will want a prize crew aboard if I'm not mistaken.' Jack grabbed the loaded pistol from his prisoner and gestured below. 'And see if he has anyone with the Spanish tongue because I know nothing of it.'

The Spaniard understood Jack's gesture and started for the companionway to his quarters, conscious that Jack had not sheathed his sword. Jack followed at a sensible distance and realized that one of his men, Jamie Hay, was behind him. 'Sergeant Packer told ma ta stay with you sir.' Jack grunted and stepped into the spacious cabin as the Spaniard moved to an ornate desk in front of the stern windows.

'Tomará una copa de vino señor?' The man indicated a half-full decanter in a fiddle on his desk. A glass could not harm, he thought, and nodded acceptance. Behind him, Corporal Hay sniffed loudly.

After taking the offered glass, he hesitated momentarily while the man in front of him smiled wryly and took a large mouthful of the red liquid. Jack raised the glass politely as a knock on the cabin door disturbed them. 'Come in,' Jack acknowledged, and half turned in his seat as a midshipman he barely knew stood uncomfortably in front of him. 'Buckley, sir, Andrew Buckley. Captain Moore's compliments and I am to be your interpreter, sir.'

'Are you proficient in the Spanish, Mister Buckley?' Jack asked.

'Oh yes sir,' the boy answered confidently. 'My mother is Portuguese and from a port-making family, she is fluent in

Spanish, sir. She insisted that my sisters and I master the language, sir. Also, I am to tell you that Sergeant Major Packer has the prisoners under guard and that Mister Harcourt is appointed as Prize Master and has come aboard, sir.'

The final piece of the boy's news caused Jack to pause and Corporal Hay to visibly stiffen. 'Very well, Mister Buckley,' he said. 'I want to know this ship's business. You may start by asking this man,' he waved his hand towards the Spanish officer, 'precisely what his business is in these waters. I wish to know what he has been up to, where he has come from, where he is bound, and what his plans are.'

The midshipman started nervously but gained confidence as he spoke to the Spaniard. In response, the man offered a lengthy answer, but Jack sensed that he was merely prevaricating, judging by the midshipman's slightly puzzled expression.

'Sir, he says he has authority from his king to search out and attack pirates operating from the Barbary Coast and destroy them, as they have been raiding villages along the Spanish coast. But sir, he is many miles from his patrol area in that case. We are a nigh on a hundred leagues from the Spanish coast.'

'Now tell him to move away from his desk and to stand aside. Jamie, keep your weapon pointed at his chest.' Jack sheathed his sword and moved closer to the desk. 'If he moves an inch, shoot him.'

At the order from the midshipman, the Spaniard looked alarmed and hesitated. 'Go on, Captain, move away,' Jack growled standing tall between the deck beams. 'Move back,' Jack growled, gesturing.

The man snatched at a drawer and pulled a small pistol. He was dead before he could raise the weapon. Jamie fired, the ball smashing into the Spaniard's right eye, spraying blood upwards to the deck-head and throwing him backwards onto the stern gallery. Smoke from Hay's musket drifted lazily among the beams on the deck-head.

'That was damned stupid of him, Jamie. He was never going to fire before you.' Jack looked at the corpse, crumpled behind the desk. 'Stupid man.'

Opening the desk drawer further, he started pulling papers out when the cabin door pushed open, and Lieutenant Harcourt bent his head and entered the small cabin. 'That is my desk now, Captain Vizzard, and I'll thank you to not interfere with its contents.' Harcourt stood with a hard-faced, muscular master's mate at his back. 'The bully has acquired a mate,' thought Jack. Captain Moore clearly wanted rid of both men; both spelled trouble for an ambitious frigate captain. He smiled at them.

'Shut your mouth, Harcourt. You stand at attention and address me as sir. I am your superior officer—in every sense of the word. I am searching the desk for matters of intelligence, which a fool like you would not recognize.'

Jamie Hay stifled a snort and Harcourt moved his hand towards his sword, but his bravado failed him, and he dropped his arm to the side.

'That is the most sensible act you have made since coming aboard, Harcourt. I do hope Captain Moore has given you some decent seamen, for you will need them. I suggest you get on deck and leave me to my business.' Jack waved him away and continued his search of the Spaniard's desk.

He unfolded a letter from which hung a large wax seal and passed it across to Buckley. 'Read that, Mister Buckley, if you would. Why are you still here, Harcourt?'

The Honourable Russell Harcourt spun on his heel, hit his head on the overhead beam, and strode from the cabin, followed by the master's mate.

'This is an order from the Spanish admiral, de Córdoba, sir,' the youngster supplied. 'It is dated two weeks ago and tells the captain of this ship that the British fleet off Cape St Vincent has only nine ships against the thirty-five of his.' Buckley read more for a minute. 'Ah, this is interesting here, sir. He instructs the captain of this ship to act as escort to three or four other Spanish ships coming from Cartagena and escort them safely into Cadiz. He records a rendezvous place.' The midshipman's eyes rose as he read on. 'He says they are of great value and importance to Spain.' Buckley placed the letter into Jack's hand. 'Why are those ships so valuable, sir?' He asked innocently.

With their true nature not contained in the Spanish captain's orders, Jack was none the wiser. 'Why, youngster, I really have no idea, but Captain Moore, and our own admiral, will want to know about this.' He folded the document and placed it inside his coat. 'Here, there is a chart and some more correspondence that looks as if it might be important. We had best get on deck and see what's happening. Jamie, get a pair of the lads to dispose of this stupid Spaniard. Just throw him over the side. I have no time or inclination to hold a service for their dead.'

As he stepped onto *Melampus'* deck he glanced back at Harcourt and the master's mate who were securing the Spanish prisoners as their prize crew of a dozen seamen forced the unfortunate captives into the hold below. The two ships were still locked together. A gang of seamen were working on the brig's foremast, rigging a jury mast to carry a sail. *Melampus'* men were starting work to separate the two vessels as Captain Moore stepped forward. 'That was well done, Vizzard. I've ordered Harcourt to keep in company astern of us while we learn what this vessel was doing out here. There are only a few survivors from the ship he burned, who may...'

'I am most dreadfully sorry to interrupt you sir,' said Midshipman Buckley stepping toward his captain, 'but I beg you to interrogate this woman urgently. She's off the Spaniard, sir. And she has a very interesting tale to tell.' Buckley was all but hopping from one foot to another in his excitement.

Moore growled at the midshipman's interruption but looked at the disheveled, exhausted woman standing next to him. She was still wet from a fall into the sea, her clothes, such as they were, clung to her slender body, revealing the fullness of her breasts and the curve of her hips. She wore a seaman's checked shirt that was too small for her, and breeches that were too short, tied around her waist with a length of line. Her near-black hair was peppered in drying salt. Moore looked about him and observed several of the crew, with lustful eyes, standing idly in the waist. 'Mister Rynne,' he spoke quietly to his first lieutenant, 'have the crew attend to their duties if you please. The people are gawping as though this is a cheap Covent Garden show.' To the other officers he said, 'Come with me gentlemen, let us see what the lady has to say for herself.' He led them into his day cabin and invited the woman to sit at the table as he ordered his servant to bring some wine.

Moore understood but a little Spanish. Andrew Buckley appeared to speak it with ease and, growing in confidence, quickly had the woman, who he said was called Adella Moreno, chattering away nineteen to the dozen. Their dialogue was interspersed with much exaggerated nodding, once or twice a shake of the head, and the occasional shrug of the shoulders. Buckley paused to explain to the other officers how the woman came to be on the brig; she was the mistress of the captain but owed him no fealty as she had been taken from her home in Cadiz against her will. She made to spit on the deck but stopped at a word from Buckley.

Moore spoke to Buckley, asking a series of probing questions, all the time watching the woman's face and eyes for clues. He asked if she knew of the Spanish ships expected from the South Americas bound for Cadiz. He noted that she hesitated and that her eyes dropped momentarily. Buckley could not avoid the quizzical expression on his face, but repeated Captain Moore's question. When she spoke again her voice was lower and more hesitant. Moore thought she was trying to be truthful but was reluctant to say too much. After a further question she spoke and confirmed that Spanish ships, but from Cartagena not South America, had been seen to the south yesterday. The brig's captain had been at first excited, then troubled when he learned from the crew of the xebec that four other Spanish ships had been delayed and separated from the others but were expected at any time. She revealed the *five* ships were armed urcas, large merchant ships that were to be escorted from Malaga to Cadiz by the Spanish fleet. Moore found her answers confusing and contradictory. He needed solid, reliable intelligence before he could report to Sir John.

Concluding the information given by the Admiralty was also flawed, Moore now doubted the ships would be carrying bullion. Yet he did not think the woman was intentionally lying; he stared into her eyes and saw compliance, a willingness to cooperate. She was no beauty but, on the other hand, she was not unappealing. She would have to be kept safe from his crew, he decided.

As her shoulders drooped, Moore felt a momentary sense of guilt: she looked exhausted. 'Have her taken below into the care of the master, please, Mister Buckley. See that she is given some dry clothes and some food. She is to be kept under guard by one of your marines.' Jack nodded his assent. 'I'll flog anyone who makes to move on her while she is under my protection.' Moore spoke earnestly. Woe betide any man who failed to take their Captain's words seriously.

'This information changes our enterprise, gentlemen,' continued Moore when the midshipman had left the cabin with the woman. 'It appears that we face four or as many as five merchantmen, all heavily armed no doubt, and very likely under a strong escort.' He stood and stepped towards the stern windows to look at the Spanish prize sailing indifferently approximately three cables astern of them. He noted that Harcourt was standing with a telescope to his eye, doubtless watching *Melampus* closely. 'We will need more support in the prize than Harcourt can offer.'

'I wonder if we should appoint another officer to command it, sir?' said Lieutenant Rynne. 'He is very junior to be offered such an honour, in my respectful opinion, sir. And the least qualified for any command.

'No, Dick. I have reasons to place him there. Ordinarily you would have the honour, naturally. He has our senior midshipman to, er, assist him, and a skilled master's mate. It is likely to be the making of the young gentleman ... but possibly not of the Honourable Harcourt. In fact, it could be his undoing.' Moore allowed himself a smile. Rynne and Jack understood the captain's intentions more clearly now.

The marine sentry at the cabin door knocked and announced the ship's carpenter, Harold Hawthorn, or 'Chips' as he was known to all, who entered with a knuckle to his forehead. 'Beg pardon, Cap'n, but I has to report a problem.' He paused and took a deep breath. 'One or two of the hits we took was on the copper and she's taking in water.' He sniffed. 'I got the pump working but it's not a good 'un. She'll start to settle afore long if we can't lighten 'er and plug some holes, sir.'

'Get a bucket chain going, Chips. I'll be down to take a look for myself.'

'Yes sir, done that already. Come as soon as you can, please. It looks bad to me.' Chips left the cabin, closing the door carefully behind him.

'I'll accompany you, sir,' said Lieutenant Rynne. 'I've not seen Chips look so troubled before.'

Moore nodded. 'We'll discuss matters further gentlemen. Let us see what is upsetting our carpenter.'

Finding their way down to the orlop deck, where no natural light permeated, Moore and Rynne fumbled behind Chips, who was carrying a lanthorn to light the way. In the lowest part of the ship the men were moving like old men, stooping low to avoid the beams overhead while they heard, rather than saw, the rats scurrying away at their approach.

Low down on the larboard side, Chips came to a sudden stop. 'Bugger,' he said, as Moore bumped into his back, 'there's another one I missed, sir. Looks like a couple of strakes has sprung.' He moved the lantern closer. 'See there, sir? I can fix the strake block but those two are badly damaged. And look here, it be worse than I thought. There's rot, lots of the bleedin' stuff.' He shook his head as Moore and Rynne leaned closer to the hull. 'The worm has got to it, Captain Moore. I can patch it, but it'll not hold for long. There's too much rot for me to tackle, sir.' He paused, measuring his words, knowing that his next comment would make the officers miserable.

'We need to get her into a dockyard, Cap'n.'

CHAPTER 9
Minerve

On the quarterdeck of *La Minerve*, Commodore Horatio Nelson studied the Rock and the Old Mole and Devil's Tongue Battery through his old telescope before looking up to focus on the developing cloud. All sea captains learned early in their career of one particular weather anomaly to be found there, called the levant.

The levant is an easterly wind that blows in the western Mediterranean Sea and southern France, an example of mountain-gap wind. In Roussillon it is called 'llevant' and in Corsica 'levante'. In the western Mediterranean, particularly when the wind blows through the Straits of Gibraltar, it is called the Viento de Levante or the Levanter. It was also known as the Solano. The Spaniards believed that one must 'ask no favour during the solano', because no one would want to help. They also thought that only pigs and Englishmen were immune to its ill effects.

Levanter comes from the Spanish 'levantar' to rise, as in the sun rising in the east. It can be a dry wind if rising from the southeast but, more often than not, it is a wind from the east or northeast which, when the air is warm, picks up moisture as it runs over the cooler waters of the Alboran Sea. When the winds are light, this gives rise to summer fogs that plague the residents of the Rock. As the winds strengthen, the fogs lift and appear as cloud.

The appearance of the Levanter cloud and how extensive it becomes depends very much on changes in the wind, humidity, the stability of the air and the depth of the moisture layer.

It can appear as a layer of low cloud, or there are the days when it is seen as a solitary cap suspended from a blue sky, forming as the wind hits the Rock and is forced upwards allowing the air to cool and then condense and form cloud. This cloud may be sculpted by the Rock itself. Under normal atmospheric conditions temperatures cool with increasing altitude. However, there are times when this changes, for example when warmer air passes over cooler air overlying the sea's surface. This rise in temperature then acts as a lid on the flow of the air and affects the depth of the cloud, giving it a flattened appearance.

Snapping the telescope shut and placing it under his left arm, he paced across the holystoned deck, now almost white in the morning sun. Nelson was troubled. He lacked detailed information and that always caused his mind to become a fertile field of activity. As the morning sun climbed over the Rock and spilled down onto the busy harbour, he blinked as his right eye reacted to the light. He reflected on the activities of the last few weeks; immediately before Christmas, when in command of *La Minerve,* he had captured *La Sabina* and fought, and beaten, a second, and larger, Spanish frigate, *Ceres.* That ship escaped him, but he, in turn, had to escape the clutches of a small enemy squadron of two frigates and two large line of battle ships. It had been a close-run affair. Nelson revelled in both the action and the subsequent escape from certain capture.

Looking up at his broad pennant, deployed on the larboard yardarm, flapping, lifting and falling in the breeze, he felt growing pride. The broad, swallow-tailed ribbon of silk, reinforced with cotton netting, had been lovingly made by his wife, Frances. It signified his command of a small squadron of warships—one that had acquitted itself well in the recent action. He was now but a short step from reaching flag rank, which must come within the year, he thought. Old Jarvie had elevated him ahead of other captains with more seniority and for that he was grateful, even if the other captains were not; doubtless some bore him resentment, even jealousy perhaps. However, to secure his own flag and a full independent command, he needed something to distinguish him from his brother officers, some deed to set him apart. He had to make his name. Now the Dons were confirmed to be at sea, there would be a major battle, the only questions being when and where. And it was a battle that he was determined to be at the heart of.

The Dons had switched sides a year since so there had to be a major fleet encounter with them soon. Nelson wanted one; Jervis wanted it too, as did England. Indeed, England needed it: needed a victory. Morale at home was low. Last year's harvest was poor. Prices were rising, and the invasion of his beloved country was a real threat. If the Dons were able to combine with the Frogs, they would present a formidable force. Better that Jervis should meet the Dons first and annihilate them. Nothing less than a total defeat of the Spanish would do. Although that would still leave the Frogs.

But a report had reached him only this morning that the Spaniards had slipped through the Straits four days before. It was why he paced the deck in agitation, hands clasped behind his back, eager to be gone. Frustration was etched on his earnest face.

The government in London determined the Royal Navy's presence in the Mediterranean had become untenable. Nelson supervised the evacuation of British people and others from, firstly, Corsica, then Elba, which made him angry. The Navy would have no presence or influence in that sea for the first time in centuries. Having fought and captured enemy frigates and been forced to abandon his beloved *Agamemnon,* which was worn out and which Jervis had sent home, he complained bitterly at the decision to abandon the Mediterranean, which would now become a French lake. Without the bases England had built and developed in Malta and Majorca, the British fleet could not seek shelter nor obtain stores and supplies, making it inevitable that the fleet must withdraw.

'Good afternoon, sir. May I ask, how is the eye today?' Nelson's thoughts were interrupted by *La Minerve's* captain, George Cockburn, and he ignored the polite enquiry.

In the evacuation of Calvi in '94, Nelson had been supervising a gun battery during the bombardment of Fort Mozello, when his right eye was injured by flying stone fragments. It increasingly troubled him, causing near complete loss of vision in that eye, and he could do without well-intentioned reminders of the disability.

'Are we ready to sail, George?' he said. 'I am anxious to find Jervis. The Spanish have passed through the Straits these four days past. Please, we must reach our rendezvous with Jervis without delay.'

'Very well, sir. The water lighter will have completed our watering shortly. I'll have to do my rounds to satisfy myself and will pass the word when all is ready, sir.'

Built in Toulon for the French navy and captured in June '95, *La Minerve* had been taken into His Majesty's service. Cockburn had commanded her since August of the previous year. He fought her, under Nelson's direction, in company with *Blanch,* against the Spanish ships, *Santa Sabina* and *Ceres.* Under Cockburn, *La Minerve* had captured the former sustaining battle damage in the action, much of which had been repaired by the crew. She carried 40 guns: twenty-eight 18-pounders and twelve 8-pounders. A well-built and fast frigate, Cockburn was happy with her. And Nelson was content with Cockburn, mentioning him in his despatch to Jervis following the action.

However, the *Santa Sabina*, had been recaptured by the Spaniards with her prize crew, including two fine officers, Lieutenants Hardy and Culverhouse. Nelson wanted Hardy back and an exchange had been negotiated with the Spanish, returning the captain of *Santa Sabrina*, Don Jacobo Stuart, to his own fleet. Both Hardy and Culverhouse were returned to Nelson.

La Minerve weighed anchor and Nelson again wondered if his destiny was to miss the fleet battle he knew to be inevitable. He noted with interest two Spanish frigates had left Algeciras, the village across the bay, intent, no doubt, on shadowing *La Minerve* and perhaps making a prize of the fast English frigate. He smiled and quietly told the Spanish ships astern 'You will not catch me, nor *La Minerve*. Not this time,' before going below to join the ship's officers and guests at luncheon. Before doing so, however, he spent ten minutes alone in his cabin and again pulled the bundle of paper from his trunk and sat by the stern windows, turning the pages until he found the place at which he had left off the previous evening.

Sir John had passed the bundle, a faithful copy of his own, written out in a neat, copperplate hand by his secretary. Nelson recalled his commander's words: 'I kept this essay it having been loaned to me by General Debbieg, a great friend of the author. Neither gentlemen is a sailor and it is too good an essay for a landsman. However, it is a sound thesis likely to prove its value to men such as you and I. I encourage you to study it well and make use of it when you can.'

And Nelson had studied it many times since. The subject of the essay on Naval Tactics was the theory, as espoused by John Clark, a learned man and Fellow of the Royal Society in Edinburgh, that the usual system of fleet battles was inherently flawed. Clerk argued that for a fleet to range along the line of the enemy required each ship to run the gauntlet of fire from each of the opposing ships in the enemy's line. Such a manoeuvre gave the enemy vessels the advantage, the opportunity to destroy or disable each of our ships as it passed along the enemy's line.

Far better, he argued, to force an enemy's line into close action by cutting through the centre of its line, thereby separating one division from another. Such a tactic, he maintained, would enable an English commander to capture one division or to bring about a general engagement involving most of his own line of battle ships at once.

Nelson found the tactic most appealing. He loved the simplicity of it, relished the prospect of cutting through an enemy's line to bring on a pell-mell battle. It was new. It was exciting. It was original. He had his servant read it aloud to him, the better to appreciate the audacity of such manoeuvres and the confusion it must surely bring upon the enemy's commander and his captains. Jervis had confided to him at the time his intention to employ the method should the Spanish fleet be deployed in such a fashion as to ensure a reasonable prospect of success.

He marked the place where he finished reading with a ribbon and made his way to the ship's wardroom to join the officers.

'My apologies for keeping you from luncheon, gentlemen,' said Nelson. 'I am anxious to depart and locate Admiral Jervis.' He took the seat at the head of the table. 'The news, gentlemen, that I received earlier this morning, is Córdoba and his fleet have left Cartagena and passed through these very straits these four days past. We are a few days behind them.'

Murmuring rippled around the table. Sir Gilbert Eliot, a diplomat and former deputy judge advocate of Corsica, found himself a guest of Nelson and on board *La Minerve* with Colonel Drinkwater, his military secretary. 'Will you pursue them to the Caribbean, Nelson? Is that where the Spaniards are bound, do you say?' he asked.

'I think not, Sir Gilbert,' said Nelson, pouring a glass from the decanter in front of him. 'They may want to attack our possessions in the Caribbean. However, the Dons will want to meet up with the French and I surmise their admiral has orders to do so. I suspect they will be bound for Brest, so I plan to proceed in that direction and trust we encounter Sir John somewhere near here,' he pointed to a chart on the table showing a projection on which was written Cape Trafalgar, 'before any major action, though I fear we may already be too late.' He could not keep the disappointment from his voice. There was a murmur of agreement and some nodding heads around the table.

Colonel Drinkwater raised his glass and said, 'Gentlemen, may I propose a toast for the safe return of our esteemed friends, Lieutenants Hardy and Culverhouse. I am so pleased to see you back amongst us, Hardy.'

Before Tom Hardy could reply, a cry from the deck interrupted the proceedings. 'Man overboard,' shouted the midshipman of the watch.

While Eliot and Drinkwater moved to the stern gallery to learn what may be seen of the unfortunate sailor, the officers raced to the quarterdeck. Hardy was first and ordered the ship's jolly boat to be lowered—the officer on watch had omitted to do so—stepping in as it was swung outboard, with a party of four strong oarsmen. The boat quickly fell astern of *La Minerve*, with the strong easterly current pushing it back toward the Straits.

From the edge of the thin sea mist the two Spanish two-deckers appeared. The departure of *La Minerve* had not gone unnoticed by the ever-watchful Spanish in Algeciras Bay and Nelson's pennant fluttered as he watched the small jolly boat struggling against the tide while the enemy ships slowly drew closer.

Nelson paced across the quarterdeck. 'By God, I'll not lose Hardy again. Back that mizzen topsail,' he roared to Captain Cockburn. Within a minute, *La Minerve*'s forward motion slowed, and she lost way, drifting down to the jolly boat. The leading Spanish ship hesitated assuming that *La Minerve* was challenging her as the vanguard of the British fleet, and promptly abandoned any pursuit, turning away to the southwest. Hardy and the jolly boat were recovered, and Nelson ordered Cockburn to turn southward immediately.

The adventures of the evening were far from over, however. The easterly wind that gave rise to the Levanter brought with it other weather components in the Straits of Gibraltar—increasing humidity, mist, and then fog. A thick fog developed as the evening progressed into darkness, a fog made when warm air, flowing out of the Mediterranean, met the colder air coming in from the Atlantic, causing the frigate to progress slowly and stealthily through the thickening, enveloping night. In the dark, the officers and crew of *La Minerve* gradually became aware of the presence of other ships. The watch on deck heard the sighs of sails and creak of rigging, the discharge of minute guns—clearly the Spaniards signaling—and the soft wallow and wash as they passed very close to a particularly large vessel.

Orders from the officer of the watch were given in whispers as the crew moved about the frigate like prowling cats of the night. All lights were extinguished, men instructed to be silent on pain of a flogging. The sounds of ships' rigging creaking, and the soft slap of the sea against hulls, told the silent officers that they were in the midst of a large fleet. A fleet that was providing protection to a valuable convoy of mercury destined for the Spanish colonies in South America, where it was to be used in the amalgamation of silver ore. A fleet ordered to meet with its new French ally's fleet. The fleet had been blown out into the Atlantic by the same Levanter that had taken Nelson out of the Mediterranean. The Spanish fleet was beating back towards Cadiz when Nelson unwittingly sailed through it, entirely concealed by a cloaking fog of invisibility. Nelson and Hardy stood silently behind the helmsman, listening with ears straining.

La Minerve cruised soundlessly through the Spanish vessels, as silent as ghosts, the duty watch holding its collective breath as it did so. A very large ship passed by only yards away, towering above the frigate like a cathedral overlooking a parish church. A babble of voices floated across the short stretch of water as Nelson stood steady in anticipation of a challenge.

None came.

CHAPTER 10
Prince George

Yes, Admiral, I do understand, but ...'

Captain Moore reviewed the carpenter's written report following their inspection and, along with the returns from the other standing warrant officers, sent copies over to Admiral Parker with his own observations and suggestions. He found himself summoned to Parker's flagship, *Prince George*, to explain matters in person before his senior decided his fate.

'No buts, Captain Moore,' said Rear Admiral William Parker. 'Those are my orders. I note your submissions and applaud your devotion to duty. However, you will return to England with all possible speed and have your ship's defects addressed by the dockyard. You will be of no service to me or Sir John if your *Melampus* should flounder in the midst of a battle. And your marines will transfer to my flagship and the squadron. My orders from the Admiralty did not allow time to embark any and we will need them. Who commands them?'

'Captain Jack Vizzard, sir. A first-class officer, inclined to be unorthodox but his men won't have an ill word of him spoken in their presence.' Moore uncrossed his legs. 'Will that be all, sir?' Moore could not conceal his bitterness any longer and wished only to return to his ship.

Admiral Parker returned the quill to its polished brass well, sprinkled fine sand on the letter he had been writing, then blew on the paper passing it across to Captain Moore.

'I believe so, Moore. Here is my formal order. If you will have the marines sent across, I shall have my boats for them in, say, an hour. Thank you.'

Melampus and Parker's small squadron had heaved to while Captain Moore relayed the news to the admiral that two shots on the waterline had caused greater damage than originally thought and his frigate was in worse condition than he had understood, with a great deal of rot. The pump was barely keeping the water level low. In attempting to repair the damage, Chips discovered that several of the ship's knees were rotting. He cut out and scarfed new timber where he could, but *Melampus* was in need of more work than could be undertaken at sea. Much of the stores had spoiled and several water barrels were damaged during heavy weather earlier in the cruise.

Moore left Admiral Parker's cabin in a downcast state of mind but was forced to accept the admiral's decision. He knew it to be the correct one. The bitterness showed on his face and his coxswain wisely withheld any greeting, simply ordering the boat's crew to, 'Sight your oars,' then to, 'Bear off.' As the stroke oarsman raised his head to look up at the huge, second-rate flagship, *Prince George* of 98 guns, towering over the boat like a majestic cathedral, the coxswain shouted, 'Eyes in the boat,' to bring the man back to his duty.

Moore was piped aboard and met by Lieutenant Rynne, to whom he issued the curt command, 'Please have Captain Vizzard report to me in my cabin. You too, Dick.' He stamped aft, shaking the spray from his hat, pulling off his boat cloak and calling for his servant.

Pouring a large measure of claret into a glass goblet, he sat at his desk and started to read the returns he had demanded from the gunner, the bosun, and the purser. He frowned as he read, his thoughts interrupted by the marine sentry knocking on his door and announcing Vizzard's arrival.

'Come in, Jack,' he said. 'Sit, please. I have news that affects you and your men, er, imminently.' Moore shifted uncomfortably in his chair.

He proffered a glass to Jack, who slowly shook his head as the captain of *Melampus* relayed the news that the marines on board must immediately transfer to *Prince George* in readiness to join with the fleet commanded by Sir John Jervis. Also, that *Melampus* was not thought to be sufficiently seaworthy to serve any useful purpose in the forthcoming battle.

'I am, naturally, disappointed that we must part company. However, *Melampus* cannot perform any useful service in her present condition. The admiral's requirement to transfer you and your company to his squadron is a sensible one; you would not wish to be returned to England, now would you, Vizzard?

'I'll take that glass now, sir,' said Jack, dismayed at the news. He drained it in two gulps. 'Clearly this is not a matter in which I have any say.' Moore slowly shook his head. 'In that case, if you will excuse me sir, I had better get the men organized. I am sorry that we will not be fighting the Dons with *Melampus*, sir. Your absence from the fleet is to be regretted, and you will be greatly missed.' Jack stood and walked out of the cabin, genuinely sad for Moore's disappointment.

As he reached the lower deck, he bellowed for Sergeant Packer in a voice that the entire watch below deck heard. Within minutes, the marines' quarters became like a disturbed ants' nest, with men dashing around seeking out items of kit and gathering personal weapons. Sailors gawped and wondered at the activity until Dick Rynne intervened and found tasks for them to attend to.

'I shall be sorry to see you leave us, Jack,' he said as the last of Vizzard's detachment climbed the companionway to the ship's waist. 'I fancy we will be missed if, or when, Jervis finds the Spanish and brings them to battle. Do take care, Jack, and I hope to see you in England before too long.'

They shook hands and Jack turned away, saddened to be leaving a ship he had grown fond of and men who had become his brothers in arms. Rynne had a parting shot for him. 'Watch your back with Harcourt, Jack. I've learned something of the part you played in his little drama.'

Jack half turned and smiled, before saluting the ensign and lowered himself down to the long boat to wonder what awaited him and his men on the *Prince George*.

* * * * *

'Welcome, welcome, Captain Vizzard.' Rear Admiral William Parker waved Jack to a chair as his servant poured a glass of ruby red wine for the rear admiral.

'I daresay you are troubled, er, perhaps concerned, at the sudden change in your circumstances. Your detachment will be unsettled, I surmise. I have ordered Captain Moore to return to the nearest English dockyard for urgently needed repairs.' Jack nodded, waiting for the rear admiral to continue. 'I carry fresh orders for Sir John that, indirectly, affect your circumstances and the detachment you command. With my flagship, I bring five line of battle ships to strengthen Sir John's fleet. The Lords of Admiralty received news the Spanish have left Cartagena and may soon be into the Atlantic. It is a much larger force. If they leave the Mediterranean there may be the devil to pay if we miss 'em, do you see?'

'I do understand that sir. However, I am naturally interested to learn how their Lordships, or yourself, wish to deploy my company.' Jack was only just able to conceal his irritation at the upheaval.

'I was coming to that, Captain. I confess, I did not know of the condition that *Melampus* was in until Captain Moore reported to me. My orders are that Sir John's fleet is deficient in marines. He has companies of the 69th Foot on some ships of his command. In my own command I have no more than a handful of marines under the command of a sergeant which is all that Chatham Division had readily available. As I anticipate having the honour of commanding the van squadron under Jervis, I wish to have some of your men amongst my ships. I am informed that you have some excellent sharpshooters in your company. I leave it to you to determine the distribution amongst my squadron.'

'My men have been well trained, sir. We train daily with all weapons so that when we are engaged in battle we will not be found wanting.' Jack took a long pull on the wine.

'Excellent Captain, quite splendid. We must find the Spanish and quickly. If they junction with the damned French before we can intervene, I very much fear that an invasion of our country is threatened. The Admiralty has advised His Majesty that the Navy will do all it can to prevent that, but the army should prepare to defend the country.'

Jack gazed at the white-haired man seated across the desk. His mind had been working hard since Graham Moore ordered him to prepare to transfer to *Prince George*. He accepted his fate to be deployed as admirals desired but resented that his company was now to be dispersed amongst a squadron of several warships. He resented being powerless to prevent that. He resented not being free to deploy his men as he chose.

'Very well, sir. Then with your permission I shall report to Captain Irvin and see to the needs of my men.' Jack got to his feet, the admiral nodding his agreement, saluted and left the great cabin.

Rear Admiral Parker stared at the sea through the stern gallery and wondered when he might locate Jervis. And whether he could depend on his newly acquired and rather surly Captain of Marines.

* * * * *

'Farewell, er, Alfonso, and safe passage.' Jervis showed his visitor, a Portuguese trader who had stumbled into the patrol area of the British fleet, to the door of his day cabin, where a smartly attired midshipman waited.

Sir John Jervis was 62 years old, and salt-water ran in his veins. Not a tall man, he stood with a slight stoop. Silvery hair curled at the sides and was tied in a short tail at the back of his head while heavy eyebrows were pulled together in a frown. He removed the uniform coat, the shoulders heavy with gold braid and the broad lapels similarly adorned. His deep blue eyes stared directly through the stern gallery of his flagship, *Victory*.

Some men hated him, others—just a few—loved him. All men under his command quickly learned to do his bidding, and they respected him; in a little over a year, he had dramatically transformed the Mediterranean Fleet to which he had been appointed commander in chief. It was a reduced fleet, more akin to a large squadron, but now it was a highly trained, very efficient, disciplined, and powerful fleet. Every ship's company trained to the highest standards in gunnery and sail drill. That included his officers.

Now that Jervis was patrolling near Cadiz, having abandoned the Mediterranean, the French and Spanish alliance, tenuous as it might be, had made the fleet's continued presence in that ancient sea untenable. Jervis still harboured bitterness towards his subordinate, Admiral Mann, whose unauthorized withdrawal from the region and misguided decision to return to England Jervis viewed as a severe failure of his duty, worthy of a Court Martial. Jervis had also lost four ships during the extraction from the Mediterranean, further weakening his command. The *Courageux* had been lost with all hands in a gale, the *Gibraltar* was so badly damaged in the same storm she had to return to England, the *Zealous* had been driven ashore, and the *Bombay Castle* totally lost while negotiating the entrance to the Tagus. All of them line of battle ships that were sorely needed. He badly required reinforcements, yet none had been sent from England.

Now, at last, word had come from the Portuguese trader he had just entertained, of a small squadron of warships flying the pennant of a rear admiral or commodore, he did not know which, seen sailing south-by-west, some twenty leagues from Brest only five days ago. His spirits improved marginally: Lord Spencer may have finally made allowance for his difficult circumstances. He sighed.

Jervis was not a healthy man. He had risen to his present rank, Admiral of the Blue, after fifty years of service, having started as an able seaman. He was tough; tough on sailors and even more tough on officers who fell short of his standards ... his very high standards.

'Reinforcements at last, Sir John,' said George Grey, captain of the *Victory*, now seated by the admiral's desk. 'I wonder how many their Lordships have sent us, and which ships they may be. One trusts they will be well commanded, sir.' Grey understood very well Sir John's opinions of captains unsuited to command. He had sent one or two he judged unfit for command home.

Jervis paced the chequerboard-pattern canvas that covered his cabin's floor. He paused and half turned to face his flagship's captain. 'Yes, by God, George. Half a dozen fresh line of battle ships will strengthen this fleet and share in the destruction of the enemy.' He continued his pacing. 'It will be Parker, I am sure. Sir William Parker. A competent if unimaginative officer, George. Pray God, he joins us before we meet the Spanish.'

As he moved to his desk he said, 'Now if you will excuse me, George, I must attend to my correspondence.' Captain Grey stood. 'Of course, Sir John. I have some prisoners come on board from *Melampus* I must see to, including a talkative woman, I am told.' He nodded to an unseeing admiral, and quietly left his cabin, knowing that Jervis would burn the candles until late into the night, his correspondence known to be prolific.

Jervis dipped the quill and started writing.

To Lord Garlies. Victory, 6th February, 1797.

My Lord, I have received intelligence of the Spanish fleet from Carthagena having passed the Straits, and probably put into Cadiz. You are, therefore, to join me with the squadron under your orders, off Cape St. Vincent; or, not falling in with me on that rendezvous before the 15th, you are to proceed to Lisbon.

I am, my lord,
J. JERVIS.

He drafted a short signal, to be issued to the fleet at the start of the forenoon watch, for all ships to practice sail drill. He thought to instruct his captains to engage in live gunnery practice but decided against that. They could practice without powder and shot.

With the immediate correspondence off his desk, Jervis moved to his armchair, poured a small measure of port, a gift from the Portuguese, and picked up John Clerk's manuscript on Naval Tactics, reading it yet again by the lights of flickering tallow lamps. 'How will they be deployed?' he thought.

'They will appear in the southwest and, as likely as not, will be in a very loose formation. That will serve quite well.'

Jervis padded through to his dining room where he had laid out a chart of the Bay of Cadiz and studied the course of the fleet. Picking up a pair parallel rulers, he adjusted them to plot the most likely course of the Spanish fleet. He extended the line of his own fleet's track during the last twelve hours and, with a sharpened pencil – he always demanded sharp pencils—he extended the line. It intersected the Spanish course approximately 25 miles from Cabo de São Vicente. 'That will do,' he thought.

The fleet was ready. The men were ready. The ships well provisioned with powder and shot.

'We will need plenty of both,' he thought, before his eyes closed for an hour or two.

CHAPTER II
Sainte Antoine

Half a league windward of *Melampus*, the seized Spanish brig, *Saint Antoine*, was under orders to act as the frigate's escort for the voyage to Portsmouth. For two days Harcourt held to the course, two days in which he tried to learn something more of sailing. Croker told him the vessel was in fact an 18-gun brig-sloop of the 6-pounder class. The prize crew was inadequate to manage both sailing and gunnery, but if fully manned she would make a worthy addition to the British fleet so Croker busied the crew in cleaning the vessel, making it more appealing to any senior officer minded to take her into service. Harcourt mulled that over in his mind.

As the watches changed, the more confused he became until, leaving the running of the vessel entirely to the master's mate, Croker, he retreated to his cabin. There he spent too much time seeking to banish his worries in cheap Spanish wine.

The confidence he'd enjoyed when ashore as Lieutenant Harcourt was evaporating; he was unhappily aware that he was out of his depth and should have purchased a commission in the army. What he needed was something to mark him out as a man of courage and imagination.

Vizzard was to blame, of course: he poisoned Captain Moore's mind. Why else would he have been given this ship crammed with Spanish prisoners of war that he was supposed to take back to England? His place was aboard the frigate where there was a prospect of fame and glory, even promotion. One of the senior lieutenants should have been assigned the task.

Then the wind had increased from the east causing the brig to be forced further into the Atlantic. He paced the deck, anxiety mounting in the pit of his stomach, staring at the sails and surveying the spray as it crashed over the bows, scouring the horizon with the telescope—a gift from his father. Captain Moore and *Melampus* were nowhere to be seen. His spirits sank lower, and his anxiety increased.

Whenever Croker asked permission to make some change to the way the sails were set, or whether a particular man should undertake a task, Harcourt simply agreed. Croker had proved himself to be useful; he could read and write and even knew how to use a sextant, calculate a position, and read a chart. Why, had he been born a gentleman he would have certainly been commissioned by now.

Harcourt concluded he needed an ally. Someone to support him and his actions. He knew where Sir John Jervis was patrolling his fleet, searching for the Spanish. Who better as a supporter than the commander in chief of the Mediterranean Fleet? If he could only join him, surely he would be welcomed and praised for his initiative in adding a ship to the fleet. He was determined to try.

'Mister Croker. I have been considering our situation. I wish to change course for Cape St Vincent. I intend to take this vessel to Admiral Jervis. Arrange that for me if you would please.'

'What, fer … sir?' stuttered Croker, who was looking forward to a spell ashore in Pompey, and maybe a berth on a proper warship where a skilled master's mate was appreciated. Even, perhaps, a shot at obtaining a warrant as master. Now, that would be something. 'If I spoke like this toff, I could try for a commission,' he thought. It was why he enjoyed running this brig, for that stupid nob in the cabin knew bugger all about sailing, or navigation. How the bastard got his commission, well who knows?

'It's quite simple, Croker,' said Harcourt. 'Captain Moore has no choice but to take *Melampus* back to Portsmouth. She needs dockyard attention. We, however, are more fortunate. This vessel may not take a position in the line of battle, but we may yet prove to be of service to Admiral Jervis. The fleet is ever in need of frigates and small, fast vessels.'

Croker strode into the shelter of the wheelhouse and pulled the chart toward him. He looked at the brig's track. 'A course of east-southeast-by-south should fetch us up in the admiral's patrol area off Cabo de São Vicente,' he said carefully. 'Cape St Vincent, sir,' he translated hesitatingly. 'But our orders is …' His objection tailed away as Harcourt glared at him.

'Very well, then let's do it. Please issue the necessary orders.' Harcourt rocked on his heels. 'Also, see if any of the Spaniards want to live and pick a few to help you. Make it clear that if they try anything, I will personally throw them overboard to feed the sharks.'

Croker grunted an acknowledgement and moved forward barking at the handful of seamen on deck. 'Ready to come about,' he shouted at the helmsman.

The topsails on both masts swung through ninety degrees as the mainsail shivered and crackled but followed. The brig was in irons for a few moments, the few crewmen struggling with the sheets until, at last, she settled on her new course, and Croker relaxed a little. He sent the tough gunner's mate into the hold with another of the prize crew to question the prisoners. A third man stood guard at the hatchway, armed with an axe, a musket and pistol.

At the stern, Harcourt stood gazing absently at the brig's snaking wake, wondering what reception he would have when he reported to Admiral Jervis. He imagined the Admiral's gratitude at the welcome addition and approval. He might be given the honour of delivering the admiral's despatch reporting a great victory to the Lords of the Admiralty, an honour that, by convention, often resulted in a promotion for the bearer of good news. Harcourt felt the glow of anticipated glory and the approbation of his fellows.

Inflating his chest, he looked in the small mirror on the bulkhead. His future progress was assured, of that he was certain.

* * * * *

Relaxing on the leeward side of the *Prince George*, Jack was considered to be an irrelevance to the smooth running of Parker's flagship. He gazed along the length of the second rate and marvelled at the sheer size of the vessel. Never had he served aboard one of the giants of the fleet. She carried 98 guns, eight 12-pounders having been added to the expansive quarterdeck, and she had carronades, the 'smashers' as they were known to the Navy. The ship teemed with hundreds of seamen who all hurried about their work with clear efficiency.

Lieutenant Hale was supervising musket drill that morning, shouting instructions to the men, requiring them to repeat each action, so the process became so routine it could be performed blindfolded; one half of his company were busily working through the manoeuvres, the other half were below, working with the great guns. Jack watched with approval and saw no reason to intervene. Hale knew his business well. He noticed Packer in the waist of the great ship listening intently to Corporal Hay, concern etched on the latter's face, and felt the need to discover the subject of their intense conversation. Descending the larboard companionway, he marched towards his NCOs.

'What's afoot, Sergeant Major?' he said formally, Corporal Hay coming smartly to attention on his approach.

'Sir,' began Packer, 'Corporal Hay 'as news of a troubling kind.' Packer looked unusually serious as he turned to his junior. 'Jamie, tell the Cap'n wot you 'ave learned,' he encouraged, rocking gently on the heels of his immaculate boots.

'Well, sir, it's a wee awkard y'see.' Hay hesitated. 'There's a woman stowed away, sir.'

Jack smiled. 'That's not altogether unusual. Most of the ships in this squadron will have a woman or two on board. His Majesty is not required to pay them, however. But they do get half rations!' His smile broadened into a grin.

'No sir, this one is the Spanish lass off the privateer. She's must a' bin smuggled aboard by one o' the lads an' she's bin a yakkin' a mite aboot silver 'n gold an' such. One o' the gunners speaks the lingo, sir.'

Jack remained impassive during Jamie's explanation while being inwardly intrigued; there was something incongruous about it and he wanted to get to the bottom the mystery.

'I'll go below with you. Will you find the gunner who can translate for me?'

Followed by Packer and Hay, he made off to the companionway leading to the marines' mess.

An hour later, Jack was sat at the stern in one of the ship's boats, hooking on to the larboard side of the flagship, *Victory*. He stared up at the cliff that formed the wooden wall of the largest ship he had ever been aboard. The little boat rose and fell against the leviathan's side as he timed his move and grasped the handholds either side of the wooden steps on the tumblehome. A thoughtful sailor above threw a line over to assist the marine officer.

He climbed until he came to the open entry port in the middle gun deck and, carefully holding the line, pulled himself aboard to be greeted by an immaculately attired midshipman, no more than 15 years of age. The deck was crowded with sailors working the 24-pounders at a practice drill. Each was manned by a crew of 10 men. Weighing a ton and a half, these guns, could fire a 24-pound round shot as far as a mile at maximum elevation; readily two cables when fired at level attitude. Jack knew their effect on a ship's timbers was to shatter planks and send splinters flying, cutting down any crew seeking shelter behind the wooden walls. The midshipman led him silently up companionways to the upper deck, past the sailmaker's work area and into the admiral's quarters.

Five minutes later, Jack was sitting a little stiffly in front of the large, highly waxed, oak desk, occupied by a severe looking Sir John Jervis. The admiral listened to the marine's thoughtfully given reasons for his visit, his lined, impassive face betrayed nothing of his own feelings.

The interrogation over, Jack concluded with, 'I've questioned the girl very carefully, sir. She is adamant the ships will have entered Cadiz this evening or will be there on to-morrow's morning tide at the latest. That's what she learned from the Spanish privateer. The girl's captain was told to expect four urcas, or armed merchantmen, and a warship, detached from Córdoba's fleet. They have been keeping close to shore to avoid your fleet, sir. They may soon be busy unloading the mercury. In my opinion, Sir John, time is of the essence—there is not a moment to lose.' He licked his lips, now dry from his lengthy explanation.

The admiral was leaning forward, his eyes drilling into Jack's, searching for any signs of doubt, of uncertainty. He had questioned Jack thoroughly and found his answers to be patently honest and thoughtful. The marine captain had sought the audience to present him with a proposition; that the admiral authorize him to lead an expedition into Cadiz Harbour itself, with the men and means to capture, or burn and destroy, the ships. What he was proposing was a bold attack into the very heart of the enemy. Bold and extremely hazardous. Yet this earnest captain of marines harboured no reservations.

The venture this marine proposed was a side issue to the principal reason for Jervis' cruise in these waters; Jervis wanted England to have a victory to celebrate. It was essential to the populace and his career had prepared him for this battle. He wanted to locate the Spanish fleet and destroy it. His Majesty's marines were integral to that aim. They were desperately needed to fight the great guns, to deal with boarders, to provide sharpshooters, and to form the backbone of boarding parties to capture enemy vessels. 'And to act as his amphibious force for shore-based actions,' the admiral reminded himself.

Loathed to lose any of his force, he could spare a small contingent to make the attempt. If it failed, the loss of men would be a matter of regret, of course, but if it succeeded what a triumph that would be. What a blow to the enemy. It was the kind of enterprise Commodore Nelson relished. Jervis could appoint one of his captains to lead the expedition ... but if – no when – he met the Spanish, he would need all his captains. He studied the marine officer: was this another young Nelson? Was he capable of leading and succeeding in a mission such as he proposed? Certainly, he did not lack for confidence.

'You wish to singe the King of Spain's beard, to emulate Drake, is that your intention, Vizzard?' The admiral's stare was cold and steely.

'As you put it that way then, yes, indeed I do, sir. If you could spare a brig or one of the smaller frigates, we could get to the Spanish vessels and hit them fast and hard. The ships are bound to be berthed close together and my marines could attack them simultaneously.' He shifted in his chair. 'My men are highly trained and keen as mustard to take the war to the enemy, sir.'

'Frigates are damned valuable and cannot be spared. I need more of them, not less. It sounds highly risky to me Captain Vizzard. A very hazardous undertaking. Any of a dozen matters could jeopardize your venture and result in the death or capture of you and all your men. Some would say it is destined to fail.' Jervis tapped his fingers on the desk and continued to stare at the stone-faced marine in front of him before he finally reached his decision.

'Very well, I shall give orders for you to have the sloop, *Raven*, at your disposal. Commander Prowse is a fine, steady officer and will be of assistance to you I have no doubt. He has risen to command from the lower deck, but do not let that colour your judgement. He is an excellent sailor and a man of a quick mind. I can allow you to take a force of no more than fifty of your men and a handful of seamen to support you. But I will need you back with the fleet with all despatch. You should report back to me no later than, shall we say, Monday? That is the 13th. Sooner would be desirable.'

'Thank you, sir.' Jack stood and saluted. 'I am very grateful to you. We will destroy those ships or be damned in the attempt.' He turned on his heel and left the great cabin, his mind racing with loose plans and compiling a mental list of his needs.

A midshipman commanded the jolly boat that took him back to *Prince George*. Sitting next to him, Jack suddenly felt the Atlantic wind bite, the low weak sun providing no warmth, as the small boat rose and dropped on the choppy sea, jarring his spine. He wrapped a boat cloak closer around his shoulders. 'I heard a whisper that you may be commanding a detachment to attack some ships in Cadiz, sir,' ventured the midshipman. At Jack's startled expression he continued.

'Word travels fast, sir, even when it originates from an admiral's quarters. Most particularly when Old Jarvie approves a course of action. When a well-known marine captain asks to see the admiral, tongues wag and ambitions are heightened.'

Jack stared at him. 'Why do you mention this, Mister ...'

'Bedford, sir. Joshua Bedford, at your service. Mind your stroke, Thompson!' he bellowed at the inattentive sailor. 'If my lieutenant agrees, would you allow me to accompany you, sir? I know some Spanish and have visited Cadiz before, in the *Agamemnon* with Captain Nelson, sir. That was before the Spanish decided to throw in their lot with the Frogs.' He grinned until an oarsman's careless stroke splashed cold seawater over his face. The unfortunate seaman received a colourful admonishment, surprising from one so young.

'Very well, Mister Bedford, if your lieutenant agrees I will expect you to make your way to the *Raven* at the appointed hour. I anticipate it will be before 'down hammocks', but await my signal.'

The jolly boat hooked onto the side of *Prince George* and Jack took care as he timed his egress from the pitching boat, stepping smartly onto the oak steps and eventually reaching the quarterdeck to report to the officer of the watch.

Seeking out Packer in the marines' mess, he whispered they would be involved in an important mission ashore on mainland Spain. He then dismissed the half dozen marines from the mess area and sent a messenger to find Lieutenant Hale and Sergeant Docherty. Both reported within a few minutes, and Jack outlined the purpose of their mission; to destroy the Spanish urcas carrying cargoes of mercury. He broadly explained how he proposed to conduct the attack, emphasizing the need for speed and stealth.

'And what does mercury have to do with Spanish silver, sir?' asked Sergeant Docherty when Jack had finished speaking.

'I would tell you, S'arnt Docherty, but I have no idea. I studied jurisprudence not the mysterious ways of apothecaries.' He laughed. 'What I can tell you is that each ship's cargo is worth a king's ransom to the Spaniards. It is our task to find and destroy them. It would be better to cut them out, but we will have neither the time nor the manpower for that.'

One of the marine guards from the admiral's cabin stamped into the mess. 'Beg pardon, sir, but Admiral Parker requires your presence in his quarters as soon as may be convenient, sir.'

Jack stood. 'That means without delay. I'll return as soon as I can as we have details to discuss and plan,' and he followed the marine guard to the admiral's quarters. There he found a naval commander seated in front of Parker who stood to face Jack and limped towards him with an extended hand. 'William,' said Admiral Parker to the commander, 'this is Captain Vizzard of the Corps of Marines, who will command the shore party. Vizzard, meet William Prowse, captain of the *Raven*, who will assist you and your men.'

'Delighted to meet you at last Vizzard,' said Prowse. 'I heard of your exploits back in '94 when I served on *Barfleur* as her third, under Captain Collingwood. We were busy but heard of your fight on the *Vengeur*. Lost my leg that day when a shot hit the gun I was laying.' The knuckle tap to his leg sounded like a door knocker. He laughed. 'Admiral Jervis appointed me to *Raven* last year, for which I am forever in

Sir John's debt.' He glanced towards Admiral Parker who was distracted by a despatch he was reading.

'Hmm, what did you say, William? Oh, never mind. Now look you two, I suggest you go below to get acquainted and put your heads together about this raid of yours. Let me have the details when you know them. You should pay especial attention to signals. Commander Prowse will help with that.' He bent his head to study the paper more closely, and waved an arm in their direction, clearly indicating they should leave.

* * * * *

'With the gunner's assistance, sir, I have been questioning the Spanish woman. She knows more than she would have us believe,' Lieutenant Hale said when Jack had taken a seat at the wardroom table. 'We now have the name of at least one of the ships, and probably know which merchants in Cadiz they belong to. I trust we will cause them great upset, to say nothing of the loss to Spain.'

'Tell me what you have learned,' said Jack.

Commander Prowse pulled up a chair and sat next to him, watching, and listening carefully. Jack accepted the wooden tankard of ale offered to him by Packer, took a swig, made a sour face, and asked for a bottle of blackstrap.

'The cargoes are destined for Casa Lonja de Mercadores, which in plain English, sir, is the House of the Merchants. The Spanish woman also had a port book concealed on her person. I have looked at it and deduce there will have been more such books on board the prize. They may still be there,

175

sitting in the dead captain's cabin.' Hale made to continue but Jack signalled for him to pause.

'What, may I ask, is the significance of these port books?' he asked.

'For our purpose, all too little, sir. They detail the cargo being carried, the port of departure, the destination, the merchant who owns the goods, the duty paid, the ship's master and suchlike information.' With an exaggerated flourish Hale produced a spoiled, soggy book and passed it across the table.

'It is largely ruined, sir, but the woman obviously thought it important enough to hold onto.'

Jack thumbed through the book, the pages glued together from immersion in seawater, and saw columns with meaningless names and numbers. 'What you are telling me is that the urcas will be berthed or moored close to the Merchant's House?'

'Indeed, I am, sir. The Spanish woman mentioned that a key merchant is a Juan Bautista de Lacoa. From what she said, he is the principal merchant or trader, or possibly an underwriter for the ships' voyages—she appeared uncertain. The ships will be close to his residence, which will be close to the waterfront. It has a very tall tower, but I am told there are a great many towers in the city.'

Jack stood up and stretched. 'We need to know how to identify the right vessels, Martin. The sooner we do that the sooner we can do what we intend and get out.'

Commander Prowse spoke for the first time. 'I can probably help with that, Jack. The port may be full of vessels at this time. Once ashore, if the light is good enough, I should be able to pick them out. The Spaniards' fleet is somewhere at sea, which means there should only be merchantmen within the harbour. In truth, the vessels should be relatively easy to identify.'

Prowse pulled a rolled chart from the boat cloak he was wearing. 'This is a chart of Cadiz Harbour.' He spread it across the table and placed a finger at a point near the entrance to the port. 'My best guess is that they will be tied up along the wharf on the south side of the entrance, just along here, for protection. The buildings along here are the merchants' properties, I believe. It is there you will find many merchantmen and, I have little doubt, the ships you seek.'

Jack wrote a list of those marines he wanted for the raid, with a note of the ships to which they were currently deployed.

'Jamie,' he said to his corporal, 'please take this to the signal lieutenant and ask him to pass the requests to the ships. I wish them to report to me here within the hour. Oh, and ask the lieutenant to make certain the flagship is included. It must be done in code and not in plain language. Got that?'

'In code not plain language. Aye, sir,' he said and took off to the quarterdeck to make sure the boss's order was sent.

There was going to be a fight at last, and Corporal Hay wondered how the Spanish would react. He wondered if he would survive. Who would die and who would live? He resolved to visit the blacksmith and get his bayonet sharpened, along with his father's lucky dirk. His father had used it at Culloden nearly fifty years ago. What would his da say if he could see him now, dressed in a red coat and taking the King of England's coin? Would he understand? Probably not, he decided.

When he returned, Jack was concluding his verbal instructions to Lieutenant Hale. 'We are agreed then, Martin? If necessary—if we are discovered—you will cause mayhem around the 'Castillo' and keep the Dons occupied. The rest of us will attack the urcas and set about destroying them. Joe, I leave you to ensure that both groups have as much ball and powder as they can carry. And grenades—as many as you can get. Designate four of the strongest men to carry bags of black powder, as many as they can carry. I checked with the gunner earlier and he grudgingly agreed to let us have one hundred pounds of Priddy's finest. Martin, I suggest your group carry some of the powder and a good supply of quick match. Remember, the powder burns at about one yard per second, so make sure you have ample.' He smiled at the intense faces. 'And keep well away from the vessels when you light them.' This raised a few laughs.

Jack had indeed secured a small supply of the gunpowder made at Priddy's Hard in Gosport. The gunner, who cherished his stock with a passion, had made it abundantly clear that it was a highly prized and expensive commodity which Admiral Parker added to the ship's store at his own expense to ensure he had more than the Admiralty allowance.

All this had been explained to the eager and demanding marine officer and the message was not lost on Jack, who parted with a handful of gold coins to soothe the gunner's conscience and ensure his company had what it needed to cause the maximum damage in the shortest time. He wanted a display of firepower to shock the Spaniards to the core, to make them regret turning against England and disrupting the recent, uneasy alliance with Revolutionary France. To strike a blow that would upset the financing of the Spanish navy made the mission even more appealing. 'Singe the King of Spain's beard,' Admiral Jervis had said. He liked the phrase. Yes, he would certainly do that.

As the minute hand moved around the face of his Half Hunter timepiece, small groups of marines arrived at *Prince George* and were directed by the officer of the watch to the marines' mess where Jack and William Prowse waited for them. They were, in the main, a well-turned-out collection of soldiers, but each of them had survived harsh conditions and exhausting battles while fighting with Captain Vizzard. Jack knew them all; more than a few had been in New South Wales with him and Packer. Mostly they were survivors from the desperate, bloody battle with *Vengeur du Peuple* in 1794. He noticed the midshipman from the flagship, Joshua Bedford, and nodded to him in recognition.

Prowse's large chart, published by Dalrymple, spread out on the large, battered table, attracted the interest of the marines. It was less than three years old and believed to be accurate. It appeared to be informative with some helpful detail.

'Captain Vizzard and I have discussed the delicate matter of our approach to Cadiz harbour,' began Commander Prowse. As you might expect, it is heavily defended. I will approach from the south for the landing, then one of my boats will move round into the port and try to create a diversion if or when needed.' He looked at Lieutenant Hale. 'You will have the responsibility of keeping any Spanish military distracted and will provide protection to the raiding group.

Mister Vizzard considers he may need twenty to thirty minutes to locate and destroy the vessels.' He looked at Jack and nodded. 'As to those vessels, they are most likely to be found ... here.'

Prowse's finger moved across the paper and stopped at a wharf a short distance behind the town hall.

'I had thought, Mister Hale, that your men be landed on this beach, which is called La Caleta.' He took a glass of blackstrap from the wardroom servant. 'However, the old city is surrounded by walls and forts, and, on further reflection, I recommend, Captain Vizzard, that all boats should land here. It is not directly overlooked by any of the forts. If I have remembered correctly, it is a blind area from the forts. A landing here should be all but invisible to the Spanish.' He was pointing to a length of beach to the east in front of the city's cathedral. 'From there, it is a short distance to the port where the vessels should be located.'

Prowse sounded confident and knowledgeable. 'I hope I am right, or these men will face a problem,' he thought, before continuing aloud. 'To the east of that point is the Castillo de San Sebastian, which I understand will be occupied by Spanish forces. The isthmus is quite narrow at that point and, I venture to say, more easily defended from any attempt to interfere. Remember, the city is a rabbit warren of narrow streets, so be careful.'

'You talk as though we are to be taking a summer picnic in the Cotswolds,' retorted Jack. 'Make no mistake, Commander Prowse, this will be an endeavour requiring raw courage and determination. Mister Hale's group are to provide a cordon around the demolition party. We must use stealth to work through the streets. If we are attacked, he will keep the enemy occupied until we reach the vessels, but only if I judge the mission to be viable. Then we move fast. But if we are engaged by a large force ... very few of us may make it back to the boats.' Jack let his final words hit the mark. 'Stealth and speed are vital, lads.'

The light-hearted mood quickly dissipated, as the majority took the information on board with sombre expressions. Some faces around the table looked concerned and anxious; a few, the reckless ones, wore smiles.

'Officers and NCOs,' said Jack, 'please gather round and study this chart. The rest of you go and prepare your kit and make ready to depart. Remember, lads, no red tunics. You wear those old canvas coats. I do not want us to stand out like tin soldiers trooping the colour on the King's birthday.'

No more than fifteen minutes had passed when a midshipman appeared out of the gloom and addressed Commander Prowse. 'The First Lieutenant's respects sir, and your ship's boats have been summoned as ordered and are now approaching, sir.'

'Very well, youngster. My compliments to the first lieutenant, and we will be assembled as soon as possible.' Prowse folded his chart and stood. Turning to Jack he extended his hand. 'I wish you the very best of good fortune. Is there anything more we can do?'

Shaking hands with the commander, Jack delivered a final, sombre request. 'We need to move fast in everything. We cannot afford any delays. If the mission must be abandoned, and in any event when we return to the beach, one of my lads will show a red light three times. If you could manage to distract any Spaniards that may be pursuing us ...'

'I understand your meaning, Vizzard,' said Prowse. 'We will be there and ready to take you off. Good luck. Let us get to the boats and have my *Raven* take us to Cadiz.'

Prowse, Jack and Packer supervised the raiding party into the collection of ships' boats being trailed astern, each ferrying heavily armed men to the sloop, *Raven*. The Atlantic was surprisingly smooth as the squadron cruised through the Gulf of Cadiz with the Spanish coast barely visible. As the dying sun gradually sank beneath the waves and darkness began to fall, the last of the sun's rays painted the western sea with bands of gold and purple. The fleet's vessels tacked and, to any watchers on the shore, disappeared into the growing murk of the western horizon.

Except one.

Raven headed southeast-by-south towards the ancient city passing the entrance to the port at a distance of three leagues. All lights extinguished and the ship's complement working in complete silence, she passed unseen, and gently hove to. A ragged collection of boats, their oars muffled by tarred rags in the rowlocks, swept silently to the beach south of the port's entrance, each commanded by a midshipman or an experienced leading hand, as the marines nursed their weapons and wondered what the coming night would bring.

* * * * *

The lookout reported a clear horizon; the little brig was alone in the Bay of Cadiz with the fleet it sought nowhere in sight. It was not the smartest vessel and would need a great deal of work if the Admiralty were to take it into service, pondered Harcourt, yet already he began to think of it as his own. He admitted Croker had improved the general appearance of the vessel with the limited manpower available. 'Yes, Admiral Jervis would be pleased,' he thought.

Looking at the chart he estimated they were approximately due south of Faro. They had seen a xebec earlier in the watch that scuttled swiftly away to hug the shelter of the coast. Croker persuaded Harcourt to abandon the fifty or so prisoners on a remote beach after rounding Cape St Vincent and, though he felt it foolhardy, he sailed away with a sense of relief from the burden of guarding so many prisoners. Having been consuming food and water that could ill be spared, they were left with a barrel of water and a sack of old bread. Some had been vocal in protesting but became more compliant when told where they were. Croker even discovered six of them wished to stay on board as able hands, so he had them entered on the ship's muster book. Captain Moore had assigned ten men to the prize crew—no doubt the ones he wanted to be rid of—so now Harcourt had enough men to sail the ship. In addition, he need not worry about an attempt to retake the vessel, something which had troubled him a good deal during the last few days.

He paced across the deck self-importantly, telescope tucked under his arm and wearing his best uniform coat; he wanted the admiral to see he was a smart and efficient officer, deserving of preferential treatment. 'Perhaps I may even be given permanent command of this unimportant brig,' he thought. Then, when he returned to the fleet, he would be closer to Vizzard, who had yet to be dealt with.

The tough marine had poisoned Lord Bridport against him and put him aboard *Melampus* and against Captain

Moore ... another senior officer who also disliked and belittled him. Well Moore was gone and would wait. It was Vizzard who must perish or be discredited and his disrespectful sergeant too.

'Where is Jervis and his damned fleet?' worried Harcourt, reasoning he should have found them between Cape St Vincent and Faro. He had Croker calculate the course to bring him to the patrol area, but Jervis was missing. Now he was undecided again; perhaps the fleet were closer to Cadiz? He pulled open his telescope and looked south and southeast. Yes, that would be right. Jervis would want to watch Cadiz to see what ships were in harbour. He would make his way to Cadiz, find Jervis and undoubtedly receive the admiral's approbation for his actions and initiative.

'Well, Mister Harcourt, what do you want to do now?' Croker intruded on his thoughts, his voice heavy with sarcasm. 'I got to tell you that the lads are getting twitchy about this jaunt of yours.'

Harcourt bristled. 'Remember who you are talking to, Croker. I am the King's officer and representative on this ship and the men will do as I say.'

'Aye sir,' Croker replied. 'But if you don't tell 'em what's happening they ain't gonna be too willing to do your bidding ... sir.'

Harcourt shrugged. 'Tell them we will find Admiral Jervis and the fleet in the morning.' He looked to the western horizon as the sun dipped into an oily sea, throwing streaks of orange and red across the dying sky. 'We have to find Jervis,' he thought, 'otherwise, my career will be ruined.'

He gave Croker the order to take him to Cadiz.

* * * * *

Captain Vizzard's boat was the first to hit the mixed sand and shingle of the beach with a heavy crunch and his feet the first to plant themselves on Spanish soil. He crouched, watching the boats silently reach the shelf of sand and disgorge their marines, his eyes searching for potential enemies and ears on full alert for any warning sounds.

The beach appeared to have been well chosen by Prowse. The fort on the southern entrance to the port was constructed with its armaments facing seaward, and the wall at the top of the beach looked deserted, at least he could not discern any guards. All was quiet. As quiet as a grave. 'Cadiz will not be my grave,' he vowed, his pledge to Mary in his mind.

Acknowledging Lieutenant Hale's signal from a hundred yards' distance, he waved him onwards. The section moved forward slowly, boots sounding loud on the wet sand. They slowed as they worked upward through the fine, dry sand, using well-honed skills to help each other scale the low wall. As they disappeared, Jack signalled his group to follow, and they ran forward at a crouch to quickly make their way over the wall, noting Hale's men moving along both sides of one of the wider streets.

It was quiet with only a pair of drunken seamen staggering along a street they knew not where. A bawdy house to the right had just ejected them and a dishevelled, more elderly, man followed them, straightening his coat and walking slowly with the aid of a stick. Jack signalled a pause in the advance and pulled his father's old Half Hunter from his pocket. He had fifteen minutes until Prowse started the distraction agreed upon. Time to move on.

Prowse had drawn him a crude plan, though he could not see the name of the road they were in, but he knew the general direction he must go and silently signalled everyone to follow. They padded quietly through the near-empty streets and collected at a narrow intersection where the shadows were darkest. Jack signalled them to move apart and go forward in small groups along both sides of the narrow road.

It opened onto a larger square lined with banyan and dragon trees, and with elaborately decorated merchants' houses, several with tall towers. Jack gazed at them momentarily, wondering at the architecture, then again waved his group through the square and along a short, wide street. At the end of the street, he saw masts and realised they had found the port.

'There they are, boss,' said Packer, a degree of surprise in his voice.

He signalled Lieutenant Hale to spread out, and watched as they disappeared into the shadows, then called his men forward and made directly for the middle of three merchantmen. Midshipman Bedford, who had commanded one of the boats, led a second group to the ship moored directly astern and a young marine second lieutenant, Marsden, from the flagship, who was unknown to Jack, had charge of the last group that made for the third vessel. Jack wondered where the fourth vessel was. He did not have time to explore the port to find it but thought it odd all four merchantmen were not moored together. 'Why only three?' He wondered.

All three vessels were dark shapes with only a harbour watch on board. As he ran up the gangway leading to his target ship, Jack heard a voice; a singing, drunken sailor was relieving his expanded bladder into the still waters of the harbour on the larboard side. Jack reached the deck and swiftly made his way forward. The stream of urine was interrupted when Jack's sword skewered the man, who obligingly fell headfirst into the harbour with little more than a gentle splash.

Noting a hatch had been left open, he told Corporal Munday to place fuses in the sacks of powder he was carrying and drop them into the ship's hold, but as he did so, another man appeared on deck calling out. Jack froze as three armed men appeared on the main deck. One called out orders in Spanish and pulled a cutlass from the rack to his left, but he was met with a pike, thrust into him by one of Packer's toughest men. His scream rent the still night air, and men started to appear on the other ships.

An officer—a man in middle age with a swollen belly poorly concealed beneath a crumpled nightshirt—quickly followed holding a sword and inviting a duel.

'I don't have time to fight you, señor,' Jack shouted at the man. 'Your ship is going to explode. Now put that sword away and get running.' He gestured to the officer to run while he had time, but the man simply stood his ground, silently circling the point of his sword.

'Hurry up, Corporal, let's get those charges lit and start some fires.' The surprise attack was now compromised, and Jack knew they had to work fast. Men began striking flint and steel to create hot sparks with which to ignite the tarred rigging, untidy piles of rope casually left on the deck, with a few poorly maintained ratlines taking fire quickly. The tar provided ready fuel to feed the flames. As they took hold and licked upwards, crackling and spitting towards the reefed sails, the increasing noise attracted more attention.

The overweight officer stared at the marines on his deck with his mouth wide open, but no sounds came. Slowly, full realisation reached his numb brain and he started shouting and ran directly at Jack, the sword now raised, his voice shrieking in fury, his face turning red and contorted. As he reached Jack the sword swung down and cut the air. Jack simply side-stepped and instinctively slashed at the figure, opening a wound across his abdomen that instantly turned his nightshirt red as the blood flowed. Jack turned from the screaming man to check on his other targets. Packer and two other marines quickly despatched the officer's men as they followed their leader to a quick death.

Along the quay, Hale's ship also now emitted flames. Hale and his men, silhouetted against the bright orange and red background, became invisible as the growing clouds of smoke slowly shielded them from view, and they fled from the scene of devastation.

Jack looked astern at the third ship, where shouting had startled nearby residents. It was time to leave, he decided. Satchels of powder could be heard sizzling and spitting, starting their work in the hold.

'Packer, time to go. The fires will finish the job. Our work is done.' A small group of three or four Spanish sailors had surrendered and were being ushered over the side to swim or sink, the marines cared not which. Packer and another marine, anonymous in the smoke, dropped two grenades each into the hold, as Jack and his party ran down the gangway to the dockside.

People were emerging onto the streets, attracted by the growing noise of the three burning ships, the light of which was now spreading across the night sky and reflecting off the low clouds. Residents were running towards the port as Hale and his party walked nonchalantly away from the havoc, heads lowered, keeping to shadows and trying hard to be inconspicuous. They attracted a few curious glances, but the local people were more concerned with the ships on fire in their port.

Midshipman Bedford had similarly thrown grenades into the hold and the officers' quarters at the stern of the ship, before running from the explosions. One of the sailors with him was too slow and was sent sprawling. Bedford halted and turned. 'It's no good, Mister Bedford, don't go back, he's a goner,' panted a marine, grasping the young midshipman by the arm. 'He'll have not survived that, sir.'

Lieutenant Hale reached the wall protecting the town from the sea. As he deployed a defensive screen, a marine on the beach opened a red-glassed oil lantern, lit the wick inside, and started the agreed signal. Hale squatted and scanned the streets. 'Come on Vizzard, where the hell are you?' He was growing concerned and his anxiety increased tenfold when he heard musket fire from the street in front of his position. 'Make ready, lads,' he shouted. 'We've finally woken up the buggers and Mister Vizzard has probably stopped off somewhere for a drink.' A couple of nervous laughs greeted his remarks just as Jack and his group came running from the street.

The sound of cannon fire caused them to turn and stare seawards, and there, close inshore, was the dark shape of

Raven, her larboard guns rippling fire and smoke, balls dropping into the streets ahead, adding to the growing noise rising from the port.

'Let's get the men into the boats, Martin,' Jack shouted, and to his own group bellowed, 'Two ranks of four in open order to give volley fire and cover the withdrawal.'

Jack left Hale to get the men into the boats as the marines opened fire on a gaggle of disorganised Spanish soldiers. The two ranks of Vizzard's Vandals, each rank alternating their disciplined and accurate fire, kept the Spaniards on the far side of the street, huddled in doorways, trying to avoid the lethal onslaught.

'Come along, sir,' said Docherty. 'It's getting a bit too warm for us here.' The rear guard was slowly falling back as the enemy increased in number and were now being led by a Spanish teniente, determined to capture the British invaders.

'One moment, Docherty. That man in front, the bearded one with the large sword. I think we should eliminate him before we join the men in the boats. He glanced to his rear and noted only one boat left with his marines calling him, his rear guard splashing in the sea to board the boat.

The Spaniards were now at the wall with all the protection it afforded while their officer called on them to attack the two British marines. Both men loaded muskets and knelt in the wet sand at the edge of the beach.

''Old on sir, not without me you don't,' shouted Packer, who knelt on Jack's right. 'I'm guessing you want their officer dead?' Sporadic fire from the Spanish threw up small fountains of sand and shingle in front of them, none finding its target.

'As soon as we have a clear shot, Joe. Yes. Then we go.'

The unfortunate officer raised his head, immediately generating three shots, one of which sent stone splinters flying from the sea wall. The other two found their mark, throwing the Spaniard's head backwards in a spray of crimson as his hirsute face exploded. The enemy's firing reduced immediately, but Jack and his two sergeants jumped for the last boat which pulled away as they took their places, the men laughing at their good fortune; they had caused the Spanish much damage for no loss to their group. One of his corporals had been hit, the shot grazing his neck, but none had been killed or maimed.

A gentle offshore breeze blew, assisting the raiders in their rapid escape from the beach, the oarsmen pulling hard, as more shot from *Raven* whistled over their heads. It struck the sea wall scattering the small Spanish force away from the killing ground.

* * * * *

The blaze in the city could be seen from two leagues at sea level. As the brig approached Cadiz, the glow in the Eastern sky became flames and smoke from substantial fires. The shout from the lookout brought Harcourt up on deck and, intrigued, he climbed the shrouds to the mainmast. From his position in the mast's lookout, Harcourt saw the flames dancing behind the silhouettes of the taller buildings and towers of the city. What he could not see, however, was Sir John's fleet. Surely it should be close now. As he moved the glass across the sea, he found a ship, close inshore and nearly hidden by the darkness. A small sloop it may be, but comparable to his own command, perhaps smaller. If he could destroy or capture that, his future was assured. It was quite obviously a Spaniard trying to escape the inferno in the port, he concluded.

He made his way carefully via the lubber's hole to the deck calling for Croker.

'Take a look, man. There's a Spaniard trying to slip away. We could destroy her or seize her. Would be worth a tidy sum as a prize, don't you think?'

Croker looked at the lieutenant and saw the man was serious. 'He's got no bleedin' idea,' he thought and patiently, as though talking to a child, started to explain. 'Sir, you know nothing about her, excepting she's a small sloop. She might have a crew of eighty, a hundred or more, Mister Harcourt. We are outgunned and outmanned. Wot we should be doin' is turnin' about an' makin' some sea room. Then you can find the admiral.' He shook his head in disbelief several times.

Harcourt stared at him for a long time. 'Croker, understand this. I command here and your job is to do my bidding. I say we clear the ship for action. Now!'

Several crew members had stopped working to watch the tension rising between the two men.

'You're mad,' Croker protested. 'You ain't thought about this, Mister Harcourt. We got to learn somethin' about 'er first,' and he started to move away.

'If you are not with me, you are against me, you dog,' bellowed a furious Harcourt and, seizing up a belaying pin, he struck Croker across the back of the head. The man collapsed in a heap. A low murmuring began amongst the men on deck, joined by the hands tending to the yards. 'Silence on deck you scum,' he shouted. 'You there at the helm, steer to intercept that brig.' He ordered vaguely. The man looked askance and, with no other authority to turn to, passed the wheel through his hands, pointing the vessel in the direction suggested by Harcourt's outstretched arm.

While the sails shivered and the vessel started to lose way, Harcourt paced, agitatedly wringing his hands behind his back. 'What are the correct orders for the sails?' he wondered, before shouting out, 'Stop gawping you men and look sharp. Get those sails under control.' To his surprise, they knew what needed doing without more precise orders and slowly brought the vessel under control. 'Now what's my next move?' he pondered and called, 'Get those larboard guns loaded and ready to roll out.'

One man stood and faced him. 'We ain't got enough 'ands to man the guns and the sails, sir,' he spoke respectfully, lacking confidence. 'No offence, sir.'

This was not going the way he wanted. He should not have struck Croker, needing him now more than he had understood. Looking down at the man, who was beginning to moan and stir, he leaned over to talk to him. Just then, out of the darkness a gun fired, and a moment later a small fountain of seawater fell across the bows.

'What the hell ...?'

'It's that Spaniard, sir,' the seaman said. 'She's fired across our bows. We must heave to, sir.'

'Really man, I can see that. I am not about to surrender to a poxed Spaniard. Let me think damn you!'

He stared into the darkness at the Spanish vessel. She probably was better manned, after all she was in home waters and probably part of the fleet Jarvis was hunting. Should he make a run for it? How could he meet Jarvis and report he had done no more than avoid the battle? He could allow the Spaniard to capture his vessel, release the Spanish prisoners, and agree to exchange him for a Spanish officer, allowing him to claim a valiant, but vain, defeat, and gain honour that way? No; he could be kept a prisoner for years. Better to run and avoid battle. He could persuade Jarvis he had faced a larger force.

'What's your name man?' He growled at the seaman.

'Spurling, sir. William Spurling. Able seaman and a top-man on *Melampus*, sir.'

'Well, Spurling, let's get the ship away from here before the Spaniard takes us. Get the men to work and have some-one get Croker below.'

Harcourt moved to the windward side and felt the light offshore breeze on his face. He took up his glass and looked across to Cadiz and the oncoming Spaniard. As he focused the lens on her, a bow gun spat fire and smoke. The ball passed through his mainsail, and he instinctively flinched and ducked.

'We need more sail, Spurling. The bugger is closing the gap between us.'

Spurling shouted at two men.

'I ... er ... we must get away from here.' Harcourt's voice trembled a little but if Spurling detected that, he did not show it.

He looked again at the oncoming enemy for a long time. She was perhaps two, maybe three cables distant and closing to fire at him again. He was sure they had him in their sights and was seeking him out specifically. He looked up at the brig's sails and realised they were not drawing well. Why was the Spaniard able to sail so fast?

A third ball smashed into the side of his ship, and he heard a scream from below. Stop, stop, his brain thought. We cannot escape. He looked all around as men started to gather towards him, as if threatening him.

'You ain't flying proper colours, Mister Harcourt, sir,' said Spurling. You could tie on the Spanish flag. That might stop 'em firing at us.'

Harcourt gave no response.

'I'll go do it then, sir,' and quickly he pulled the Spanish flag from the locker and tied it on the jack staff. The red and yellow stripes, with the coat of arms of Spain off-centred toward the hoist, fluttered in the weak wind. To show the flag more clearly, Spurling lit a stern lamp, looking nervously at Harcourt, half expecting a howl of protest.

Harcourt looked to the sloop which appeared to have luffed and turned its broadside towards him. 'Hah, Spurling, that has worked indeed. Well done man. They have stopped firing.'

His excitement gave voice to the growing sense of elation he felt at having avoided a battle and possible death or maiming ... until another shot spat out from the sloop, striking the larboard bulwark. He raised his glass again and swore. 'Hell's teeth. She's English and she is full of damned marines.' He swore again. 'Spurling, remove that Spanish rag at once, and replace it with the blue ensign.' If the sloop had marines on board, he would wager Vizzard was among them. And he would be wrong-footed, unable to seek his revenge.

The more he thought about his situation, the more despondent he became.

'We ain't got a blue ensign, sir,' said Spurling. Spanish ships don't carry British admirals' flags.'

'Belay that man. Just lower the Spanish flag. That will be all the signal needed,' and for the first time Lieutenant Harcourt began to understand that his actions may have been in error.

* * * * *

Jack Vizzard was below when he heard a lookout shout something muffled and unintelligible to his ears. He was tired as were his men. Tired from the exertions of the night, and tired from the release of emotions that followed a fierce action against a determined enemy. He would stay where he was for now. Whatever it was, it would not concern him. He closed his eyes again.

But sleep eluded him and, as the hubbub on deck increased, with feet thrumming as sailors ran to their posts, he sighed and climbed the companionway to the main deck to investigate. He glanced around and approached the sloop's commander, William Prowse. 'Why all the activity, William? Can a gentleman not sleep on your ship?' He stretched and yawned.

'Use this and look to starboard, a league or so to the west-by-southwest.' He kept his eyes on the object of his instruction and handed the telescope to Jack.

A moment or two later, with the vessel in the lens, Jack exclaimed, 'Why, if I did not know better, I would say that is the Spanish prize we took and was given to that fool, Harcourt. However, I am no expert.' He continued looking, as the sloop rose and fell on a rising swell.

'Just so, Jack. Just so,' confirmed Prowse. 'But what is she doing in these waters when she should by now be in Portsmouth, or the Channel?'

'The fool has lost control, I'll wager, and she has been re-taken by the prisoners. That man is a liability to the service and a disgrace to the uniform he wears.' Jack was shaking his head.

Prowse luffed to allow his starboard guns to bear and or-dered them to load and run out in readiness as he continued to watch the unusual sailing behaviour of the Spanish vessel. 'Place a shot in front of him, Mister Bedford,' he shouted to the young midshipman, who sighted the gun himself.

The shot had effect, as the enemy vessel seem to stall. Prowse wondered what his opponent might do next. He ex-pected it to heave to, but it might put up some resistance. 'Let her have another, Mister Bedford. Closer if you can.' Bedford duly obliged and placed the next ball into the ene-my's sail, if no real damage were done it would at least demonstrate that the *Raven* had her range and could pour fire on to her with accuracy.

Prowse refocused his glass again and saw his enemy was in irons, her captain clearly not in full command of his ship. 'Mister Bedford, he has had two chances, I will not give him another. You may fire one into his deck.'

Joshua Bedford gave the orders to the gun's crew and again, sighted the weapon personally. Standing aside he brought the slow match to the touch hole. Moments later he saw, with great satisfaction, that he had hit her low down amidships and done some damage.

Prowse saw a flag break out at her stern, revealed to be the flag of Spain. So, she was enemy. He ordered Bedford to have all guns loaded and manned on the larboard side.

'Just a moment, William,' Jack interrupted. 'She's no Spaniard. Well, she is not under Spanish command. I can see Harcourt. What's the fool playing at?' Both men stood and stared. There was no activity on the opposite deck. A few crew members were in the rigging and three or four on the deck. As they continued to stare at their opponent, they saw the Spanish flag hauled down. 'By God she's struck her colours, she's yours, William.' He slapped him on the shoulder. 'Although, if she is now an English vessel, you may not claim her as a prize, I regret to say.'

Prowse grinned. 'Jack, would you take Mister Bedford and an armed party to go and possess her, please. I suggest Mister Bedford deserves the honour, and I fancy you would enjoy the pleasure of boarding and talking to Mister Harcourt.' He smiled.

'Unless you have strong objection,' said Jack, 'I would prefer to remain here and send Mister Hale in my place. He will stand no nonsense from Harcourt or his crew.'

Prowse eyed Jack, his mind wondering what the marine was about. 'As you wish, Jack. Although I suspect you are making mischief. Mister Bedford,' he shouted, 'Mister Hale and you have the honour of taking possession if you would. Take command of her until we find Sir John and the fleet. I am extremely interested to learn why it has been necessary to capture this vessel twice, and why she should be approaching Cadiz when she is supposed to be in Portsmouth.'

He gazed at the young man. 'Are you ready to take the responsibility, Bedford?

A broad grin spread across the young man's face. 'Aye, sir. Most certainly. I will not forget your faith and confidence in me, sir.'

'Get her under way as soon as you can in case the Dons should have something in pursuit, and take station five cables abreast of me so we can search a greater area.' Prowse stomped around his deck, relieved that he was not facing a real enemy.

The midshipman organised a crew for the ship's launch and to assist with the prize. Jack called for Lieutenant Hale and Joe Packer along with a dozen of his best marines to form the boarding party, giving his subaltern quiet instructions. As the boat crossed the shortening stretch of sea between the two vessels, Lieutenant Hale warned his men to be ready for any sign of treacherous behaviour and checked his pair of pistols for the second time.

The brig was wallowing in the gentle swell and Jack studied her through the glass. He could make out Harcourt, strutting on the deck. Had he himself taken the men across, there was a danger of violence erupting. He thought it best that Hale take control and conduct an impartial discussion with the man in advance of his own interrogation.

Jack watched as the launch hooked on and the men quickly clambered aboard as though they were boarding a prize. Hale deployed the marines and Bedford started issuing orders to the seamen to get the vessel under way. As expected, Harcourt appeared to object to a midshipman taking command and, as they drifted closer, his voice could be heard remonstrating with the young officer, until his subaltern, Martin Hale, intervened. Jack smiled, enjoying the scene. Harcourt's voice heightened and became a bullying rant, directed at both the marine officer, and the midshipman who was busy giving instructions to a stocky sailor.

A shouted order was heard from the brig and Jack saw that Martin had drawn a pistol. It was pointed at Harcourt who fell quiet for a moment, before continuing to harangue the young officer. Evidently Martin reached a point of exasperation and swung a fist at Harcourt, who collapsed and disappeared from Jack's view.

Commander Prowse returned to the deck in time to see his ship's launch returning with two seamen and two marine guards, pointing muskets at the furious-faced Harcourt. 'What the devil has happened, Jack?'

'May I suggest that I defer comment for fear of causing you prejudice and wait for Lieutenant Harcourt to present his report? I believe he is still unaware of my presence here and I shall retreat to the refuge of your cabin and await you both there, if you are agreeable? Prowse nodded, intrigued as to what must have happened between the two men, but now certain that Jack had been responsible for some mischief.

He did not have long to wait. Lieutenant Harcourt all but ran up the scrambling net in his haste to reach the quarterdeck. 'Commander Prowse, I understand.' Not waiting for an acknowledgement, he continued in a strident voice, 'I must demand a Court Martial, er, sir. One of your junior officers, a mere midshipman, has taken command of my ship, on your orders it appears, and I have been assaulted, violently assaulted sir, by a junior marine officer under your command. It is an outrage, and I will have a Court Martial to see these men kicked out of the service and be reinstated to my command.'

Harcourt paused for breath at which a calm and patient William Prowse raised a hand. 'One moment lieutenant, if you will. There will be no Court Martial of those officers, Mister Harcourt. Both men were acting under orders, my specific orders in fact. However, there may well be a Court Martial once Captain Moore and Sir John Jervis have my report on the episode, together with that of another officer.' Noting the unspoken question in the lieutenant's eyes, Prowse continued, 'Follow me to my quarters, if you will, and all will be explained to you.'

Without waiting for any further protest, Prowse walked away and surprised the marine sentry on duty at the door to his cabin. Pushing the door open, he lowered his head and strode forward, followed immediately by Harcourt, whose head promptly struck a deck-head beam. Prowse went to his desk and watched the interplay on the faces of the captain of marines and the lieutenant.

'You!' Harcourt visibly sagged, his aggression dissipating immediately. 'I did not expect to see you again. It all makes sense now. You staged it all to humiliate me. I see that. What do you propose now, Vizzard?'

Jack thought of standing to face his enemy, but decided to remain seated by the stern windows, partly because of the cramped space in the cabin. 'You are here because you have chosen to ignore Captain Moore's orders. As I understand matters, you have no discretion; you were ordered to escort *Melampus* to England. Accordingly, Commander Prowse and I will recommend to Admiral Jervis that you face a Court

Martial.' Jack sat grim faced watching a range of emotions play across Harcourt's face. 'Mister Bedford will no doubt pass his board examination for lieutenant at the next opportunity. A brief period in command of yonder prize will enhance his skills and prospects, will it not Commander Prowse?'

'My very reasons for appointing him, Captain Vizzard,' he replied with exaggerated politeness. Then to Harcourt, 'Your request for a Court Martial is denied. I expect the commander in chief will be unlikely to accede to your request also. He is less keen on Courts Martial and more inclined to send home any officer who brings dishonour on the service or displeasure to him personally. It is my understanding that you were ordered by Captain Moore, to return to Portsmouth?'

'But sir, I judged it of greater benefit to the fleet to return and add the prize to Sir John's fleet,' protested Harcourt. 'Captain Moore was in error in sending me home, damn it.'

Prowse was in no mood for argument. His sloop was under way, heading northwest and he was required on deck. 'That, Harcourt, was not a decision for you to make. The matter of prizes is for the Admiralty Court. The disposition of the fleet is a matter for Sir John. You disobeyed a direct order and will face the consequences, man. Sir John will receive a report from me once Mister Hale has made enquiries of the crew of the prize and I doubt he will look favourably on you. I will not place you under arrest, but I strongly recommend that you keep out of my way. You may go, sir.' The anger was evident in Prowse's voice.

'This is your doing, Vizzard, I know it, and know this, I shall make you regret it, if it is the last thing I do.' Harcourt stamped from the cabin.

Prowse turned to Jack and said, 'Watch your back with that one, Jack. I would not trust the man. I must attend to my duties but do help yourself to a bottle.' He gestured to a rack, 'I believe you have earned it this night.'

By the end of the middle watch, the sea had taken on a calmness Prowse had rarely seen in these waters. The night air seemed clear with a myriad of stars forming a glittering canopy over the two small ships. He sat in a chair watching the Dutch bosun, Pieter Hanraets, teaching the younger midshipman something of the night sky, pointing out constellations he needed to master in order to become a navigator. The boy, Phillip Colledge, now aged twelve, was on his first voyage.

Prowse listened to the lad box the compass confidently and without hesitation, and raised his own telescope to better study Cassiopeia and Cepheus. He had learned these constellations, and more, from his mentor, Captain Bowyer. Of humble birth, Prowse worked hard to reach his present rank, something his father would have thought impossible.

Following the sky down to the sea, he paused. The horizon was suddenly closer and now appeared grey, uneven and it was moving. Fog: warmer air from the land passing over the colder water of Cadiz Bay. He sighed, that would make matters difficult. By rights he should display lights and fire off a gun at periodic intervals to give warning to any other vessels in the area. But the Spanish could be nearby, and he would not want to alert them to his two ships.

'Piet, take a look ahead,' he called to the bosun, handing over his telescope. 'Do you see?'

'Fog,' said Hanraets. 'That is a nuisance, sir. Will you be sounding a gun? I'll have the lads load and make ready.'

'I think not, Piet. The Spanish fleet could be near, and I would not wish to alert them to our presence. Have the men warned and make sure all lights are out. No singing and certainly no noise, please.' He looked across at the prize and saw the midshipman, Bedford, standing proud, ensuring that his craft kept exact station. 'Have a signal to that effect sent to the prize so Mister Bedford is aware and does what I want him to do and not what his Steel's book of seamanship tells him to do!'

Prowse made a tour of the ship with the bosun, leaving his first lieutenant, Matthew Ingram, on watch. He growled at the ship's gunner, who had failed to fully close a gunport, before looking into his cabin to see Captain Vizzard asleep in his bunk; an empty bottle still secured by his right hand. He smiled, retrieved his boat cloak from the hook on the door, and left the man to his slumber. Closing the door silently behind him, he returned to the deck.

Lieutenant Ingram reported nothing untoward and moved to the leeward side, just as the silent, suppressing fog slowly enveloped the ship. The two officers stared ahead until their eyes ached. The only sounds to reach their straining ears were the creak of the stays and sheets, in discordant conjunction with the sound of the sea caressing the wooden walls of the *Raven*.

CHAPTER 12
Captain

She was the last of the four Canada class 74-gun ships of the line, designed by William Bateley and built at Limehouse by Robert Batson. Of the lighter or common class, she carried twenty-eight of the less powerful 18-pounder guns on her upper gun deck, as opposed to the heavier 24-pounders. On her main gun deck she carried twenty-eight of the heavy 32-pounders. On the quarterdeck, where several officers would be stationed during action, she had 9-pounders, fourteen of them in total, with another four of that weight on the fo'c's'le. Today however, she was lacking a few, but not enough to be significant. What she truly lacked was marines, or so thought her captain. A few soldiers from the 69th Foot had been deployed on board with a marine officer and a small section of marines. 'And a good thing it was too,' pondered the captain. However, if it came to boarding the Spanish ships, he would rather have a full platoon of marines. They were better shots than the regular infantry, more accurate, nimble, and faster at moving about a ship. In short, they were skilled at killing.

Ralph Willett Miller looked along her upper deck and reminded himself how fortunate he was to command such a fine vessel. Miller was of American birth, the son of a loyalist. Having distinguished himself in previous commands and as a frigate captain, it was Jervis who appointed him to *Captain* one of the two-deckers which formed the backbone of the Royal Navy. His ship was the finest type in the Navy and Miller loved her.

Miller had come to know Horatio Nelson when the commodore flew his pennant from *Captain's* mizzen, after his old ship, the *Agamemnon*, had succumbed to the ravages of time and the sea with extensive wear and rot, and was sent home. For all its faults, Nelson loved the *Agamemnon*, as indeed he loved all ships he commanded. To Nelson, every naval ship was an object of beauty.

Aboard once more and wearing out the quarterdeck with his constant pacing, Miller found it both an honour to carry the broad pennant of a commodore, and a pleasure, because Nelson was a man given to inspirational conversation and leadership. He was unlike other men; he thought noble thoughts and was known to place honour and duty above all things. He also valued physical courage highly. Indeed, Miller remembered a phrase of Nelson's that had planted itself in his mind and taken firm root: 'courage alone will not lead to conquest without the aid and direction of exact discipline and order.'

Miller learned discipline and order during his years in the Navy, as had Nelson, so Miller hoped for an opportunity to prove his courage, too. Now there was the certainty of a battle; Jervis knew it, Nelson knew it, the men below deck knew it, too. The fleet that had been formed by Hood, shaped, polished, and disciplined by Jervis, now sailed fully poised and, though reduced in number, confident of a victory against England's new enemy, Spain.

It was still dark in the west as he watched the fleet ahead through the early morning haze to the eastern sky. The flagship, which had just hoisted his ship's number, caught his eye. Brenton, the signals lieutenant, ordered the acknowledgement even before Miller opened his mouth to alert him. A short signal followed. Which both he and Brenton started to read aloud almost simultaneously.

'Prepare to take on board a party of marines to add to your force.'

How odd, thought Miller, having a handful of infantrymen from the 69th and half a dozen marines already on board. So be it. If there was a battle to be fought, a boatful of marines could only be of benefit. Were they trained, they could fill gaps at the guns—gaps caused by the thunder of death as iron balls smashed through the wooden walls, spraying splinters, some the size of the beams supporting the deck above, sweeping men off their feet and turning their sweating bodies to pulped meat. Such weapons tore limbs from young men, removed heads, and cut people in two. He shuddered, shook the morbid thoughts from his mind and continued watching as Brenton repeated the signal, as was his duty.

'Very good, Brenton. Thank you.'

As he spoke, he saw a boat lowered and make its way between the two lines of the fleet. It was carrying a dozen or so stocky men in a hotchpotch of uniforms ... if they could indeed be called uniforms. There was a splash or two of red among them. Perhaps Jervis did not approve of such a rag-tag collection of misfits and shabby soldiers and had elected to remove them from his flagship.

'Good morning, Ralph.' The ubiquitous Commander Edward Berry, on board as a supernumerary, interrupted his thoughts. He was likely to appear at any time and in any place. Like Miller, he was known as an energetic and fearless officer. Jervis regarded him as an officer of 'talents, great courage and laudable ambition', according to his recent report to the Admiralty. Berry was on board as an observer, awaiting a new command.

'Good morning, Edward. Nelson has said that Sir John appears not to sleep. He's been throwing out signals since first light. Now he has despatched some marines to assist us in the coming fight,' said Miller, pointing in the direction of the flagship's launch.

Berry grunted. 'We will be fighting the Dons. They are likely to run as not, and I expect will not put up much resistance. Why, your *Captains* will capture two or three of the enemy, I have no doubt. They are a fine crew, Ralph.'

Miller smiled. 'Aye, they are as fine a crew as a captain could wish for, yet should we have a chance at boarding one, it will be to our benefit to have some marines to assist.'

'What you say is true enough, Ralph. I hear they have a sergeant major who escaped the noose in Portsmouth having punched a lieutenant. Lord knows how that happened. Old Jervie would have hanged the man without breaking wind.'

Together they watched the boat quickly make its way and the midshipman commanding it neatly turned into *Captain's* leeward side and hooked on. Minutes later a lean, hard-faced officer in full uniform was first aboard, adjusted his hat and paused momentarily as a sergeant major with a stern, sun-stained face jumped down behind him and growled an order over the side.

The officer, he was a captain, stepped forward and saluted. 'Which of you gentlemen is Miller?' he enquired.

'I am Ralph Miller,' replied the captain, 'and you are?'

'Vizzard, Jack Vizzard, commanding the marine detachment. Sir John feels you may require us in the coming battle.' He extended a hand, taken by Miller and Berry in turn.

''Tis true we lack a full complement of marines, Captain Vizzard, but the few we do have aboard have a commander. Did Admiral Jervis not inform you of this? Major William Morris commands our detachment.' Miller's face wore an honest expression of puzzlement.

Jack had been warned by Jervis, who had taken him into his confidence. 'I am placing you in a position likely to be of some hazard, Captain Vizzard,' the admiral had said. 'There is a major of marines on board *Captain*, I have not met him, but he is reported to be of limited ability and has ... ahem ... shall I say, been promoted above his appropriate station. It may prove an embarrassment to you however, if *Captain* is to be involved in boarding any enemy vessel, or in defending the ship, as she most certainly will be. Her marines and seamen will require exemplar leadership; someone willing and capable of fighting from the front. I believe you to be such a man. Major Morris is, er, said to be more reticent in action.'

'Sir, Admiral Jervis instructed me to hand you this note for your confidential information, explaining my deployment to your ship.'

Miller broke the wax seal of the note and quickly ran his eyes over the neat, copperplate-style writing in Sir John's own hand. He raised his eyes to look at Jack's expressionless face. 'I understand the admiral's reasons, Captain. I shall do all that I must to support you.'

'I will need to make arrangements for my men, if you could task someone to assist, please, Captain Miller.'

Miller called a middie forward, directing him to escort the marines below, and asking his first lieutenant to arrange a bunk for Captain Vizzard.

'I have to say, Miller, that your new captain of marines appears not to be, shall I say, enthusiastic to be joining our happy crew.' Berry, a man of natural bonhomie, had immediately formed an adverse opinion of the marine. 'What is Old Jervie thinking of, sending us a junior marine captain when we have a senior major aboard?'

Ralph Miller looked at Commander Berry with a meaningful expression, what might have been observed as a warning. 'Marines can make for surly messmates. He probably had a comfortable berth on the flagship and resents being deployed to a third rate. Who can fathom Sir John's mind, eh? Let us try to welcome him and provide an opportunity for him to become one of us *Captains*.'

The note informed Captain Miller that Sir John fully expected *Captain,* as Commodore Nelson's flagship, to be engaged in close action with the Spanish and that Captain Vizzard had demonstrated superior leadership and initiative. Marines from Captain Vizzard's company had been distributed to other ships of the line to strengthen those expected to be involved in boarding actions.

Miller wondered if Jervis was trying to provide additional protection for his rising star, knowing that Nelson's physical courage would undoubtedly see him exposed on the quarterdeck. There was no denying that both he and Nelson would take *Captain* into close action against the enemy. Miller had nothing to prove to his adopted country; he had fought the French at the Chesapeake under Admiral Tom Graves after his family's property had been lost because of their allegiance to the British crown and King George. He had been wounded three times during various engagements. The forthcoming battle might see him wounded or in some way mutilated, or even meet his death. He would do his duty, whatever the outcome.

Ralph Miller crumpled the note in his right hand and threw it over the side into the sea.

* * * * *

Below, on the gun deck, Sergeant Major Joe Packer was directing his men to the messing area used by the embarked infantry, the 69th Regiment, several of them audibly grumbling at the intrusion of marines into their domain.

'Right, you lot, no carping or bemoaning your miserable existence. We're all 'ere to kick the shit out of the Dons, whenever we find the buggers, so get used to each other. Where's your officer?' Packer asked.

'That'll be Lieutenant Pearson. He's sick.' Came a voice from the shadows.

'He's sick, Company S'arn't Major Packer, you poor excuse for a soldier. What's your name, boy?'

'Johnson, Sarn't Major. William Johnson, 69th. We weren't told we was getting more lobsters, Sarn't Major.' Johnson grinned in the gloom.

'Well now, Johnson, I am that surprised Old Jervie didn't take you into his confidence in planning the demise of the Dons,' growled Packer. 'Coz he consulted me personally and said, Packer, you make sure you knock those blockheads of the 69th into shape for me! Just be grateful to whoever you call your God that you have the best fighters on your side to look after your sorry arse.' Packer was not smiling. 'So, make room for Vizzard's Vandals, or we'll make space our way. Go on, shift yer ballast.' Slowly meeting the eyes of each of the infantrymen in turn, he glowered.

Packer was a man used to getting his way.

There was a pause as the infantrymen weighed matters and their chances against the burly, hard-faced marines confronting them in a menacing manner. Then there was shuffling and movement as the men of the 69th realized they were facing Captain Vizzard's best men. Some of the 69th had been amongst Howe's fleet on the 1st of June, three years before, when Captain Vizzard's courage, daring and sheer fighting ability had become spoken of in the fleet. Few marine officers were well known to the common seaman, but amongst the men of Jervis's fleet, his reputation had spread.

'Time for some grub lads and some purser's swipes. Get yourselves settled in and Jamie, you're in charge of messing so hop along to the galley. If Mister Vizzard is going to breakfast with the Navy, I don't see why we can't eat with the South Lincs children.'

Joe Packer had little time for the regular line regiments.

* * * * *

'Welcome, Captain Vizzard,' said Miller. 'We are delighted to add you and your men to our force. Your reputation precedes you, so you are doubly welcome as few of our men have been bloodied in battle.'

'Yes indeed,' agreed another officer clad in a scarlet coat, his tone lacking any semblance of sincerity. 'Welcome aboard, Captain. I am William Morris, Chatham Division. Delighted that you are joining my detachment, though it comes as a surprise to me,' he said, offering his hand. Morris thought it extraordinary but kept his own counsel.

'Thank you, Major. I confess I did not expect another secondment quite so soon. Sir John appears to have taken command of my detachment and distributed them among the fleet. I had no say in his dispositions.'

Jack lifted a cup of lukewarm, bitter coffee to his lips while he pondered the unasked question. 'My reputation is what it is, although likely undeserved. I have merely been fortunate to survive. Do you have any knowledge when we will meet the Spanish? Is there any intelligence as to their whereabouts?'

The steward hovered to place servers of fried liver and onions and cold hams on the table and rocked on his heels as the ship rolled, and the lanterns swung.

'It will be soon, Vizzard. Old Jervie had a council of war yesterday. One of his Portuguese friends spotted them beating back on an easterly course. He's been moving officers and men amongst the fleet, including you and your fellows.'

Berry grinned: he was keen to meet the Dons and prove his worth. 'I hear you managed to destroy some valuable ships inside Cadiz harbour. What an extraordinary thing. I should like to have been involved in that adventure. Also, I learn that you and Commander Prowse retrieved a prize that was somewhat off course. One that Captain Moore and you captured and had been ordered home?'

Jack had ignored the liver and onions—he disliked liver—and attacked the alternative course placed in front of him: a large bowl of burgoo. 'We were fortunate; the Spanish were asleep, and we had surprise on our side.' Jack drained the rest of the coffee. 'Yes, a Spanish brig. The fool in command of it thought to distinguish himself by returning it to the fleet in disobedience of Captain Moore's clear order to return to Portsmouth. The man was seeking approbation from the admiral for adding to his available vessels, although my sergeant major tells me that most of the work was undertaken by a master's mate. The lieutenant spent much time below with little knowledge of commanding the vessel.'

'I heard such,' interjected Captain Miller. 'Sir John gave him a drubbing that was heard throughout the flagship apparently. Chewed him up and spat him out. Sir John has no time for officers, or men, who disobey orders or are simply incompetent. He removed a few from this fleet when he took command.'

'I'll say he did,' exclaimed the first lieutenant, James Anderson. 'Said he needed lessons in seamanship, discipline, and navigation, and, upon my word, sent the unfortunate chap to us to learn from Captain Miller, with my assistance, sir.' He nodded at Ralph Miller, as if inviting comment, but the captain merely nodded.

Jack froze. 'He is here? Harcourt is on this ship?' He could barely conceal his anger.

'You look most alarmed, Vizzard. What on earth is the matter?' Miller's puzzlement was plain to see.

Jack suddenly lost the appetite with which he started the meal and pushed the bowl away. 'I can say only that he and I do not enjoy a convivial relationship and never will. Mark my words gentlemen, that man is more a danger to us than to the Spanish. He wishes to see me and my Sergeant Major dead. Be very wary of him. I shall say no more. I thank you for the hospitality of your table and for your company, but I must excuse myself as I have a duty to attend to.' With that, Jack nodded to Ralph Miller and left the cabin.

He strode from the cabin seeking Joe Packer, his boots loud on the deck timbers. The first marine he saw told him the Sergeant Major had gone to the heads and would likely be found there or on the marines' walk with a pipe. Jack left his men to their own activities and climbed the companion-way to the foredeck and the marines' walk by the bowsprit.

Packer was sitting cross-legged on the deck pulling on a clay pipe, the smoke plucked from his mouth by a breeze blowing from the southwest.

'Joe, I hesitate to interrupt you, particularly as it is with dark news that I must do so.' Jack squatted on a protrusion from the cathead. Packer looked puzzled and adjusted his position facing his captain.

'Go on, sir. We're bein' moved agin? Now Old Jervie has changed 'is mind an' wants us back wiv 'im on the flagship?'

'Harcourt is back, Joe.' Jack saw no purpose in talking around the subject. 'Not only is he back with the fleet, but Sir

John has also seen fit to send him to *Captain*, ostensibly to learn discipline and seamanship. He's on board this very ship, skulking below somewhere.'

Packer grunted. 'Bleedin' typical. I reckon we wait till dark then throw the bastard overboard.' The smile didn't reach his eyes, and, in his heart, he knew he could do just that. Packer had killed many men, all in the performance of his duty. One more would not trouble his conscience. He hated Harcourt and had often wished the man dead.

Jack smiled. 'It's a tempting prospect, Joe. However, I could not countenance such a thing. Just beware and pass the word along to the men. We must bide our time. Who knows, Joe, the Dons might provide a solution to the present problem.' His facial expression gave nothing away, but Packer sensed exactly what the boss meant by that comment.

Packer's attention was drawn away. 'Captain, look, isn't that the *Minerve* joining the fleet? Does that mean Commodore Nelson is now with us? Packer had never seen Nelson but, like many in the fleet, he was known as a fighting captain.

'I believe you are correct, Joe. It certainly looks like *Le Minerve*. Ah, look there, the flagship is signaling. Damn, I still can't read the things. When this thing is done I will spend time with the signal book. Let me see what the officer on watch makes of it. You had best get below and let the men know about Harcourt. If, or when, you see him, Joe, he is not to be touched, understand? Not under any circumstances.'

'Aye, sir,' said Joe. 'Not to be touched. Understand you perfectly, Captain Vizzard, sir.' He snapped to attention and threw an untypically smart salute to Jack, who grinned and swore quietly at his senior marine.

Jack strode quickly to the quarterdeck where Captain Miller now stood watching events at the flagship, and ordered his lieutenant to prepare to heave to, on the admiral's command. A further signal broke out from the flagship and, with one flowing movement, the fifteen ships of the line forming the fleet that Jervis would lead to battle heaved to and awaited further orders.

A turn of the glass later, a boat was lowered from the flagship and started pulling in the rising swell of the sea towards *Captain*. As it drew closer, the figure in the stern sheets acquired clear form; slightly built—almost diminutive—it was overshadowed by the heavily built men forming the boat's crew.

The officer of the watch called for the bosun, who rapidly stood ready by the ship's side with a party of able men. Jack called those marines on watch to the deck, to form up in readiness to greet Commodore Nelson.

'Hah, so that explains the signals,' said Captain Miller, to nobody in particular. 'Nelson is to shift his broad pennant back to *Captain*. Excellent news, quite excellent.' Miller was beaming.

'Why so?' asked Jack.

'Simply because, Captain Vizzard, where Nelson sails, we can be sure of being in the thick of it. Make no mistake, when we find the Dons, Nelson will go straight for them when he can. He may have news as to their whereabouts too.'

As the pipe's final note faded, the broad pennant of a commodore broke out from the maintop, and the small figure of Horatio Nelson strode forward, hand extended. 'Ralph, good morning to you. I am delighted to be hoisting my pennant back on the *Captain*. So very good to see you again. Come, my friend, I must tell you my news as I have just provided to Sir John. I have had a feast of adventures and misadventures.' The Commodore's voice was soft and pitched far from the usual stentorian tone of a senior naval officer in command of hardened fighting men.

Nelson led the way to the cabin that he would now occupy. The commodore and Captain Miller sat at the long mahogany table and Nelson revelled in telling his story, of how the little *Minerve* found herself sailing in a heavy sea fog while officers and men on deck slowly realized they were not alone in the sea, and how the silent *Minerve* crept, like a mouse seeking escape from a hunting cat, through the spectral shapes in the milky darkness of the night.

'An unnerving experience for you, sir.' Miller let his imagination take him to the deck of the small frigate, sailing silently, hidden in the sea fog of the night through the middle of the mightiest fleet that Spain had put to sea since the Armada, and felt the tension rising in him, much as Nelson must have done that night.

'They were in this area the night before last, Ralph.' Nelson placed a finger on the chart in front of them. 'That is some seventeen leagues from our present position. They were in two very loose formations.' He picked up the stub of a pencil and quickly sketched a series of lines, showing how the enemy vessels were grouped. 'As we know, Ralph, the Spanish are poor, undisciplined sailors and they are, or were, in much disarray.'

'Do you know how Sir John proposes to use our small force against the Spanish, sir?' Miller asked.

'No, Ralph. Much will depend on the Dons' formation when we meet them, if indeed they manage to form up at all. I hold a low opinion of the Spanish fleet, as you well know. Poorly manned and with inferior officers. But when we do meet, it will be Sir John's wish to create such a melee as to throw them into great confusion. Certainly, it is what I would do. Never mind manoeuvring, just go straight at 'em. They are sure to break their line and we simply get in amongst them and destroy them.'

'That's departing from the Admiralty's Fighting Instructions, sir. A captain might find himself viewed with considerable displeasure by their Lordships for behaving in such fashion, do you not think, sir?'

Nelson, with a twinkle in his eye, answered, 'That depends on the captain. Now, let us take a tour of your ship, Ralph, and see how the people are faring.'

They left the cabin, catching the marine sentinel by surprise, and descended to the gun deck where they walked forward slowly on the larboard side, pausing to address a few words to clusters of men at each mess. The commotion of laughter, disputes, and arguments died away at the sight of the captain and a commodore on the gun deck. The lower deck men, used to the regular sight of their captain, were taken aback to see the diminutive commodore walking amongst them.

As they turned to make their way back on the starboard side, Nelson stopped. A face he knew was caught in the beam of light coming through an open gunport.

'It's Porter, is it not? We were on *Albemarle* together, if my recollection is sound.' Nelson was quite certain he was correct.

'Aye, sir. Jim Porter,' said the man. 'Topman on the *Albemarle*. A grand crew we had there.' Porter knuckled his temple. 'Good of you to remember, sir, given it's thirteen or fourteen year gone since them days.'

'Are you still a topman, Porter?'

'Aye, sir. No place like it when the weather's fine, as it be today. Not so good in a bit of weather.' He chuckled.

Nelson smiled. 'Fine enough for a fight with the Dons, eh, Porter?'

Another voice, an older one, belonging to a wizened man with a straggly white beard, spoke out. 'You find 'em for us, your honour, and we'll be givin' them a fight like they never had afore. We'll blow 'em out of the water.'

'Well said that man,' Nelson replied. 'What is your name?'

'Roberts, your honour. Leading man for twenty years, sir. Ordinary for five year afore that.' The life spent at sea had not diluted his Welsh lilt. With difficulty, Roberts refrained from spitting a well-chewed piece of tobacco through the gunport.

'Admiral Jervis will find them and between us we'll sink them or capture them. Carry on men.' A small cheer went up from the men.

'You have good recall for a face, sir,' said Miller. 'A lot of sea has been covered since you commanded the *Albemarle*.'

When the two officers reached the companion way leading to the weather deck, Nelson stopped, half-turned to Miller and said, 'When you order a man to be flogged for insubordination to an officer, one tends to remember the face, Ralph. I ain't a flogger, never was, but on that occasion, it was necessary to maintain discipline. The officer, however, was later found to be in error and my letter at the end of the commission was probably responsible for his never being employed in the service again. Porter appears to have forgiven me, for which I am indeed grateful.'

They ascended to the weather deck and quickly climbed to their usual stations, pacing across the quarterdeck. 'Sir John is signaling, Ralph, are you able to read it?' Nelson put the telescope to his eye. 'Damn, this light is playing the devil with my vision. Ah, I think I have it. The fleet is to prepare for action and to maintain two divisions and keep in close order during the night.'

'Then we shall have our battle on the morrow, sir.'

CHAPTER 13
Victory

Her keel was laid on 23rd July 1759 in the Old Single Dock at Chatham Royal Dockyard in Kent, to a design and specification of Sir Thomas Slade. The new first rate's specification called for 100 guns on three gun decks. In the making of her, she had consumed six thousand oak trees from a hundred acres of woodland, some of the oak obtained from the Baltic because English oak was becoming scarce. One hundred and fifty men built her frame and another hundred worked on other parts of her construction. Her hull was completed on Saint George's Day, 1765. When built she displaced 3,500 tons, making her the largest warship ever built for the Royal Navy. She was called *Victory*, the seventh of that name in the service of Britain.

The middle watch had reported the sound of signal guns during the night. They were not sounded consistently, and the watch on deck thought they were very distant. Nonetheless, the log confirmed what the lookouts heard and the officers on watch confirmed the sounds clearly came from the southwest. Sounds travel well at night. The Spanish were near.

Sir John Jervis moved to the room at the entrance to his day cabin and examined the line on the chart depicting his fleet's course during the last twenty-four hours. He pulled a gold watch from his waistcoat and studied it, as if doubting the information it imparted. Two o'clock in the morning. He had not slept and would not sleep until he had found and beaten the Spanish. He held a parallel rule, and his pencil drew another line, then picked up a pair of dividers and estimated a point of interception, noting it to be approximately 30 miles west from the Cape St Vincent. Don Córdoba was further north than he had reckoned, if Nelson's information was correct. And Nelson would never be in error about his own ship's position.

'Good,' thought Sir John. 'Córdoba is looking to avoid battle. He wants to get to Cadiz before joining the French with his ships intact. Probably has intelligence that my fleet has only ten or a dozen line of battle ships. How many does he have at sea? Twenty, twenty-five, thirty? The more, the merrier because he will never exercise control over a fleet of that size. It would take the Spaniard a full day of manoeuvring to get all his vessels into readiness for a fleet battle, and still not achieve it.'

Jervis had questioned the two lieutenants Nelson lost in an action with Spanish warships shortly before Christmas 1796, subsequently recovered in an exchange at Gibraltar for Don Jacobo Stuart. Lieutenants Hardy and Culverhouse had briefly been prisoners of war until Nelson negotiated the exchange and they had much to tell Sir John on the conditions of the Spanish fleet and its crews. The Spanish built large, strong, powerful ships. They were larger than British ships and heavily armed. He knew the Spanish fleet had few experienced hands manning its ships and was poorly led with few officers having any real knowledge of the business of seamanship and naval warfare.

Further intelligence concerning the Spanish fleet's position and course was received from the commander of the sloop of war *La Bonne Citoyenne*, Captain Lindsey, who had briefly exchanged shots with a Spanish frigate. Weighing all the snippets of intelligence, Jervis formed a very clear understanding of when, and where, he would meet the enemy. A major battle would take place on the morrow—that much he knew with certainty—and England badly needed a victory.

Amongst the population there was a fear of a Franco-Spanish invasion. In December a small French force had landed on the west coast of Ireland. Unsettling both the public and the government, it created a falling away of confidence in the Navy's ability to protect British coasts. The momentum of the war was with the French and their ally, Spain. England needed a victory that only the Navy could deliver. If the Navy did not prevail, and the French and Spanish managed to become masters of the Channel, their armies would land on English soil for the first time since the Normans. Jervis was not willing to be the man convicted by history of responsibility for such a catastrophe.

'I shall cut them in half, keep the wind gauge, and we can tackle them one by one,' he vowed. 'One alteration of course, I think, more to the south, and we should sight them by morning.'

He stepped out onto the quarterdeck issuing the necessary order to his pessimistic Captain of the Fleet, Robert Calder. Having exchanged a few words with Calder, he turned to retire to his bunk for a couple of hours when a lookout called, 'Below on the deck. Sail on the starboard beam. Looks to be in a hurry, sir.'

Jervis pulled his telescope from its place near the binnacle. It was a fine, if plain, instrument, little more than two feet in length, the size and shape of a cook's rolling pin. At one end, a sliding eyepiece made from brass, at the other, a tightly fitting brass cover for the objective lens. Unlike other officers, his preference was for an instrument that had no embellishments, no maker's name or elaborate engraving, no flowers, or waves or sea creatures. It was utilitarian. It was an object to be looked through, not to be looked at.

He looked through it now and after a few moments made the approaching vessel: a Portuguese frigate. It closed to within hailing distance and a short exchange took place between Calder's watch officer and the frigate's captain who offered the simple message that a large Spanish fleet was near, about fifteen miles to the southwest, then resumed her run to Lisbon.

With that news, Sir John decided some sleep was necessary after all and left instruction to be called if the situation should change. He crept into his bunk, pausing only to remove his uniform coat and shoes.

However, sleep eluded him, and his febrile mind continued to consider the coming battle and the tactical directions he must give to his ships as the battle evolved.

* * * * *

His servant brought the admiral breakfast shortly after four bells in the morning watch, to find him sitting at his

225

desk writing. He knew he would meet the Spanish today and wished to ensure he had addressed all his correspondence.

An immaculately dressed midshipman of some eighteen years of age knocked on the door at the entrance to the admiral's quarters. A gruff voice instructed him to enter, and he stood at attention to repeat the ship's captain, George Grey's, order, verbatim:

'The captain's respects, Sir John, and the enemy is in sight to the southwest.' He waited for a response.

'Very well, Mister Waite, I shall come at once.'

Jervis stood and stretched, picked up his coat and hat, and strode out to the quarterdeck to survey the unfolding scene. The wind, which had been blowing strongly from the east for some days, had now come right round to the southwest. It was a cold morning and a light fog lingered on the sea. 'Once the sun warms the air, that will disappear,' he thought. He studied the enemy ships with his telescope. Much as he thought, only five of them were visible in the southwest-by-south quarter; many more would be out of his sight. He continued watching patiently as the two fleets slowly converged on a point, the point predicted by Jervis at two o'clock this morning. He despatched Captain Lindsey in *La Bonne Citoyenne* to reconnoitre.

Eventually, Jervis spoke to those officers on deck with him, and there were many now that word of the enemy had spread. 'A victory to England is essential at this moment, gentlemen.'

He continued to watch the Spanish. Their admiral, Córdoba, was trying to get his fleet in order. It appeared to Jervis' experienced eye that his opponent was attempting to reverse the order of his fleet by ordering the whole fleet onto the larboard tack. Such a manoeuvre would enable him to keep the weather gauge. The manoeuvre would have challenged even the best trained fleet, and now the Spanish fleet's lack of experience became manifest. As they slowly came round onto a heading, the ships began to lose their order, bunching together and masking each other's broadsides. Jervis watched as a gap began to open up and realised at once he had been presented with an opportunity. He looked to the southeast and saw what appeared to be a division of nine ships detached from Córdoba's main body. If he could keep them apart, he would reduce the odds against him considerably.

As the wind had now shifted to west by north, he adjusted his tactics. Turning to Calder, he said, 'Please signal the fleet to form line of battle ahead and astern of the flag as most convenient.' He had the opportunity to put John Clerk's theory on tactics to a real test.

Within a minute of the signal flags breaking out, the British fleet, with a precision honed through frequent practice and discipline, manoeuvred swiftly into a single line. The Spanish admiral, Córdoba, would be watching open mouthed at the spectacle of a squadron of disparate ships moving as one.

The early morning haze slowly evaporated revealing a sky of pale cornflower blue, liberally peppered with clumps of white and grey clouds. The sea was calm with a light breeze brushing over it, the kind seamen called a top-sail breeze. There was enough movement in the air to clear the smoke of battle, enough light airs to enable a ship to manoeuvre and engage an enemy ship or escape from an overwhelming force.

Ahead lay the enemy, in disarray as he fully expected of the Spanish. He could see a larger group to the north of his line, a smaller straggling group of warships and, it appeared to his experienced eye, a group of four merchantmen, all but hidden from view by an escort of powerful warships. It crossed his mind they should not be there with this fleet.

'They have left a large gap and appear to be unable to close it,' thought Jervis. By the time we converge, our line must be in tight order as it will be like threading the fleet through the eye of a moving needle while under concentrated fire.'

'A fine day,' thought Jervis. 'A fine day for dying. A fine day for a slaughter. For that is what it will be.'

Preventing the two irregular Spanish groups from closing the gap was now his first goal. Thus, by three bells in the forenoon watch, he ordered three of his vessels into a chase to the south-by-west quarter: *Culloden, Prince George*, and *Blenheim*. Shortly afterwards, he strengthened the chase with the addition of *Irresistible, Colossus*, and *Orion*.

A little past six bells of the forenoon watch, *La Minerve* frigate made the signal reporting twenty sail in the southwest quarter, and a few minutes after, of eight sail in the south-by-west. Half an hour afterwards the *Bonne Citoyenne* made the signal that she distinguished sixteen of the strange ships, and immediately afterwards twenty-five, to be of the line. The enemy's fleet was indeed now visible to all in the English squadron. A gaggle of gigantic ships, it resembled a confused and swaying forest of masts and sails.

Calder and another supernumerary, Captain Benjamin Hallowell, a Canadian, were counting the enemy vessels as they came into view. Once he realised he was outnumbered two to one, he cut the counting short with a snapped command and declared his intention to sail right through them no matter how many ships he faced.

Jervis ordered a change of course for the fleet, to steer south-by-southwest, aiming his fleet like a spear straight at the Spanish throat. Then, shortly before seven bells, he again adjusted the fleet's course such that others could close up and ordered his large standard and battle ensigns be hoisted. Each ship in the English fleet now flew the meteor flag, the ensign of an admiral of the red. They sailed, gliding majestically onwards like cathedrals of sails, bowsprit to stern with little sea space between them.

Having correctly anticipated the enemy's position, he had done all that he could to bring about the battle. The enemy's numbers would have justified his refusing to engage, as a lesser admiral might have done, but he determined to risk a general engagement. The enemy may lack cohesion and be poorly led but he could still punch hard. Now it was for the wooden walls of England and the men of steel who stood behind them, to fight the battle.

To fight and to win. Or to die in the attempt.

* * * * *

Prince George

Lieutenant Hale and Sergeant Docherty ensured the marines in their charge had been allotted space adjacent to the gunroom, which on a ship as large as *Prince George* was, by frigate standards, quite commodious. Once the men were settled, Lieutenant Hale climbed to the ship's waist with his sergeant.

'The vagaries of the service, sergeant. One never knows where one's fate may lie. We are fortunate to be on a flagship and very likely to see some serious action. Had we been deployed to a frigate, we should be limited to the role of by-standers, mere spectators to the battle.'

Sergeant Docherty nodded. ''Tis true sir, however, in some strange sense I feel we may be detached from the very centre of affairs.' He placed a foot on a cannon's truck, adopting a casual stance. 'Mister Vizzard may be regretting the admiral's decision to place him on one of the 74s at the rear of the squadron. When we meet the Dons, the *Captain* may come in for something of a pounding. I am told she is one of the smaller 74s in the fleet, too.'

'If the Dons show any spirit, we in *Prince George*, will surely attract their attention, as *Prince George* is a large ship, even as a second rate, and we are flying a rear admiral's piece of bunting, sergeant.' He looked up at the admiral's flag.

Docherty reflected on this and nodded agreement. 'Aye, sir. That is true. We should have small arms drill as soon as the men have had their breakfast, to get their eyes ready. They will need all the skill they can muster.'

The two marines moved toward the fo'c's'l as Admiral Parker appeared on the quarterdeck.

'Good morning, sir,' Captain Irwin said as his admiral walked toward him. 'Sir John's last signal instructed us of his intention to pass through the Dons' line. It is a bold move.'

They walked slowly away from the helmsmen to the windward side.

'Will this weather hold, John, do you think?' Parker asked of the captain of *Prince George*. 'The haze is lifting but the sky is yet still a little grey.'

'We will prevail, Sir William. I have every confidence in our fleet, reduced as it may be, and in the men we command.' They turned together near the larboard gunwale and reversed course across the deck.

'I share your views, John. However, unless Jervis gives me the honour of leading the van, I fear we may be left on the edge of things. We shall see how he arranges the fleet.'

As he spoke, the signal flags broke out from *Victory*.

'The fleet will form a single line of battle, taking station ahead or astern of the flag as most convenient,' shouted the signals lieutenant.

Captain Irwin smiled. 'That's very considerate of Sir John,' he thought and ordered the helmsman to execute the order and guide *Prince George* into the line, immediately astern of *Blenheim,* captained by Thomas Frederik, and ahead of *Orion*, with Sir James Saumarez, the feisty Channel Islander, in command.

The first lieutenant was busy preparing the ship for battle. Chain slings were being fitted and netting fixed above the heads of crews manning guns on the exposed weather deck. A chain of seamen were throwing buckets of seawater on the topsails, the courses having been reefed in to prevent them being caught by sparks from the guns and marine sharpshooters in the tops. They sailed inexorably towards the enemy, an agonizingly slow progress, watching the sun climb and wash the blue sky with gold light.

'Look, sir.' Captain Irwin pointed. 'The Spanish are trying to close the gap in the line, but 'tis too late. Why, there must be a league or more of sea between their divisions. We shall cut through them as a hot knife through butter. Drummer, sound all hands to their stations.'

The opening rat-a-tat from the boy's instrument was enough to send the waiting men scampering barefoot to their positions in readiness for battle. While those below, often bare chested too, knew that within minutes they would be sweating from continuous strenuous exertion, mixed with perhaps an element of anxiety. Jack Tar would face off with his country's enemy, and work hard to keep his gun firing, even should the guns on either side be put out of action. He might have to do that for hours until his body ached and his mouth was desiccated, his tongue feeling twice its normal size. There was rarely time to take a drink from the water butt during the heat and frenzy of battle.

Further signal flags broke out from the *Victory's* peak, ordering the windward leading ships to make for the greater mass of Spanish line of battle ships. The *Culloden* 74 led, Thomas Troubridge proudly in the van, thrusting his ship between the trailing Spanish three-deckers, spewing thunder, smoke and flames from both sides. His critical opening broadside was disciplined, deadly accurate gunnery, bringing death and mutilation to the Spanish crews who tried in vain to return fire.

Minutes later and *Blenheim* followed with *Prince George* in her wake. The enemy's return of fire was slow, undisciplined, and sporadic.

'Sergeant Docherty, I think we may dispense with small arms drill for today,' shouted Lieutenant Hale, his voice competing with the noise of the battle. 'Let's get the men busy with the real thing. Target their officers. They may also dispense with their uniform coats if they wish,' Hale growled as he picked up a spare musket, a case of ball and cartridges. He ran up the companionway, taking up position behind the hammocks on the quarterdeck, throwing his scarlet coat and his hat into a corner so that his long fair hair rose from his head with the breeze. Without the hat, the Dons' soldiers might not take him for an officer, he reasoned.

Sergeant Docherty had taken station in the waist with two sections of his men and cases of musket cartridges and ball. He sent two sections to the fore and main masts with instructions to seek out the Spanish officers, readily identified by their colourful uniforms. Captain Irwin had ordered the lower courses to be brailed up out of the reach of chain or bar shot and musket flashes, and to give the marines a clear field of fire.

The lieutenant commanding the larboard guns nearest to him started the sequence of orders to fire the first broadside. Here on the upper gun deck, *Prince George* carried thirty 12-pounders: fifteen a side.

'Cast loose your gun,' he shouted, freeing the weapon from its securing tackle.

'Level your gun and remove your tampion.' That brought the cannon to the loading position.

'Prime.' The gun captain, a muscular man of 30 years, inserted his primer, a goose quill filled with fine powder, into the cannon's vent.

'Load with cartridge!' The gun's loader moved nimbly to insert the charge; a cylindrical bag filled tight with powder.

Docherty was watching the crew at work, never having seen ships' cannons fired in anger. And was impressed with the speed and apparent efficiency with which they worked.

'Load with shot and wad to shot!' The loader rolled a ball down the muzzle followed by another wad.

The rammer, a short man with red hair, inserted the ram into the muzzle and caught the lieutenant's eye as the order was given. 'Ram home your shot and wad.'

'Two-six ho!' The shout told guns two and six to heave on the side tackles to run the guns out again.

At the order, 'Fire,' timed by the lieutenant perfectly, the gun captains, standing aside from the cannon, sharply pulled a lanyard to release the flintlock mechanism, creating the necessary spark thus igniting the powder in the quill tube which, in turn, ignited the powder in the charge.

A near simultaneous release of iron spewed from the guns. The calm of their initial approach changed to the thunderous roar and fires of hell as *Prince George's* main armament commenced, taking toll of the Spanish, turning spars and sails to splinters and rags, and turning the deck of its closest opponent red as Spanish blood was ejected from bodies violently scythed down by iron balls and grapeshot. Huge splinters of timber were sent flying, some ripped from the ship's side by the cannon balls were the size of men. The screams of those ripped apart and maimed by iron and timber were enough to make any man shudder.

Docherty was brought back from his state of idle spectating when a ball thudded into the side of *Prince George*, just level with his feet. Looking out over the side, he saw it stuck, half in and half out of the ship's timbers. Docherty knew enough of gunnery to understand the cannon that fired it could not have had a full charge, that or the powder used was poor quality. Otherwise, he would have had his feet blown off and be bleeding slowly to death.

He pulled his head back in and brought his breathing under control, levelling his weapon and searched for a target. He found himself looking at the face of a Spanish gunner. They were so close he could see the fear in the man's eyes. He fired, and when the smoke cleared, the man had gone. Turning his back, he leaned against the gunwale to reload his musket. He pulled a cartridge from his case, bit off the end of paper, tipped just enough into the open pan which he then snapped shut, poured the remainder down the barrel with the lead ball, pulled the ramrod from beneath the weapon and rammed the ball home rapidly two or three times, then turned and levelled the musket again.

The ships had moved and now he had the enemy's quarterdeck hanging above his sight. Two or three officers were visible within the thinning smoke. He fired. One fell out of sight. Docherty grinned. Quickly reloading, he found another target. This time a soldier. He could see several of them, with their odd, pointed helmets. He tracked one as the Spaniard was loading his weapon, a clumsy looking blunderbuss. The man fell, his helmet pierced, and a small spurt of blood the proof of his accuracy. This is like shooting fish in a barrel he thought.

Again, he repeated the loading procedure, and this time, rather than crouching, he stood clear of the gunwale, in plain sight of the enemy. He saw a second group of soldiers, standing with a variety of weapons, shouting at each other. As he fired one of them turned and fired in a swift move, and Docherty found himself on the deck, blood oozing from a small flap of loose skin on his right cheek.

A marine knelt by his side. 'Am I going to die?' Docherty asked.

'We should be so lucky, sarge. You've got a small wound. The ball just grazed you. Another inch to the left and you would be bleedin' dead. 'Ang on, I'll wrap this around it an' you'll be right as rain.' The private wrapped a large kerchief around Docherty's head tying the loose corners together into a knot above his right ear.

Docherty was feeling shaken and dazed. He reached for his water bottle and realised it had been hit, either by a ball or a splinter; whichever it was the bottle was now empty. The lack of it made him thirstier.

'Oh bloody 'ell, sarge, 'ere, drink this.' A wooden bottle was thrust under his mouth, and he took it, swallowing hard. Then he realised it was grog, part of the man's daily allowance and greatly prized. He gulped a large mouthful, feeling the warming liquid descend to his stomach, bringing with it a warm glow and renewed eagerness for the fight. He garnered his senses and realised the lieutenant was continuing his calm, but much louder, direction of the guns' crews.

'Worm and sponge,' he bellowed. The rammer thrust the worm down the muzzle first to remove any solid embers, followed quickly by the wet sponge to extinguish any hot spots left. The gun crew worked rapidly, in an orchestrated, practiced and smooth sequence, like a complex dance, to bring the gun back to readiness for firing. The process was repeated all along the gun deck, crews working without pause or hesitation on each gun, trained to a perfect pitch, seamlessly. Little fire was coming back from the Spaniards.

All the time, the lieutenant was keeping an eye on his pocket watch, smiling with satisfaction as the crews maintained the rhythm and released a second broadside within three minutes of the first.

Lieutenant Hale was firing repeatedly, with a coolness that surprised him. He spied a Spanish officer waving a sword, giving encouragement to a few cowering gunners – or possibly threatening them – who, as the guns rolled out ready to fire, threw themselves prostrate to the deck. A spasmodic, ragged, ineffectual fire striking the side of *Prince George* that found no human target. Hale fired, and once the smoke from his weapon had cleared, he was gratified to see the officer had disappeared. Resuming his crouching behind the protection of the gunwale, he felt the wind of a shot as it whistled past his ear and struck the deck by his knee. 'Hell, and damnation,' he shouted to nobody, realising the hunter had become the hunted. 'That was too close.'

He found another target, a sharpshooter in the mizzen top, probably the man who had targeted him, trying to remain concealed behind the mast. Hale was pleased to see that he, too, fell with a scream into the sea. Such marksmanship under the pressure of battle, with the deafening roar of cannon and the flames and smoke, should please even Mister Vizzard. 'I just hope we both survive to argue about the wager agreed on,' he thought, his smoke-stained face breaking into a grin.

Docherty was directing his sections of marines to fire on targets he picked out, still shooting when he could, using the time during reloading to identify officers or any enemy brave enough to show his face. Having abandoned the protection of the ship's bulwarks, he moved along the ranks of his marines, shouting orders and encouragement. All were shooting with as much accuracy as their weapons could provide, firing with a rhythm that only frequent practice that training imbues in a soldier.

He paused midway along the line to reload, when he was hit a hammer blow in the left arm and fell to the deck from the force of the shot. 'The bastard. I've been hit again,' he groaned, his words superfluous.

A young marine knelt beside him. 'You alright, sarge? Let me help you below and get that arm seen to.' The lad grabbed his right arm and lifted him to his feet, with strength that surprised him.

'I think not youngster. I ain't letting any sawbones anywhere near my arm. It didn't hit bone, but Christ on the cross it felt like a hammer blow.' Hale winced in pain. 'Get me something to keep it clean and tie it up. Let me sit down. It's sheltered here.' Docherty sat heavily, groaning as the pain increased, holding his wounded arm as the blood dripped to the deck.

Lieutenant Hale's supply of cartridge was nearly exhausted. He looked over to the marines in the waist and saw Docherty sitting with his arm covered in blood. Sliding down the companionway onto the deck, Hale ran to him. 'You must stop bleeding, Pat. You're making a mess of Admiral Parker's flagship and you know how fussy he is about cleanliness.' Docherty smiled weakly. Hale removed Docherty's uniform coat, pulled a length of cord from his own jacket pocket, and deftly tied it around the bloody arm, above the wound. With his pencil he twisted the cord tighter and tighter, stopping only when Docherty shouted in pain. 'Is that comfortable, Pat? Or shall I tweak it a little more?'

'You sir are a right bastard. Thank you, that is tight enough. Look, the bleeding has stopped.'

'Now, get below to the surgeon and get that seen to. Don't worry, I don't see that arm as lost. He'll not amputate.' Hale encouraged.

Docherty sat where he was, shaking his head. 'No sir. I'll stay with the men. One of the drummers can load for me. I'll keep firing as long as I can.'

Lieutenant Hale gave his sergeant a long, hard look. He realised further instructions would be a waste of breath, and reloaded Docherty's musket for him, before turning his own weapon toward the Spanish ship, which was now slipping out of range. 'Hold off, Patrick,' Hale shouted at the marines in the waist. 'Hold your fire, lads. That one is out of range.' He dropped down and crossed his legs, breathing hard, thinking of the last half an hour or so of intense activity and the noise of battle ringing in his ears.

* * * * *

Victory

Embroiled in the battle, the floating batteries sprayed flames of death and destruction at each other. However, the guns of the English fleet despatched their iron much faster, and with greater accuracy than their enemy's. Jervis estimated his fleet was firing five or six times as fast as his enemy, possibly more. It confirmed his opinion that the Spanish fleet was under manned and lacked essential training and discipline.

Now that Jervis and *Victory* had passed through the Spanish line, he ordered the fleet to tack in succession, under the very guns of the Spaniards. Knowing his fleet had the collective skill to undertake the difficult manoeuvre, he hoped to encourage the Spaniard's southernmost division to break the British fleet's line. When they duly obliged, each attempt was beaten off with withering, accurate and sustained gunfire.

Having observed the northern division attempting to reunite with the southern division, Jervis grunted and determined to frustrate the attempt. Signalling his rear division to tack to counter the Spanish manoeuvre. *Britannia*, flagship of Vice Admiral Sir Charles Thompson in command of the rear squadron, however, ignored his specific order. Jervis looked at the masthead and decided the signal had been clear, witnessing *Minerve*, out of the battle's smoke, repeating it. Gripping the rail, his knuckles whitened as he struggled to contain his anger. What was the man doing? Is he blind? 'Make his number, please,' he ordered. Yet *Britannia* continued sailing straight ahead, and Jervis' anger continued to increase.

Thompson's small division followed his lead in the way subordinates do when faced with conflicting information, not knowing whether to follow the commander in chief's order, or Thompson's actions. Their respective captains could not be criticised or censured, but confusion was abroad on the decks of them all.

Except one. On board *Captain*, Nelson had clearly seen the signal. He was observing the Spanish fleet's attempt and foresaw events about to unfold; the main body of the Spanish fleet would pass by the rear of the English fleet to re-join its disconnected southern division, without early interference from the English fleet.

Jervis, focusing his glass on his rear division, saw *Captain* suddenly wear ship away from the enemy, then swing in a tight arc to turn and steer northwest on the port tack straight towards it, passing between the two rearmost vessels, *Excellent* and *Diadem*. Nelson's pennant fluttered bravely in the breeze as *Captain* sailed directly at the enemy. He traversed the glass and saw a cluster of large Spanish ships, including the largest he had ever seen: a leviathan with four gun decks. Jervis smiled and lowered his glass. His favoured captain had discerned the situation, understood that Thompson was not complying with the order for reasons unknown, and courageously decided to act on his own responsibility, attack the enemy and prevent them meeting the southernmost division. His 74-gun *Captain* looked like a David to the Spaniard's Goliath.

'My word, sir,' exclaimed Captain Calder. 'What the devil does Nelson think he is doing? You must issue the recall to him at once, Sir John, he has left the line of battle and disobeyed your orders.' Calder spoke with clear anger at the breach of discipline shown by Nelson.

'I most certainly will not, and I'll thank you not to tell me what orders or signals to issue to my ships, sir!' He paced across the deck, hands firmly clasped behind him. 'I can see perfectly well what the Commodore is seeking to do, and that is to attack the enemy, sir, to prevent its reunion with its southerly division,' Jervis snorted in derision. 'Do you not see how matters are evolving?'

Next, he turned his glass on *Prince George*, his eye attracted to a signal breaking out from Parker's flagship. 'What is Admiral Parker signalling, youngster?' he bellowed at the signals' midshipman. 'Quickly now.'

'Sssir, yes Sir John,' stammered the lad, nervous under the eye of his commander in chief. 'Admiral Parker's signal reads, 'Fill and stand on in support of *Captain*', Sir John.' The youth was clearly relieved to have read it correctly, and his lieutenant smiled at his young protégé.

Jervis might well be fighting a major sea action, but he still took time to check on young gentlemen seeking to become lieutenants.

'Very good, youngster, very good. Now I have one for you, if you will. Signal to *Excellent, Culloden, Blenheim*, and *Orion* to support *Captain*. Thank you.'

As he issued the order, *Captain* all but disappeared, surrounded by some five or six Spanish vessels, most of them larger and more powerful than she. The sound of her guns reached them moments after the smoke flew from the gunports on both sides.

'Damned fool,' thought Jervis. 'If he survives this, I shall be greatly surprised. If he dies, we will have lost a splendid officer and gifted leader. Courage there was aplenty amongst his officers, but to charge alone, without orders, into a mass of the enemy. That showed a disregard for one's own life in the service of the King.'

Resuming his scrutiny of manoeuvres, he watched as *Victory* drew closer to the enemy. He did not have to wait long before *Victory* reached the point at which Jervis' order to tack was to be executed. Just then, a Spanish three-decker, later established to be the *Principe de Asturias* flying a vice admiral's flag and heavily armed with 112 guns, made a brave and determined attempt to break through the British line. It came too close to *Victory* and was forced to tack, for which manoeuvre she was rewarded with two well-timed, disciplined and devastating broadsides. There followed a terrible rolling thunder, with fire, smoke and death causing carnage amongst her crew, before she fell away out of reach of the British guns, her sails in shreds, yards shattered, wounded men screaming and her officers helpless to bring their ship under control.

And Spanish blood slowly staining her battered sides.

* * * * *

Captain

Jack had managed only three hours' sleep and woke with a jerk of his head as though his unconscious being had been struck hard on the jaw. The wardroom servant was shaking him, talking gibberish.

'What? What did you say, man?' he spluttered, shaking the fog from his still-sleeping brain. He lowered a leg to the deck.

'The captain's respects sir, and he would be grateful if you would join him on the quarterdeck. The commodore is with him, sir.'

'Very well. Thank you. Is there any coffee?'

'As you like it sir, black and strong, with a tot of rum.' The servant passed over a pewter mug. 'By the by, sir, the Spanish fleet is in sight to the southwest.' He grinned at the marine officer who was talked about by some on the lower deck with the kind of respect not shown to many officers, and rarely, if ever, shown to officers of marines.

Jack swung both legs out of the hammock and rubbed his chin, then reached for his uniform coat. Ignoring the gorget, which he loathed, he quickly buckled on his sword and pulled his hat from the protruding trenail in the overhead beam, before making his way to the quarterdeck, now fully awake. The sea mist was thinning, a weak winter's sun slowly breaking through, and the line of the British fleet could be seen stretching ahead.

'Ah, good morning, Vizzard. Thought you would wish to see the enemy we are to fight this day,' said Captain Miller, extending an arm toward the gathering Spanish.

'Good morning, sir, indeed I would like to, very much,' Jack replied, searching the horizon ahead. 'There does seem to be a great many of them. What are the admiral's intentions, sir, would you know?' He wondered if Jervis would turn the fleet and sail broadside to broadside, so each British ship could immediately commence firing at the nearest Spanish ship. 'That's how sea fights are usually fought,' he thought. But Jervis appeared to have no such intention.

'Why, as you may observe, the enemy appears to be some miles apart in two divisions, we have counted twenty of them, but there are likely more. Now, do you see the gap between them?' He extended his arm. 'The admiral will take us through that, then doubtless tack, and prevent the main body from closing the gap and bringing the two divisions together. It will be hot work as we pass through and, with our position in the line, I fear we may be late to the dance.' He grinned at Jack, quite obviously viewing the forthcoming battle with some relish. That, Miller thought to himself, was what the fleet had trained for during the last year or more. A major battle could lead to his death, admittedly, but it could also lead to fame, distinguishing oneself and obtaining preferment in the matter of promotion.

In addition, there was always the chance of prize money, but he chose not to discuss that subject with junior officers. He relished the prospect of capturing a major Spanish warship, but with three admirals and a commodore in the fleet, his share would be greatly diluted.

Jack took the offered telescope and stared at the line of ships, some of them very large indeed. If they were properly manned the potential weight and volume of fire to be poured on the British fleet was enormous. Jack was not easily frightened, but the sheer size of the enemy's fleet and the destruction it might be capable of made him wonder, 'This could be as bloody as Howe's action of the 1st of June, back in '94.' He thought of Mary and her concern for his wellbeing. 'I might die today.' The thought entered his mind unbidden and was just as quickly dismissed. 'Not today, Jack! You will survive this day and you will return home.'

Jack acknowledged Miller's comment. 'I understand that sir,' he said, before voicing his alarm. 'Do we not then run the risk of being under fire from the Spanish with no possibility of fighting back until after we break their line? They have plenty of time to prepare for us. It strikes me as a very risky enterprise.'

'Oh, granted that may be true, Vizzard. My fear is that the enemy will be much dispersed before we can get into action. The sea is quite calm and with this light breeze it will take us time to reach their line but, once there, we will pound them with rapid, disciplined fire from both broadsides at once. I doubt they will be as well organised as us. Remember, until a few months back, we were allies. We had the opportunity to see their ships and meet some of their officers.'

'Ah ha,' continued Miller. 'There you have it, Vizzard. See the signal? 'Admiral intends to pass through enemy's line.' No doubt about Old Jervie's intentions now. He's departing from the regular system, by God! We will divide and conquer, you'll see.'

'I shall see about something to eat and instruct my men. Thank you for your candour, Captain Miller.'

Before he left the deck in search of something to eat, Jack looked at Nelson, whose whole being was fixed on the enemy fleet. The commodore was standing with a long glass studying the oncoming Spanish and the line of British men o' war stretched out ahead of *Captain*, before suddenly changing the object of his interest to all signals from *Victory*. Studiously watching and waiting, Nelson dearly wanted to know what tactics Jervis would employ. In the back of his mind, however, was the essay on tactics Jervis had encouraged him to study. The simplicity and audacious nature of that style of attack captivated him.

The prospect of an imminent action always gave Jack a hunger. In the wardroom he met the other marine officer, Major William Morris, who, a marine reported, had been 'indisposed' in his bunk. Meeting him again this morning, Jack immediately understood why. The man was already swaying, and not from the rolling motion of the frigate. He had been drinking.

'Ah, so you are here,' the man spluttered. 'You are sent by Jervis to torment me!' The major sat heavily at the table, fumbling, and searching for a glass that was not there.

Jack stood still as if slapped in the face. He searched his superior's face for some explanation of this extraordinary outburst. Having never so much as heard of this officer before this deployment, he now stood accused as his tormentor.

'I am at a loss to understand you, sir. I am here with my men to provide reinforcement to your command.'

If only Jervis had informed him of the character of this officer, though perhaps Jervis did not know he was a drunkard. Or perhaps he did, which might better explain the decision to send a strong cadre of men to support Commodore Nelson. Jack had received one too many shocking revelations since coming aboard. First, his nemesis Harcourt, and now a senior marine officer who was drunk, or deranged, or possibly both.

'Hah,' said the Major. 'Do not inshult me, damn you. Jervis conshiders me incompetent and has shent the famous Captain Vizzard to undermine my position, to supplant me. I know preshisely why you are here.' He coughed, clasping a kerchief to his mouth. 'Spratt, where are you damn it. Bring me a bottle of wine, now,' he bellowed in the general direction of the servant's pantry.

'I can assure you, sir, that is not my purpose.' Jack's initial anger fell away to disappointment, followed by a sense of embarrassment and, finally, a degree of sympathy. The man had lost respect. If not the respect of Admiral Jervis, then without question he had lost any sense of self-respect. How easily an officer could lose the confidence of his seniors. Fortunately, Jack enjoyed the confidence and, he hoped, respect of his commanding officers, but had seen others falter and become ineffective in the face of seniors who bullied from the rear, rather than led from the front.

Jack always strove to be one of the latter: a positive leader. It was a trait that came effortlessly. Bullying, arrogant officers were anathema to him. He had experienced the type at school, and then the snobby kind at Oxford, who in their particular manner sought to belittle people deemed to be of lower social status. Jack, as the son of a plain, albeit successful, country lawyer, was considered as such by the sons of bishops, earls, or even baronets. If that is what was required to be a member of the aristocracy, then Jack had decided early in life it was not for him. From the back of his mind the conversation with Doctor Jenner came to the fore. Perhaps he was a minor member with an inherited baronetcy. If his brother George, was in fact dead, then yes, the baronetcy would surely pass to him. His London agent had been instructed to make enquiry of the College of Heralds and to advise him. He shook his head to clear the irrelevant thoughts crowding his mind.

'You are gravely mistaken, sir,' he said. 'Let me repeat, my instructions are to provide Captain Miller, and naturally, yourself, with additional men capable of defending this ship, of fighting the Spaniards and winning. That, sir, is why I am here. I will assist you as much as I can but,' he paused, 'do not try to prevent me from performing my duties. That will not serve at all. Now, I suggest, sir, you have a shave and report to Captain Miller ready to perform your duty.'

The major's eyes were bloodshot and glazed, and Jack was uncertain whether the man had any comprehension of what he had said. His chin dropped heavily onto his chest, and an unsightly trickle of saliva seeped from the corner of his mouth.

All thoughts of breakfast had dissipated, his hunger vanished, and Jack left the wardroom with a sour taste in his mouth, seeking more amenable company. He returned to the deck and saw Packer organizing sections for the fighting tops and the waist. He had deployed marines to all the companionways to prevent any men leaving their stations without good cause. Others had been sent to the liquor store and the magazine, deep in the bowels of the ship. The liquor store, in the purser's domain, was out of bounds, although the hands always seemed to acquire alcohol before an action. Only barefoot powder monkeys, young ship's boys, were permitted in the magazine. A single spark could turn the great ship into a million fragments of matchwood, and its occupants to a similar state.

Jack went to his station on the quarterdeck and stood beside Commander Berry. 'You might have told me that your Major Morris is a drunkard. I've just left him below and he was in his cups.'

'One moment, Vizzard, the admiral is signalling again.' He waited for the signals lieutenant to decipher the flags, which read, 'Take suitable stations for mutual support and engage the enemy as coming up in succession.'

Berry gave a grunt. 'Ah, now that is unfortunate, Vizzard. The Major is known to be fond of his wine, and spirits, but I for one have never seen him incapable through drink or, as you put it, in his cups. Are you suggesting he is unfit for duty?'

'He could barely stand and was damn near incoherent. I advised him to wash and shave and report for duty, but I doubt we will see him. He outranks me, else I would immediately remove him from his command.' Jack was still angry that a senior officer could let his men, and himself, down in such a manner. 'The man brings dishonour to the Corps and the uniform he wears.'

'I hold no position on this ship, Vizzard, other than as a supernumerary, a mere observer of events. You might raise the matter with Captain Miller if you are that concerned. He is receptive to matters of discipline and good order, in officers as well as the hands.'

Jack reflected for a moment, 'This is probably not the time ...' but the rest was left unfinished as Commodore Nelson turned around and addressed Captain Miller.

'Ralph, Admiral Jervis is signalling Britannia.' Nelson focused his telescope on the flags breaking out from *Victory*. 'Leading ship to tack and others in succession.' He turned the telescope to study *Britannia*, flagship of Vice Admiral Sir Charles Thompson. Nelson was waiting for the acknowledging signal and for *Britannia* to commence to tack. He grunted and was heard to mumble something to himself. Thompson must surely have seen the signal. Why has he not acted? He waited for half a minute.

'I have come to a decision, Ralph. I require you to wear ship immediately and reverse course and make for the enemy over there,' he said, pointing to a pair of the largest Spanish ships.

'Sir, may I respectfully direct you to the admiral's orders, we should ...'

'The responsibility is entirely mine, Captain Miller,' he responded, with a formality that prohibited any argument. 'I am aware of the Admiral's general orders. However, what is plain to me, perhaps less so to Sir Charles Thompson, is that if we all continue this course and await our turn to tack, all may be lost. In the time that will take, the enemy's northern division will pass to our rear and link up with its southern group. I cannot allow that to happen. Please, wear ship now.' Nelson turned on his heel and continued to watch the enemy.

Miller passed the order to the first lieutenant, who, clutching a speaking trumpet, bellowed, 'Hands will prepare to wear ship.' He watched as the men looked askance at the unusual and unexpected order, discipline forcing them to take hold of the necessary halyards and sheets in preparation.

'Wear ship,' bellowed the first lieutenant sending the hands into a frenzy of activity. Within half a minute, *Captain* was heeling over, her wake describing a neatly drawn semi-circle, sending her back to the last two ships of the rear division, *Diadem* and *Excellent,* the crews of which called and shouted at the men on *Captain* as she steered swiftly but neatly through the narrow gap between the two. It was immediately apparent to the crews of the two warships exactly what the commodore was attempting, their commanders having watched the evolving battle carefully.

'Well done helmsman,' shouted Ralph Miller. 'That was handsomely done.' Turning to Berry and Vizzard, he said, 'I do hope our Commodore survives this and pray that Jervis does not censure our Nel. It is a bold but courageous manoeuvre.'

'He means to take on those two thumpers,' exclaimed Berry, pointing at two magnificent vessels, one a four-decked monster, larger than any ship ever seen by anyone in the British fleet. They were in a cluster of five line of battle ships. 'We shall be in the thick of it after all, gentlemen.'

'I see what he is about now,' exclaimed Jack. 'He means to sail into the bows of that group to prevent them getting astern of us. My God, we shall be very much in the cauldron of fire. He will either make us heroes, or ...' Jack left the word unsaid, as visions of dead and dying, mutilated men came into both his and Berry's minds.

A marine officer's hat appeared at the top of the companionway, followed by a voice, still slurred by wine or rum, which bellowed, 'What's to do this morn? Are we to fight the Dons or run from them?' Major Morris stumbled as he took a position on the quarterdeck to the far side of Captain Miller.

Jack looked at the man. Unable to form appropriate words for the situation, he raised his hand in salute to his superior. 'It would seem, Major, that our gallant Commodore is intent on taking on the Spanish Armada single handed,' he found himself saying drily. 'We best make ready for we are nearly upon them.' With that, he collected his musket, fitted a bayonet to it, looked down at Sergeant Major Packer—who turned toward the quarterdeck and threw Jack a smart salute —before turning his eyes toward the oncoming Spanish.

'This will soon become warm work, gentlemen. My lads have a standing order to dispense with their scarlet coats and their hats during battle. They are more comfortable that way.' Jack hung his coat on a belaying pin, placed his hat neatly on top of it, and proceeded to load the musket. Then he checked his holster pistols, made for him by Ketland &

Company in Birmingham. They were primed and loaded and felt reassuring in his hands. Balanced and effective at short range, he prized them greatly.

Nelson paced across the deck, joined by Ralph Miller, and looked over the larboard beam at *Victory* and Jervis, whom he believed he could now see on his deck. There was a signal being hoisted but not a signal of recall. Nelson clenched his jaw. 'I am set on a course and will see it through, signal or no signal,' he thought.

His vision for the evolving battle was as swift and as keen as his solitary eye. Despite breaching his orders, which left a gap in the British line he hoped would be plugged by *Diadem* and *Excellent*, his bold move had been worthy and daring. Or so he thought. Yet now the great Spanish three-deckers in the Spanish van came sweeping down to cross his stern.

'Ah, excellent,' said Nelson to the men on the quarter-deck. 'It appears Jervis has fully appreciated the changing positions and is signalling *Excellent, Culloden, Blenheim,* and *Orion* to support us.'

Then hell was let loose, and *Captain* opened up with all her guns, attacking the enormous four-decker, identified as the *Santissima Trinidad*, with 136 guns, as well as the *San Josef*, the *Salvador del Mundo*, the *San Nicolas*, and the *San Isidoro* all heavyweight line of battle ships, bristling with hundreds of cannons between them. Within minutes, *Captain* found herself surrounded and receiving fire, some of it effective, from five enemy ships. All of them were larger vessels.

Jack looked up as the sound of tearing timber broke in above the repeated explosions from *Captain's* guns and, through the burgeoning smoke, saw the foretopmast fall over the side, dragging two of his marines with it. *Captain* was all but immobile. Her guns, however, were continuing to pour fire and death into her larger opponent, now no more than ten feet away from the muzzles. *Captain's* rigging and sails started to sustain damage. The enemy's fire was slow and sporadic, but some Spanish iron found a target.

The mizzen yard came crashing down, canvas spilling across the deck, sheets and blocks flying. Jack struggled with the canvas helped by a pair of sailors and quickly looked about. He saw Nelson leaning against Captain Miller, with a hand on his side. 'Are you hit, sir?' He asked Nelson.

'I am winded Mister Vizzard, 'tis nothing.' Nelson's words gave the lie to his facial features; the pain produced a grimace, which he quickly removed. Turning to Captain Miller, he said. 'Really, Ralph. I am quite uninjured. Thank you for your concern.'

Nelson ordered the helm over to starboard and alongside the nearest Spaniard, and he ran forward toward the bows, his sword held high above his head as *Captain's* bowsprit ran through the starboard quarter-gallery windows in the Spanish giant, discovered to be the *San Nicholas*. *Captain's* bowsprit caught in her mizzen shrouds, her wheel-post was shattered, much of her rigging was torn apart as if by giant hands, and several of her guns overturned, crushing the life of two of their crews and maiming others. Captain's cathead was caught in *San Nicolas'* stern gallery, forming a convenient bridge to the Spanish ship.

With a yell, Nelson called for boarders, shouting, 'Westminster Abbey or a glorious victory.' With that he jumped onto the cathead and started towards the Spanish vessel.

Captain Miller made to join the boarders, with Nelson immediately objecting and ordering him to remain in command of his ship. 'I must have the honour of boarding her, Ralph,' he said. 'To you falls the duty of managing the ship.'

Miller, a fighting man, was bitterly disappointed.

Berry was the very first to jump into the leviathan's quarter gallery, from there making his way up the side of the ship to the Spaniard's quarterdeck, followed by a line of sailors, armed with tomahawks, axes, and pikes. There were some from Nelson's old ship, *Agamemnon*, eager to support their former captain. He narrowly escaped death or injury as fire from the Spaniard found its target amongst the crush of seamen, many of whom were scythed down.

Nelson dropped into the stern gallery, assisted by a soldier of the 69th Regiment who used his musket to shatter the gallery windows. Three midshipmen and Lieutenant Pierson of that regiment followed them.

A few seconds behind Nelson, Jack was disappointed, having been in the act of firing at the very moment of Nelson's move forward. 'Damn it,' he said out loud, as he stepped carefully along *Captain's* bowsprit.

'Now then, sir, I 'ope you had no intention to leave me behind?' yelled Packer. Now get moving sir, we have Spaniards to kill.'

More seamen and marines followed, not wishing to miss the drama; one unfortunate soldier, attempting the leap from bulwark to bulwark, missed his footing and fell into the sea between the two rolling vessels. The pressure crushed the life from him before he could drown.

They pushed through into the cabin, the doors of which were closed. As it was attacked with an axe wielded by a burly seaman, Spanish officers on the far side fired pistols through the timber panelling. The doors broke open and Packer, along with a few soldiers from the 69th, fired their muskets. Some Spaniards fell, their blood adding to the general detritus littering the deck. One of the dead, they learned, was a Spanish Brigadier, equivalent to a British Commodore, with a distinguishing pennant. They pressed onwards to the Spanish quarterdeck, not meeting any further resistance, and found Berry in command of the poop deck and in the act of hauling down the Spanish flag, a broad grin across his grimy face.

Behind Berry, the crumpled body of Major William Morris was lying in a pool of his own blood. Berry turned to Jack and said, 'He followed me along the bowsprit and died defending me from the Spanish Marine officer over there.' He pointed to a dishevelled, slightly built Spaniard, looking dejected in defeat. 'He had no chance at all. How he managed the bowsprit is surprising, but then the Spaniard stepped forward to attack me. The Major simply put himself in the way. It was astonishing.' Berry shook his head, still not comprehending.

* * * * *

Lieutenant the Honourable Harcourt had kept an eye out for Vizzard for the last twenty-four hours, carefully avoiding any direct contact with the over-confident, arrogant Marine officer. He had been given command of a forward group of the 32-pounders on the larboard side of the lower gun deck.

256

With little knowledge of gunnery, it fell to one of the gunner's mates and a mature midshipman to take control, with Harcourt, most of the time, cowering behind the foremast and becoming increasingly frightened at the prospect of being struck by a cannon ball. He had witnessed as much befall the crew of one of his guns. The gun was blown upwards into the deck-head wiping out most of the crew and sending body parts sliding across the bloody deck.

A man had called to him, pleading with him to take charge but the gunner's mate intervened. 'Leave him mate, he's no bleedin' use to us. Tend to your duties.'

Harcourt eventually found the courage to flee the noise and carnage of the lower deck. In a dazed state he appeared on the upper deck where firing was ongoing. He watched as Vizzard dropped into the Spaniard's stern gallery behind the Commodore. Finding an area by the *Captain's* foremast where he was not easily seen from the quarterdeck, Harcourt picked up a musket from a dead marine. From there he watched Captain Miller, and others, whose attention was focused on the Spanish ships.

Moving slowly, Harcourt climbed the larboard ratlines to the foretop and positioned himself on the far side away from the quarterdeck, praying he was not seen by Miller or anyone else. From this vantage point he saw a growing number of men in a variety of uniforms. He waited until he saw a red uniform on the opposite quarterdeck amongst a group of officers, both British and Spanish, in blues, and reds, and one in yellow or gold. Levelling the musket, he took careful aim.

The ball passed so close over Joe Packer's head that he felt the wind of it. It continued its trajectory across the

Spaniard's quarterdeck, cleared Jack Vizzard and eventually struck the upperworks of a second, powerful Spanish warship on the far side. From the trajectory Packer realized the shot must have come from *Captain*, alongside. He stepped across to the ship's side, saw the face he detested in the foretop, the face that now looked back in shock. Packer understood immediately that Jack Vizzard had been the target. The man who would have seen Packer hang, now held a musket from which smoke exuded and, as the noise of battle came across the Spanish deck from a second ship on the far side and the Commodore shouted back to *Captain* calling for more boarders, Joe Packer raised his own weapon, took aim and, and fired. He was gratified to see the hated face of Lieutenant Harcourt erupt with a crimson spray as he was thrown back and fell onto the deck.

'S'arn't Major Packer, follow me. The Commodore has taken this ship, but now wants to capture another that is still fighting. Hurry up man, what are you doing over there?' Jack turned and followed the Commodore whose flowing hair was caught in the breeze, a fresh group of sailors and more of Jack's marines supporting him. A sudden outburst of musket fire indiscriminately swept away seven of the boarding party and many Spanish sailors too.

One of Nelson's bargemen was on the Commodore's left side and Jack found himself to his right as they climbed the side of the second ship. A face appeared above them. Jack pointed his sword at the man as he reached the top and was still pointing his sword at the Spaniard as he dropped lightly to the deck next to Nelson.

What they saw before them took them both by surprise. The *San Jose* was a first rate carrying 112 guns and nigh on a thousand men: sailors, soldiers, and many untrained lands-men. In number they greatly exceeded the crew of *Captain*, yet they were lining up to surrender their swords to the slightly built English officer who passed them along to his bargeman, William Fearney.

Jack found the situation astonishing. As one of the lead-ing members of the boarding party he expected to be fighting for his life. Instead, the enemy were surrendering having abandoned their guns and decided against any further resis-tance. The release of tension and emotions relaxed him so much that he started laughing. Softly at first, then with in-creasing volume.

Packer understood. He became infected by Jack's laugh-ter and was soon joining in, the assembled Spaniards and the British sailors alike, puzzled by their behaviour. Cheers erupted from amongst *Captain's* sailors, soon joined by the crews of the others of the fleet, *Excellent, Culloden* and *Blenheim*, as news of Nelson's unique success reached them. The Commodore was later to describe it as 'Nelson's Patent Bridge for Boarding First Rates'.

As Nelson turned away from the humiliated Spanish offi-cers, Jim Porter was there, knuckling his forehead as a salute. 'Gawd bless your honour on a great victory, sir. We sure gave 'em their Valentines, didn't we sir?'

Nelson smiled and, clapping a hand on the sailor's shoul-der said, 'Yes, Mister Porter, we certainly did that. Thank you.'

Jack moved away from the group taking Packer by the shoulder. 'I saw you fire back at *Captain*. Tell me why you did that, Joe?'

'Now, sir, all I can truly say is that an enemy fired at us, and I simply returned fire as is me duty. We now got one less enemy to worry about, Captain Vizzard.' He stared at Jack, daring his commander to challenge his account.

Jack's eyes drilled into Packer's with a steely coldness while Packer's face remained devoid of any expression. It was the face he adopted when addressing senior officers. A blandness born from years of dealing with the gentlemen carrying the King's commission.

'If I did not know better, Joe ...'

'Best you don't then, innit, sir. Ask me no questions, and I'll thee no lies. Shall we join the Commodore sir, although it looks as if he's got things under control.'

THE END

Author's Note

First, a word about ship designation. At present, it is traditional to apply the honorific HMS before the name of a Royal Navy ship, but at the time of this battle it was common practice to simply refer to a ship by name. This has been verified by the findings of naval historian Sam Willis in his book *The Hour of Victory*. Willis found a cache of original dispatches from the Napoleonic era, and in these documents the ships are usually named without the appellation HMS.

The battle of Cape St Vincent delivered a crushing blow to Spanish interests. It frustrated French plans too. The battered fleet was able to retreat to Cadiz and posed very little threat to England for several years, until, that is, another battle was fought some eight years later, and not far away for that matter, near a headland called Cape Trafalgar.

During the intervening years, Horatio Nelson became a national hero, notorious perhaps for the treatment of his lawful wife, and his affair with Emma Hamilton. The latter, coupled with his country of England, were the two great passions of his life. A hero because of his leadership, personal physical courage and sheer boldness at the great sea battles of the period; the Battle of the Nile, Copenhagen, and ultimately, Trafalgar.

Cape St Vincent was not all about Nelson, however. He ensured his name and exploits became well known because he was, after all, very effective as a self-publicist and PR co-ordinator. He sought fame and honour, and St Vincent gave him the opportunity to achieve both goals. Above other qualities, the man had an incisive mind, great tactical vision, the driving desire to utterly defeat England's enemies, and immeasurable personal courage. He observed the Spanish manoeuvres and understood clearly what his mentor, Sir John Jervis, intended. Having the courage of his convictions, he acted without express consent, knowing his actions were consistent with his admiral's strategy, yet risking the severest of reprisals. A lesser captain might not have acted with the conviction and force of personality to act in such a manner. And yet there were some excellent captains in the fleet including Troubridge, Collingwood, Cockburn, Berry, and Miller. All these men were to become his 'Band of Brothers'.

The Earl St Vincent, as Jervis became in reward for his exertions, gave the eager Nelson the opportunity, by providing the training and discipline the fleet needed and in giving Nelson the independent authority as a commodore to distinguish himself. His early promotion attracted criticism and acrimony from other, older, captains and flag officers, but subsequent events certainly justified the trust Jervis placed in him.

Nelson's act in wearing the ship *Captain* and taking her out of the line of battle was in direct disobedience of orders. Robert Calder, as Flag Captain, did vehemently point this fact out. Jervis dismissed the accusation summarily, recognising—perhaps a little too late—that unless more direct action was taken the two separated divisions of the Spanish fleet might well have become one. Would that have made a difference to the outcome? In my judgement: probably. The fact the Spanish fleet was in such disarray undoubtedly helped Jervis realise his purpose, which was to give England a victory and to prevent the Spaniards from joining with the French. The country was not ready to face an invasion. But what do I know? I'm only an armchair admiral.

It is known the Spanish fleet was poorly trained. Its own officers admitted as much even before the battle. Spain had built some excellent ships but failed to train their men in how to use them. Their skill at sailing was below average and their gunnery nowhere near as good as the fleet that Jervis commanded. That is reflected in the casualty rates and in the consumption of stores of powder and shot of the principal protagonists. One observer noted that for each broadside attempted by the Spanish fleet, Jervis and his captains delivered as many as seven or eight times the number. That devastating firepower determined the outcome of a fleet action, and against a combined Spanish fleet, it is possible that Jervis and his highly trained crews would have still prevailed.

I have terminated the novel at a point before the conclusion of the battle, for no better reason than neither Horatio Nelson nor Jack Vizzard played any significant further part. It is a battle worth studying as it demonstrates the high level of skill and expertise the Mediterranean Fleet achieved in the year or so of Jervis' command. Before his appointment it had been allowed to become inefficient, some officers had become lazy and inattentive with lax attention to gunnery and sail drill. Jervis examined every aspect of the fleet he had inherited and improved every facet of it.

In my research for this novel, I have consulted many texts and include a bibliography for those interested in reading more. One of the chief primary sources is that of Colonel John Bethune Drinkwater, who sailed with Nelson on *Minerve* and *Captain,* and was permitted by Jervis to remain with the fleet until the conclusion of the battle. He was an eyewitness to many of the events described and had the benefit of talking to those officers most closely involved in the battle.

As Nelson said prior to the Battle of Cape St Vincent, 'they know not what this fleet is capable of performing; anything and everything.'

MHM

M Howard Morgan

About The Author

M Howard Morgan is a *nom de plume* of Malcolm Mendey.

Born in Carmarthen in South Wales, he spent his childhood years living in France, Belgium, Gibraltar and Germany. Following an initial career in civil law, he moved into loss adjusting, acting for and advising underwriters at Lloyd's of London and multi-national insurers. With his family he spent nearly twenty years in New Zealand, has traveled extensively on assignments within the UK and Europe, the Far East, Oceania, and North America.

An interest in genealogy resulted in the surprising discovery of an ancestor who was a marine with the First Fleet of convicts sent by Britain to Australia in 1788. Always a student of history, the discovery triggered an ever more consuming investigation into the Royal Marines and the history of the Golden Age of Sail and tangentially, the conflicts with Revolutionary and Napoleonic France.

First Fleet is a debut novel; the sequel, *The Glorious First,* set in 1794, describes the first major naval engagement between Britain and France, known in Britain as The Glorious First of June. The third novel finds the two principal characters, Jack Vizzard and Joe Packer, back at sea in 1797. They join the Mediterranean Fleet commanded by Sir John Jervis. The story concludes with the major fleet engagement known as the Battle of Cape St Vincent, in which a young captain Horatio Nelson distinguished himself and won his knighthood.

A qualified boat master, a failed golfer, enthusiast of aviation, consumer of fine wines, real ales, and spirits, the author has absolutely no interest in celery.

He lives in the beautiful Cotswolds in Southwest England with his beautiful wife, affectionately known as SWMBO (credit H Rider Haggard: *She Who Must Be Obeyed*) and a wonderful Sprollie dog called Molly.

First Fleet

By

M Howard Morgan

Love, murder, betrayal, and adventure with the transportation of convicts from Britain in 1787 and the founding of the penal colony that became Australia.

With the American colonies closed to Britain the gaols overflowed and the criminal under-class posed a growing threat to the property-owning classes. A solution was required to deal with the overcrowded prisons. The answer lay in colonising the continent on the far side of the world – *Terra Australis Incognita*; the unknown continent.

Claimed for Britain by James Cook during his first voyage of discovery in April 1770, the government of the day launched an ambitious project; to make use of the criminal class to develop a new colony. Its aim to find a new source of trade and a establish a new base for Britain's Royal Navy to support the burgeoning empire. The First Fleet of eleven ships left Portsmouth in May 1787 tasked with those objectives. The First Fleet of convicts. The great experiment so nearly failed.

Jack Vizzard, a young and raw marine officer of affluent background, becomes a member of the expedition. Lawyer, newly commissioned subaltern and a murderer, Vizzard finds his acts of betrayal follow him to New Holland. But what awaits him there? Retribution and reconciliation? Or ignominy and death?

PENMORE PRESS
www.penmorepress.com

THE GLORIOUS FIRST
BY

M HOWARD MORGAN

The second in the Jack Vizzard series of historical fiction

Lieutenant Vizzard is sent to the coast of France as that turbulent country declares war on Britain. His mission: escort and protect a government agent carrying valuable intelligence of vital importance to Prime Minister Pitt's government. Captured by a traitor, Vizzard must first escape France, then survive, then make his way home across dangerous waters. Dare he trust the beautiful Frenchwoman who befriends him? Or will treachery be repeated?

Vizzard's work leads directly to the battle known in France as Le Combat de Prairial. In Britain the engagement will become known as The Glorious First of June, but for Jack Vizzard it will be the day that heroes and cowards die together.

PENMORE PRESS
www.penmorepress.com

BLUE WATER SCARLET TIDE

BY

JOHN DANIELSKI

It's the summer of 1814, and Captain Thomas Pennywhistle of the Royal Marines is fighting in a New World war that should never have started, a war where the old rules of engagement do not apply. Here, runaway slaves are your best source of intelligence, treachery is commonplace, and rough justice is the best one can hope to meet—or mete out. The Americans are fiercely determined to defend their new nation and the Great Experiment of the Republic; British Admiral George Cockburn is resolved to exact revenge for the burning of York, and so the war drags on. Thanks to Pennywhistle's ingenuity, observant mind, and military discipline, a British strike force penetrates the critically strategic region of the Chesapeake Bay. But this fight isn't just being waged by soldiers, and the collateral damage to innocents tears at Pennywhistle's heart.

As his past catches up with him, Pennywhistle must decide what is worth fighting for, and what is worth refusing to kill for —especially when he meets his opposite number on the wrong side of a pistol.

PENMORE PRESS
www.penmorepress.com

Brewer and the Portuguese Gold
By

James Keffer

The year is 1840. Twenty-three years ago, Horatio Lord Hornblower was governor of the island of St. Helena and hailer to its only prisoner, Napoleon Bonaparte. First mutual respect and later shared tragedy forged a clandestine friendship between the two men. Now King Louis Philippe of France has requested that the remains of the late emperor be returned, and Queen Victoria has granted that request. The French have also requested that the former-Governor Lord Hornblower attend the exhumation as the official British representative! Hornblower knows the situation is a veritable powder keg; the Ultra-Royalists, led by the ruthless Duke of Angouleme, will stop at nothing to prevent Bonaparte's remains from returning to France, while the Bonapartists, led by the late-emperor's nephew Louis-Napoleon, hope to use the return to stage a coup and establish a renewed French Empire. Hornblower must do his utmost to ensure the mortal remains reach French shores safely to pay a debt he has owed for over twenty years.

Penmore Press

Challenging, Intriguing, Adventurous, Historical and Imaginative

www.penmorepress.com